THE EPIC BATTLE HAS BEGUN....

It was ten minutes before they heard the screaming. It was an unearthly sound that twisted the stomach into knots of fear and turned the blood cold. Involuntarily, the Baron and Sir Rodney reined in as they heard it. Their horses plunged wildly against the reins. It came from straight ahead of them and rose and fell, until the air quaked with the horror of it.

"Good God in heaven!" the Baron exclaimed. "What is that?"

"It's the Kalkara," Will said. "They're hunting."

Read all of the adventures of

RANGER'S APPRENTICE

RANGER'S APPRENTICE

BOOK ONE: THE RUINS OF GORLAN

JOHN FLANAGAN

PUFFIN BOOKS
An Imprint of Penguin Group (USA) Inc.

PUFFIN BOOKS

Published by the Penguin Group

Penguin Young Readers Group, 345 Hudson Street, New York, New York 10014, U.S.A.

Penguin Group (Canada), 90 Eglinton Avenue East, Suite 700, Toronto, Ontario, Canada
M4P 2Y3 (a division of Pearson Penguin Canada Inc.)

Penguin Books Ltd, 80 Strand, London WC2R 0RL, England

Penguin Ireland, 25 St Stephen's Green, Dublin 2, Ireland (a division of Penguin Books Ltd)

Penguin Group (Australia), 250 Camberwell Road, Camberwell, Victoria 3124, Australia
a division of Pearson Australia Group Pty Ltd)

Penguin Books India Pvt Ltd, 11 Community Centre, Panchsheel Park, New Delhi - 110 017, India

Penguin Group (NZ), 67 Apollo Drive, Rosedale, Auckland 0632, New Zealand
(a division of Pearson New Zealand Ltd)

Penguin Books (South Africa) (Pty) Ltd, 24 Sturdee Avenue,
Rosebank, Johannesburg 2196, South Africa

Registered Offices: Penguin Books Ltd, 80 Strand, London WC2R 0RL, England

Published in Australia by Random House Australia Children's Books
First published in the United States of America by Philomel Books,
a division of Penguin Young Readers Group, 2005
Published by Puffin Books, a division of Penguin Young Readers Group, 2006
This edition published by Puffin Books, a division of Penguin Young Readers Group, 2011

3 5 7 9 10 8 6 4 2

THE LIBRARY OF CONGRESS HAS CATALOGED THE PHILOMEL EDITION AS FOLLOWS:
Flanagan, John (John Anthony)
The ruins of Gorlan / John Flanagan.—1st American ed.
p. cm.—(ranger's apprentice)
Summary: When fifteen-year-old Will is rejected by battleschool, he becomes the reluctant
apprentice to the mysterious Ranger Halt, and winds up protecting the kingdom from danger.
[1. Heroes—Fiction. 2. Fantasy.] I. Title PZ7.F598284Ru 2005 [Fic]—dc22 2004027735
ISBN 0-399-24454-9 (hc)

Text set in Adobe Jenson
Designed by Marikka Tamura

Puffin Books ISBN 978-0-14-241744-7

Printed in the United States of America

For Michael

PROLOGUE

MORGARATH, LORD OF THE MOUNTAINS OF RAIN AND Night, former Baron of Gorlan in the Kingdom of Araluen, looked out over his bleak, rainswept domain and, for perhaps the thousandth time, cursed.

This was all that was left to him now—a jumble of rugged granite cliffs, tumbled boulders and icy mountains. Of sheer gorges and steep narrow passes. Of gravel and rock, with never a tree or a sign of green to break the monotony.

Even though it had been fifteen years since he had been driven back into this forbidding realm that had become his prison, he could still remember the pleasant green glades and thickly forested hills of his former fief. The streams filled with fish and the fields rich with crops and game. Gorlan had been a beautiful, living place. The Mountains of Rain and Night were dead and desolate.

A platoon of Wargals was drilling in the castle yard below him. Morgarath watched them for a few seconds, listening to the guttural, rhythmic chant that accompanied all their movements. They were stocky, misshapen beings, with features that were halfway human, but with a long, brutish muzzle and fangs like a bear or a large dog.

Avoiding all contact with humans, the Wargals had lived and bred in these remote mountains since ancient times. No one in living memory had ever set eyes upon one, but rumors and legends had persisted of a savage tribe of semi-intelligent beasts in the mountains. Morgarath, planning a revolt against the Kingdom of Araluen, had left Gorlan Fief to seek them out. If such creatures existed, they would give him an edge in the war that was to come.

It took him months, but he eventually found them. Aside from their wordless chant, Wargals had no spoken language, relying on a primitive form of thought awareness for communication. But their minds were simple and their intellects basic. As a result, they had been totally susceptible to domination by a superior intelligence and willpower. Morgarath bent them to his will and they became the perfect army for him—ugly beyond nightmares, utterly pitiless and bound totally to his mental orders.

Now, looking at them, he remembered the brightly dressed knights in glittering armor who used to compete in tourneys at Castle Gorlan, their silk-gowned ladies cheering them on and applauding their skills. Mentally comparing them to these black-furred, misshapen creatures, he cursed again.

The Wargals, attuned to his thoughts, sensed his disturbance and stirred uncomfortably, pausing in what they were doing. Angrily, he directed them back to their drill and the chanting resumed.

Morgarath moved away from the unglazed window, closer to the fire that seemed utterly incapable of dispelling the damp and chill from this gloomy castle. Fifteen years, he thought to himself again. Fifteen years since he had rebelled against the newly crowned King Duncan, a youth in his twenties. He had planned it all carefully as the old king's sickness progressed, banking on the indecision and confusion that would follow his death to split the other barons and give Morgarath his opportunity to seize the throne.

Secretly, he had trained his army of Wargals, massing them up here in the mountains, ready for the moment to strike. Then, in the days of confusion and grief following the king's death, when the barons traveled to Castle Araluen for the funeral rites, leaving their armies leaderless, he had attacked, overrunning the southeastern quarter of the kingdom in a matter of days, routing the confused, leaderless forces that tried to oppose him.

Duncan, young and inexperienced, could never have stood against him. The kingdom was his for the taking. The throne was his for the asking.

Then Lord Northolt, the old king's supreme army commander, had rallied some of the younger barons into a loyal confederation, giving strength to Duncan's resolve and stiffening the wavering courage of the others. The armies had met at Hackham Heath, close by the Slipsunder River, and the battle swayed in the balance for five hours, with attack and counterattack and massive loss of life. The Slipsunder was a shallow river, but its treacherous reaches of quicksand and soft mud had formed an impassable barrier, protecting Morgarath's right flank.

But then one of those gray-cloaked meddlers known as Rangers led a force of heavy cavalry across a secret ford ten kilometers up-stream. The armored horsemen appeared at the crucial moment of the battle and fell upon the rear of Morgarath's army.

The Wargals, trained in the tumbled rocks of the mountains, had one weakness. They feared horses and could never stand against such a surprise cavalry attack. They broke, retreating to the narrow confines of Three Step Pass, and back to the Mountains of Rain and Night. Morgarath, his rebellion defeated, went with them.

And here he had been exiled these fifteen years. Waiting, plotting, hating the men who had done this to him.

Now, he thought, it was time for his revenge. His spies told him the kingdom had grown slack and complacent and his presence here was all but forgotten. The name Morgarath was a name of legend nowadays, a name mothers used to hush fractious children, threatening that if they did not behave, the black lord Morgarath would come for them.

The time was ripe. Once again, he would lead his Wargals into an attack. But this time he would have allies. And this time he would sow the ground with uncertainty and confusion beforehand. This time none of those who conspired against him previously would be left alive to aid King Duncan.

For the Wargals were not the only ancient, terrifying creatures he had found in these somber mountains. He had two other allies, even more fearsome—the dreadful beasts known as the Kalkara.

The time was ripe to unleash them.

1

"TRY TO EAT SOMETHING, WILL. TOMORROW'S A BIG DAY, after all."

Jenny, blond, pretty and cheerful, gestured toward Will's barely touched plate and smiled encouragingly at him. Will made an attempt to return the smile, but it was a dismal failure. He picked at the plate before him, piled high with his favorite foods. Tonight, his stomach knotted tight with tension and anticipation, he could hardly bring himself to swallow a bite.

Tomorrow would be a big day, he knew. He knew it all too well, in fact. Tomorrow would be the biggest day in his life, because tomorrow was the Choosing Day and it would determine how he spent the rest of his life.

"Nerves, I imagine," said George, setting down his loaded fork and seizing the lapels of his jacket in a judicious manner. He was a thin, gangly and studious boy, fascinated by rules and regulations and with a penchant for examining and debating both sides of any question—sometimes at great length. "Dreadful thing, nervousness. It can just freeze you up so you can't think, can't eat, can't speak."

"I'm not nervous," Will said quickly, noticing that Horace had looked up, ready to form a sarcastic comment.

George nodded several times, considering Will's statement. "On the other hand," he added, "a little nervousness can actually improve performance. It can heighten your perceptions and sharpen your reactions. So, the fact that you are worried, if, in fact, you are, is not necessarily something to be worried about, of itself—so to speak."

In spite of himself, a wry smile touched Will's mouth. George would be a natural in the legal profession, he thought. He would almost certainly be the Scribemaster's choice on the following morning. Perhaps, Will thought, that was at the heart of his own problem. He was the only one of the wardmates who had any fears about the Choosing that would take place within twelve hours.

"He ought to be nervous!" Horace scoffed. "After all, which Craftmaster is going to want him as an apprentice?"

"I'm sure we're all nervous," Alyss said. She directed one of her rare smiles at Will. "We'd be stupid not to be."

"Well, I'm not!" Horace said, then reddened as Alyss raised one eyebrow and Jenny giggled.

It was typical of Alyss, Will thought. He knew that the tall, graceful girl had already been promised a place as an apprentice by Lady Pauline, head of Castle Redmont's Diplomatic Service. Her pretense that she was nervous about the following day, and her tact in refraining from pointing out Horace's gaffe, showed that she was already a diplomat of some skill.

Jenny, of course, would gravitate immediately to the castle kitchens, domain of Master Chubb, Redmont's head chef. He was a man renowned throughout the kingdom for the banquets served in the castle's massive dining hall. Jenny loved food and cooking, and her easygoing nature and unfailing good humor would make her an invaluable staff member in the turmoil of the castle kitchens.

Battleschool would be Horace's choice. Will glanced at his wardmate now, hungrily tucking into the roast turkey, ham and potatoes that he had heaped onto his plate. Horace was big for his age and a natural athlete. The chances that he would be refused were virtually nonexistent. Horace was exactly the type of recruit that Sir Rodney looked for in his warrior apprentices. Strong, athletic, fit. And, thought Will a trifle sourly, not too bright. Battleschool was the path to knighthood for boys like Horace—born commoners but with the physical abilities to serve as knights of the kingdom.

Which left Will. What would his choice be? More importantly, as Horace had pointed out, what Craftmaster would accept him as an apprentice?

For Choosing Day was the pivotal point in the life of the castle wards. They were orphan children raised by the generosity of Baron Arald, the Lord of Redmont Fief. For the most part, their parents had died in the service of the fief, and the Baron saw it as his responsibility to care for and raise the children of his former subjects— and to give them an opportunity to improve their station in life wherever possible.

Choosing Day provided that opportunity.

Each year, castle wards turning fifteen could apply to be apprenticed to the masters of the various crafts that served the castle and its people. Ordinarily, craft apprentices were selected by dint of their parents' occupations or influence with the Craftmasters. The castle wards usually had no such influence and this was their chance to win a future for themselves.

Those wards who weren't chosen, or for whom no openings could be found, would be assigned to farming families in the nearby village, providing farm labor to raise the crops and animals that fed the castle inhabitants. It was rare for this to happen, Will knew. The Baron and his Craftmasters usually went out of their way to fit the wards into one craft or another. But it could happen and it was a fate he feared more than anything.

Horace caught his eye now and gave him a smug smile.

"Still planning on applying for Battleschool, Will?" he asked through a mouthful of turkey and potatoes. "Better eat something then. You'll need to build yourself up a little."

He snorted with laughter and Will glowered at him. A few weeks previously, Horace had overheard Will confiding to Alyss that he desperately wanted to be selected for Battleschool, and he had made Will's life a misery ever since, pointing out on every possible occasion that Will's slight build was totally unsuited for the rigors of Battleschool training.

The fact that Horace was probably right only made matters worse. Where Horace was tall and muscular, Will was small and wiry. He was agile and fast and surprisingly strong, but he simply didn't have the size that he knew was required of Battleschool apprentices. He'd hoped against hope for the past few years that he would have what people called his "growing spurt" before the Choosing Day came around. But it had never happened and now the day was nearly here.

As Will said nothing, Horace sensed that he had scored a verbal hit. This was a rarity in their turbulent relationship. Over the past few years, he and Will had clashed repeatedly. Being the stronger of the two, Horace usually got the better of Will, although very occasionally Will's speed and agility allowed him to get in a surprise kick or a punch and then escape before Horace could catch him.

But while Horace generally had the best of their physical clashes, it was unusual for him to win any of their verbal encounters. Will's wit was as agile as the rest of him and he almost always managed to have the last word. In fact, it was this tendency that often led to trouble between them: Will was yet to learn that having the last word was not always a good idea. Horace decided now to press his advantage.

"You need muscles to get into Battleschool, Will. Real muscles," he said, glancing at the others around the table to see if anyone disagreed. The other wards, uncomfortable at the growing tension between the two boys, concentrated on their plates.

"Particularly between the ears," Will replied and, unfortunately, Jenny couldn't refrain from giggling. Horace's face flushed and he started to rise from his seat. But Will was quicker and he was already at the door before Horace could disentangle himself from his chair. He contented himself with hurling a final insult after his retreating wardmate.

"That's right! Run away, Will No-Name! You're a no-name and nobody will want you as an apprentice!"

In the anteroom outside, Will heard the parting sally and felt blood flush to his cheeks. It was the taunt he hated most, although he had tried never to let Horace know that, sensing that he would provide the bigger boy with a weapon if he did.

The truth was, nobody knew Will's second name. Nobody knew who his parents had been. Unlike his yearmates, who had lived in the fief before their parents had died and whose family histories were known, Will had appeared, virtually out of nowhere, as a newborn baby. He had been found, wrapped in a small blanket and placed in a basket, on the steps of the ward building fifteen years ago. A note had been attached to the blanket, reading simply:

His mother died in childbirth. His father died a hero.
Please care for him. His name is Will.

That year, there had been only one other ward. Alyss's father was a cavalry lieutenant who had died in the battle at Hackham Heath, when Morgarath's Wargal army had been defeated and driven back to the mountains. Alyss's mother, devastated by her loss, succumbed to a fever some weeks after giving birth. So there was plenty of room in the Ward for the unknown child, and Baron Arald was, at heart, a kindly man. Even though the circumstances were unusual, he had given permission for Will to be accepted as a ward of Castle Redmont. It seemed logical to assume that, if the note were true, Will's father had died in the war against Morgarath, and since Baron Arald had taken a leading part in that war, he felt duty bound to honor the unknown father's sacrifice.

So Will had become a Redmont ward, raised and educated by the Baron's generosity. As time passed, the others had gradually joined him and Alyss until there were five in their year group. But while the others had memories of their parents or, in Alyss's case, people who had known them and who could tell her about them, Will knew nothing of his past.

That was why he had invented the story that had sustained him throughout his childhood in the Ward. And, as the years passed and he added detail and color to the story, he eventually came to believe it himself.

His father, he knew, had died a hero's death. So it made sense to create a picture of him as a hero—a knight warrior in full armor, fighting against the Wargal hordes, cutting them down left and right until eventually he was overcome by sheer weight of numbers. Will had pictured the tall figure so often in his mind, seeing every detail of his armor and his equipment but never being able to visualize his face.

As a warrior, his father would expect him to follow in his footsteps. That was why selection for Battleschool was so important to Will. And that was why the more unlikely it became that he would be selected, the more desperately he clung to the hope that he might.

He exited from the Ward building into the darkened castle yard. The sun was long down and the torches placed every twenty meters or so on the castle walls shed a flickering, uneven light. He hesitated a moment. He would not return to the Ward and face Horace's continued taunts. To do so would only lead to another fight between them—a fight that Will knew that he would probably lose. George would probably try to analyze the situation for him, looking at both sides of the question and thoroughly confusing the issue. Alyss and Jenny might try to comfort him, he knew—Alyss particularly since they had grown up together. But at the moment he didn't want their sympathy and he couldn't face Horace's taunts, so he headed for the one place where he knew he could find solitude.

The huge fig tree growing close by the castle's central tower had often afforded him a haven. Heights held no fear for Will and he climbed smoothly into the tree, continuing long after another might have stopped, until he was in the lighter branches at the very top— branches that swayed and dipped under his weight. In the past, he had often escaped from Horace up here. The bigger boy couldn't match Will's speed in the tree and he was unwilling to follow as high as this. Will found a convenient fork and wedged himself in it, his body giving slightly to the movement of the tree as the branches swayed in the evening breeze. Below, the foreshortened figures of the watch made their rounds of the castle yard.

He heard the door of the Ward building open and, glancing down, saw Alyss emerge, looking around the yard for him in vain. The tall girl hesitated a few moments, then, seeming to shrug, turned back inside. The elongated rectangle of light that the open door threw across the yard was cut off as she closed the door softly behind her. Strange, he thought, how seldom people tend to look up.

There was a rustle of soft feathers and a barn owl landed on the next branch, its head swiveling, its huge eyes catching every last ray of the faint light. It studied him without concern, seeming to know it had nothing to fear from him. It was a hunter. A silent flyer. A ruler of the night.

"At least you know who you are," he said softly to the bird. It swiveled its head again, then launched itself off into the darkness, leaving him alone with his thoughts.

Gradually, as he sat there, the lights in the castle windows went out, one by one. The torches burnt down to smoldering husks and were replaced at midnight by the change of watch. Eventually, there was only one light left burning and that, he knew, was in the Baron's study, where the Lord of Redmont was still presumably at work, poring over reports and papers. The study was virtually level with Will's position in the tree and he could see the burly figure of the Baron seated at his desk. Finally Baron Arald rose, stretched and leaned forward to extinguish the lamp as he left the room, heading for his sleeping quarters on the floor above. Now the castle was asleep, except for the guards on the walls, who kept constant watch.

In less than nine hours, Will realized, he would face the Choosing. Silently, miserably, fearing the worst, he climbed down from the tree and made his way to his bed in the darkened boys' dormitory in the Ward.

2

"ALL RIGHT, CANDIDATES! THIS WAY! AND LOOK LIVELY!"

The speaker, or more correctly the shouter, was Martin, secretary to Baron Arald. As his voice echoed around the anteroom, the five wards rose uncertainly from the long wooden benches where they had been seated. Suddenly nervous now that the day had finally arrived, they began to shuffle forward, each one reluctant to be the first through the great ironbound door that Martin now held open for them.

"Come on, come on!" Martin bellowed impatiently. Alyss finally elected to lead the way, as Will had guessed she would. The others followed the willowy blonde girl. Now that someone had decided to lead, the rest of them were content to follow.

Will looked around curiously as he entered the Baron's study. He'd never been in this part of the castle before. This tower, containing the administrative section and the Baron's private apartments, was seldom visited by those of low rank—such as castle wards. The room was huge. The ceiling seemed to tower above him and the walls were constructed of massive stone blocks, fitted together with only the barest lines of mortar between them. On the eastern wall was a huge window space—open to the elements but with massive wooden shutters that could be closed in the event of bad weather. It was the same window he had seen through last night, he realized. Today, sunlight streamed in and fell on the huge oak table that Baron Arald used as a desk.

"Come on now! Stand in line, stand in line!" Martin seemed to be enjoying his moment of authority. The group shuffled slowly into line and he studied them, his mouth twisted in disapproval.

"In size place! Tallest this end!" He indicated the end where he wanted the tallest of the five to stand. Gradually, the group rearranged itself. Horace, of course, was the tallest. After him, Alyss took her position. Then George, half a head shorter than she and painfully thin. He stood in his usual stoop-shouldered posture. Will and Jenny hesitated. Jenny smiled at Will and gestured for him to go before her, even though she was possibly an inch taller than he was. That was typical of Jenny. She knew how Will agonized over the fact that he was the smallest of all the castle wards. As Will moved into the line, Martin's voice stopped him.

"Not you! The girl's next."

Jenny shrugged apologetically and moved into the place Martin had indicated. Will took the last place in the line, wishing Martin hadn't made his lack of height so apparent.

"Come on! Smarten up, smarten up! Let's see you at attention there," Martin continued, then broke off as a deep voice interrupted him.

"I don't believe that's totally necessary, Martin."

It was Baron Arald, who had entered, unobserved, by way of a smaller door behind his massive desk. Now it was Martin who brought himself to what he considered to be a position of attention, with his skinny elbows held out from his sides, his heels forced together so that his unmistakably bowed legs were widely separated at the knees, and his head thrown back.

Baron Arald raised his eyes to heaven. Sometimes his secretary's zeal on these occasions could be a little overwhelming. The Baron was a big man, broad in shoulder and waist and heavily muscled, as was necessary for a knight of the realm. It was well known, however, that Baron Arald was fond of his food and drink, so his considerable bulk was not totally attributable to muscle.

He had a short, neatly trimmed black beard that, like his hair, was beginning to show the traces of gray that went with his forty-two years. He had a strong jaw, a large nose and dark, piercing eyes under heavy brows. It was a powerful face, but not an unkind one, Will thought. There was a surprising hint of humor in those dark eyes. Will had noted it before, on the occasions when Arald had made his infrequent visits to the wards' quarters to see how their lessons and personal development were progressing.

"Sir!" Martin said at top volume, causing the Baron to wince slightly. "The candidates are assembled!"

"I can see that," Baron Arald replied patiently. "Perhaps you might be good enough to ask the Craftmasters to step in as well?"

"Sir!" Martin responded, making an attempt to click his heels together. As he was wearing shoes of a soft, pliable leather, the attempt was doomed to failure. He marched toward the main door of the study, all elbows and knees. Will was reminded of a rooster. As Martin laid his hand on the door handle, the Baron stopped him once more.

"Martin?" he said softly. As the secretary turned an inquiring look back at him, he continued in the same quiet tone, "Ask them. Don't bellow at them. Craftmasters don't like that."

"Yes, sir," said Martin, looking somewhat deflated. He opened the door and, making an obvious effort to speak in a lower tone, said, "Craftmasters. The Baron is ready now."

The Craftschool heads entered the room in no particular order of precedence. As a group, they admired and respected one another and so rarely stood on strict ceremonial procedure. Sir Rodney, head of the Battleschool, came first. Tall and broad-shouldered like the Baron, he wore the standard battledress of chain mail shirt under a white surcoat emblazoned with his own crest, a scarlet wolfshead. He had earned that crest as a young man, fighting the wolfships of the Skandian sea raiders who constantly harried the kingdom's east coast. He wore a sword belt and sword, of course. No knight would be seen in public without one. He was around the Baron's age, with blue eyes and a face that would have been remarkably handsome if it weren't for the massively broken nose. He sported an enormous mustache but, unlike the Baron, he had no beard.

Next came Ulf, the Horsemaster, responsible for the care and training of the castle's mighty battlehorses. He had keen brown eyes, strong, muscular forearms and heavy wrists. He wore a simple leather vest over his woolen shirt and leggings. Tall riding boots of soft leather reached up past his knees.

Lady Pauline followed Ulf. Slim, gray-haired and elegant, she had been a considerable beauty in her youth and still had the grace and style to turn men's heads. Lady Pauline, who had been awarded the title in her own right for her work in foreign policy for the kingdom, was head of the Diplomatic Service in Redmont. Baron Arald regarded her abilities highly and she was one of his close confidants and advisers. Arald often said that girls made the best recruits to the Diplomatic Service. They tended to be more subtle than boys, who gravitated naturally to Battleschool. And while boys constantly looked to physical means as the way of solving problems, girls could be depended on to use their wits.

It was perhaps only natural that Nigel, the Scribemaster, followed close behind Lady Pauline. They had been discussing matters of mutual interest while they waited for Martin to summon them. Nigel and Lady Pauline were close friends as well as professional colleagues. It was Nigel's trained scribes who prepared the official documents and communiqués that were so often delivered by Lady Pauline's diplomats. He also advised on the exact wording of such documents, having an extensive background in legal matters. Nigel was a small, wiry man with a quick, inquisitive face that reminded Will of a ferret. His hair was glossy black, his features were thin and his dark eyes never ceased roaming the room.

Master Chubb, the castle cook, came in last of all. Inevitably, he was a fat, round-bellied man, wearing a cook's white jacket and tall hat. He was known to have a terrible temper that could flare as quickly as oil spilled on a fire, and most of the wards treated him with considerable caution. Florid-faced and with red, rapidly receding hair, Master Chubb carried a wooden ladle with him wherever he went. It was an unofficial staff of office. It was also used quite often as an offensive weapon, landing with a resounding crack on the heads of careless, forgetful or slow-moving kitchen apprentices. Alone among the group, Jenny saw Chubb as something of a hero. It was her avowed intention to work for him and learn his skills, wooden ladle or no wooden ladle.

There were other Craftmasters, of course. The Armorer and the Blacksmith were two. But only those Craftmasters who currently had vacancies for new apprentices would be represented today.

"The Craftmasters are assembled, sir!" Martin said, his voice rising in volume. Martin seemed to equate volume and the importance of the occasion in direct proportion. Once again, the Baron raised his eyes to heaven.

"So I see," he said quietly, then added, in a more formal tone, "Good morning, Lady Pauline. Good morning, gentlemen."

They replied and the Baron turned to Martin once more. "Perhaps we might proceed?"

Martin nodded several times, consulted a sheaf of notes he held in one hand and marched to confront the line of candidates.

"Right, the Baron's waiting! The Baron's waiting! Who's first?"

Will, eyes down, shifting nervously from one foot to the other, suddenly had the strange sensation that someone was watching him. He looked up and actually started with surprise as he met the dark, unfathomable gaze of Halt, the Ranger.

Will hadn't seen him come into the room. He realized that the mysterious figure must have slipped in through a side door while everyone's attention was on the Craftmasters as they made their entrance. Now he stood behind the Baron's chair and slightly to one side, dressed in his usual brown and gray clothes and wrapped in his long, mottled gray and green Ranger's cloak. Halt was an unnerving person. He had a habit of coming up on you when you least expected it—and you never heard his approach. The superstitious villagers believed that Rangers practiced a form of magic that made them invisible to ordinary people. Will wasn't sure if he believed that—but he wasn't sure he disbelieved it either. He wondered why Halt was here today. He wasn't recognized as one of the Craftmasters and, as far as Will knew, he hadn't attended a Choosing session prior to this one.

Abruptly, Halt's gaze cut away from him and it was as if a light had been turned off. Will realized that Martin was talking once more. He noticed that the secretary had a habit of repeating statements, as if he were followed by his own personal echo.

"Now then, who's first? Who's first?"

The Baron sighed audibly. "Why don't we take the first in line?" he suggested in a reasonable tone, and Martin nodded several times.

"Of course, my lord. Of course. First in line, step forward and face the Baron."

After a moment's hesitation, Horace stepped forward out of the line and stood at attention. The Baron studied him for a few seconds.

"Name?" he said, and Horace answered, stumbling slightly over the correct method of address for the Baron.

"Horace Altman, sir . . . my lord."

"And do you have a preference, Horace?" the Baron asked, with the air of one who knows what the answer is going to be before hearing it.

"Battleschool, sir!" Horace said firmly.

The Baron nodded. He'd expected as much. He glanced at Rodney, who was studying the boy thoughtfully, assessing his suitability.

"Battlemaster?" the Baron said. Normally he would address Rodney by his first name, not his title. But this was a formal occasion. By the same token, Rodney would usually address the Baron as "sir." But on a day like today, "my lord" was the proper form.

The big knight stepped forward, his chain mail and spurs chinking slightly as he moved closer to Horace. He eyed the boy up and down, then moved behind him. Horace's head started to turn with him.

"Still," Sir Rodney said, and the boy ceased his movement, staring straight ahead.

"Looks strong enough, my lord, and I can always use new trainees." He rubbed one hand over his chin. "You ride, Horace Altman?"

A look of uncertainty crossed Horace's face as he realized this might be a hurdle to his selection. "Well . . . no, sir. I . . ."

He was about to add that castle wards had little chance to learn to ride, but Sir Rodney interrupted him.

"No matter. That can be taught." The big knight looked at the Baron and nodded. "Very well, my lord. I'll take him for Battleschool, subject to the usual three-month probationary period."

The Baron made a note on a sheet of paper before him and smiled briefly at the delighted, and very relieved, youth before him.

"Congratulations, Horace. Report to Battleschool tomorrow morning. Eight o'clock sharp."

"Yes, sir!" Horace replied, grinning widely. He turned to Sir Rodney and bowed slightly. "Thank you, sir!"

"Don't thank me yet," the knight replied cryptically. "You don't know what you're in for."

3

"Who's next then?" Martin was calling as Horace, grinning broadly, stepped back into the line. Alyss stepped forward gracefully, annoying Martin, who had wanted to nominate her as the next candidate.

"Alyss Mainwaring, my lord," she said in her quiet, level voice. Then, before she could be asked, she continued, "I request an appointment to the Diplomatic Service, please, my lord."

Arald smiled at the solemn-looking girl. She had an air of self-confidence and poise about her that would suit her well in the Service. He glanced at Lady Pauline.

"My lady?" he said.

She nodded her head several times. "I've already spoken to Alyss, my lord. I believe she will be an excellent candidate. Approved and accepted."

Alyss made a small bow of her head in the direction of the woman who would be her mentor. Will thought how alike they were—both tall and elegant in their movements, both grave in manner. He felt a small surge of pleasure for his oldest companion, knowing how much she had wanted this selection. Alyss stepped back in line and Martin, not to be forestalled this time, was already pointing to George.

"Right! You're next! You're next! Address the Baron."

George stepped forward. His mouth opened and closed several times, but nothing came out. The other wards watched in surprise. George, long regarded by them all as the official advocate for just about everything, was overcome with stage fright. He finally managed to say something in a low voice that nobody in the room could hear. Baron Arald leaned forward, one hand cupped behind his ear.

"I'm sorry, I didn't quite get that," he said.

George looked up at the Baron and, with an enormous effort, spoke in a just-audible voice. "G-George Carter, sir. Scribeschool, sir."

Martin, ever a stickler for the proprieties, drew breath to berate him for the truncated nature of his address. Before he could do so, and to everyone's evident relief, Baron Arald stepped in.

"Very well, Martin. Let it go." Martin looked a little aggrieved, but subsided. The Baron glanced at Nigel, his chief scribe and legal officer, one eyebrow raised in question.

"Acceptable, my lord," he said, adding, "I've seen some of George's work and he really does have a gift for calligraphy."

The Baron looked doubtful. "He's not the most forceful of speakers, though, is he, Scribemaster? That could be a problem if he has to offer legal counsel at any time in the future."

Nigel shrugged the objection aside. "I promise you, my lord, with proper training that sort of thing represents no problem. Absolutely no problem at all, my lord."

The Scribemaster folded his hands together into the wide sleeves of the monklike habit he wore as he warmed to his theme.

"I remember a boy who joined us some seven years back, rather like this one here, as a matter of fact. He had that same habit of mumbling to his shoes—but we soon showed him how to overcome it. Some of our most reluctant speakers have gone on to develop absolute eloquence, my lord, absolute eloquence."

The Baron drew breath to comment, but Nigel continued in his discourse.

"It may even surprise you to hear that as a boy, I myself suffered from a most terrible nervous stutter. Absolutely terrible, my lord. Could barely put two words together at a time."

"Hardly a problem now, I see," the Baron managed to put in dryly, and Nigel smiled, taking the point. He bowed to the Baron.

"Exactly, my lord. We'll soon help young George overcome his shyness. Nothing like the rough and tumble of Scribeschool for that. Absolutely."

The Baron smiled in spite of himself. The Scribeschool was a studious place where voices were rarely, if ever, raised and where logical, reasoned debate reigned supreme. Personally, on his visits to the place, he had found it mind-numbing in the extreme. Anything less like a rough and tumble atmosphere he could not imagine.

"I'll take your word for it," he replied, then to George he said, "Very well, George, request granted. Report to Scribeschool tomorrow."

George shuffled his feet awkwardly. "Mumble-mumble-mumble," he said and the Baron leaned forward again, frowning as he tried to make out the low-pitched words.

"What was that?" he asked.

George finally looked up and managed to whisper, "Thank you, my lord." He hurriedly shuffled back to the relative anonymity of the line.

"Oh," said the Baron, a little taken aback. "Think nothing of it. Now, next is. . . ."

Jenny was already stepping forward. Blond and pretty, she was also, it had to be admitted, a little on the chubby side. But the look suited her, and at any of the castle's social functions, she was a much sought-after dance partner with the boys in the castle, both her year-mates in the Ward and the sons of castle staff as well.

"Master Chubb, sir!" she said now, stepping forward right to the edge of the Baron's desk. The Baron looked into the round face, saw the eagerness shining there in the blue eyes, and couldn't help smiling at her.

"What about him?" he asked gently and she hesitated, realizing that, in her enthusiasm, she had breached the protocol of the Choosing.

"Oh! Your pardon, sir . . . my . . . Baron . . . your lordship," she hastily improvised, her tongue running away with her as she mangled the correct form of address.

"My lord!" Martin prompted her. Baron Arald looked at him, eyebrows raised.

"Yes, Martin?" he said. "What is it?"

Martin had the grace to look embarrassed. He knew that his master was intentionally misunderstanding his interruption. He took a deep breath, and said in an apologetic tone, "I . . . simply wanted to inform you that the candidate's name is Jennifer Dalby, sir."

The Baron nodded at him, and Martin, a devoted servant of the heavy bearded man, saw the look of approval in his lord's eyes.

"Thank you, Martin. Now, Jennifer Dalby . . ."

"Jenny, sir," said the irrepressible girl, and he shrugged resignedly.

"Jenny, then. I assume that you are applying to be apprenticed to Master Chubb?"

"Oh, yes, please, sir!" Jenny replied breathlessly, turning adoring eyes on the portly, red-haired cook. Chubb scowled thoughtfully and considered her.

"Mmmmm . . . could be, could be," he muttered, walking back and forth in front of her. She smiled winningly at him, but Chubb was beyond such feminine wiles.

"I'd work hard, sir," she told him earnestly.

"I know you would!" he replied with some spirit. "I'd make sure of it, girl. No slacking or lollygagging in my kitchen, let me tell you."

Fearing that her opportunity might be slipping away, Jenny played her trump card.

"I have the right shape for it," she said. Chubb had to agree that she was well rounded. Arald, not for the first time that morning, hid a smile.

"She has a point there, Chubb," he put in, and the cook turned to him in agreement.

"Shape is important, sir. All great cooks tend to be . . . rounded." He turned back to the girl, still considering. It was all very well for the others to accept their trainees in the wink of an eye, he thought. But cooking was something special.

"Tell me," he said to the eager girl, "what would you do with a turkey pie?"

Jenny smiled dazzlingly at him. "Eat it," she answered immediately.

Chubb rapped her on the head with the ladle he carried. "I meant what would you do about cooking it?" he asked.

Jenny hesitated, gathered her thoughts, then plunged into a lengthy technical description of how she would go about constructing such a masterpiece. The other four wards, the Baron, his Craftmasters and Martin listened in some awe, with absolutely no comprehension of what she was saying. Chubb, however, nodded several times as she spoke, interrupting as she detailed the rolling of the pastry.

"Nine times, you say?" he said curiously and Jenny nodded, sure of her ground.

"My mother always said: 'Eight times to make it flaky and once more for love,'" she said. Chubb nodded thoughtfully.

"Interesting. Interesting," he said, then, looking up at the Baron, he nodded. "I'll take her, my lord."

"What a surprise," the Baron said mildly, then added, "Very well, report to the kitchens in the morning, Jennifer."

"Jenny, sir," the girl corrected him again, her smile lighting up the room.

Baron Arald smiled. He glanced at the small group before him. "And that leaves us with one more candidate." He glanced at his list, then looked up to meet Will's agonized gaze, gesturing encouragement.

Will stepped forward, nervousness suddenly drying his throat so that his voice came out in barely a whisper.

"Will, sir. My name is Will."

4

"WILL? WILL WHO?" MARTIN ASKED IN EXASPERATION, FLICK-
ing through the sheets of paper with the candidates' details written
on them. He had only been the Baron's secretary for five years and
so knew nothing of Will's history. He realized now that there was no
family name on the boy's papers and, assuming he had let this mistake slip past, he was annoyed at himself.

"What's your family name, boy?" he asked severely. Will looked
at him, hesitating, hating this moment.

"I . . . don't have . . . ," he began, but mercifully the Baron inter-
ceded.

"Will is a special case, Martin," he said quietly, his look telling the
secretary to let the matter go. He turned back to Will, smiling encouragement.

"What school did you wish to apply for, Will?" he asked.

"Battleschool, please, my lord," Will replied, trying to sound confident in his choice. The Baron allowed a frown to crease his forehead
and Will felt his hopes sinking.

"Battleschool, Will? You don't think you're . . . a little on the small side?" the Baron asked gently. Will bit his lip. He had all but convinced himself that if he wanted this badly enough, if he believed in himself strongly enough, he would be accepted—in spite of his obvious shortcomings.

"I haven't had my growing spurt yet, sir," he said desperately. "Everybody says that."

The Baron rubbed his bearded chin with thumb and forefinger as he considered the boy before him. He glanced to his Battlemaster.

"Rodney?" he said.

The tall knight stepped forward, studied Will for a moment or two, then slowly shook his head.

"I'm afraid he's too small, my lord," he said. Will felt a cold hand clutch his heart.

"I'm stronger than I look, sir," he said. But the Battlemaster was unswayed by the plea. He glanced at the Baron, obviously not enjoying the situation, and shook his head.

"Any second choice, Will?" the Baron asked. His voice was gentle, even concerned.

Will hesitated for a long moment. He had never considered any other selection.

"Horseschool, sir?" he asked finally.

Horseschool trained and cared for the mighty battlehorses that the castle's knights rode. It was at least a link to Battleschool, Will thought. But Ulf, the Horsemaster, was shaking his head already, even before the Baron asked his opinion.

"I need apprentices, my lord," he said, "but this one's too small. He'd never control one of my battlehorses. They'd stomp him into the ground as soon as look at him."

Will could only see the Baron through a watery blur now. He fought desperately to keep the tears from sliding down his cheeks. That would be the ultimate humiliation: to be rejected from Bat-

tleschool and then to break down and cry like a baby in front of the
Baron, all the Craftmasters and his wardmates.

"What skills do you have, Will?" the Baron was asking him.

Will racked his brain. He wasn't good at lessons and languages,
as Alyss was. He couldn't form neat, perfect letters, the way George
did. Nor did he have Jenny's interest in cooking.

And he certainly didn't have Horace's muscles and strength.

"I'm a good climber, sir," he said finally, seeing that the Baron
was waiting for him to say something. It was a mistake, he realized
instantly. Chubb, the cook, glared at him angrily.

"He can climb, all right. I remember when he climbed up a drain-
pipe into my kitchen and stole a tray of sweetcakes that were cool-
ing on the windowsill."

Will's jaw dropped with the unfairness of it all. That had been
two years ago! He was a child then and it was a mere childish prank,
he wanted to say. But now the Scribemaster was talking too.

"And just this last spring he climbed up to our third-floor study
and turned two rabbits loose during one of our legal debates. Most
disruptive. Absolutely!"

"Rabbits, you say, Scribemaster?" said the Baron, and Nigel nodded emphatically.

"A male and a female rabbit, my lord, if you take my meaning?"
he replied. "Most disruptive indeed!"

Unseen by Will, the very serious Lady Pauline put one elegant
hand in front of her mouth. She might have been concealing a yawn.
But when she removed the hand, the corners of her mouth were
slightly uptilted still.

"Well, yes," said the Baron. "We all know how rabbits are."

"And, as I said, my lord, it was *spring*," Nigel went on, in case the
Baron had missed the point. Lady Pauline gave vent to an unladylike
cough. The Baron looked in her direction, in some surprise.

"I think we get the picture, Scribemaster," he said, then returned his gaze to the desperate figure who stood in front of him. Will kept his chin up and stared straight ahead. The Baron felt for the young lad in that moment. He could see the tears welling up in those lively brown eyes, held back only by an infinite determination. Willpower, he thought abstractedly, recognizing the play on the boy's name. He didn't enjoy putting the boy through all this, but it had to be done. He sighed inwardly.

"Is there any one of you who could use this boy?" he said.

Despite himself, Will allowed his head to turn and gaze pleadingly at the line of Craftmasters, praying that one of them would relent and accept him. One by one, silently, they shook their heads.

Surprisingly, it was the Ranger who broke the awful silence in the room.

"There is something you should know about this boy, my lord," he said. Will had never heard Halt speak before. His voice was deep and soft-spoken, with the slightest burr of a Hibernian accent still noticeable.

He stepped forward now and handed the Baron a sheet of paper, folded double. Arald unfolded it, studied the words written there and frowned.

"You're sure of this, Halt?" he said.

"Indeed, my lord."

The Baron carefully refolded the paper and placed it on his desk. He drummed his fingers thoughtfully on the desktop, then said:

"I'll have to think on this overnight."

Halt nodded and stepped back, seeming to fade into the background as he did so. Will stared anxiously at him, wondering what information the mysterious figure had passed on to the Baron. Like most people, Will had grown up believing that Rangers were people who were best avoided. They were a secretive, arcane group, shrouded in mystery and uncertainty, and that uncertainty led to fear.

Will didn't like the thought that Halt knew something about him—something that he felt was important enough to bring to the Baron's attention today, of all days. The sheet of paper lay there, tantalizingly close, yet impossibly far away.

He realized that there was movement around him and the Baron was speaking to the other people in the room.

"Congratulations to those who were selected here today. It's a big day for all of you, so you're free to have the rest of the day off and enjoy yourselves. The kitchens will provide a banquet for you in your quarters and for the rest of the day you have free run of the castle and the village.

"Tomorrow, you'll report to your new Craftmasters first thing in the morning. And if you'll take a tip from me, you'll make sure you're on time." He smiled at the other four, then addressed Will, with a hint of sympathy in his voice.

"Will, I'll let you know tomorrow what I've decided about you." He turned to Martin and gestured for him to show the new apprentices out. "Thank you, everyone," he said, and left the room through the door behind his desk.

The Craftmasters followed his lead, then Martin ushered the former wards to the door. They chatted together excitedly, relieved and delighted that they had been selected by the Craftmasters of their choice.

Will hung back behind the others, hesitating as he passed the desk where that sheet of paper still lay. He stared at it for a moment, as if somehow he could see through to the words written on the reverse side. Then he felt that same sensation that he had felt earlier, that someone was watching him. He looked up and found himself staring into the dark eyes of the Ranger, who remained behind the Baron's high-backed chair, almost invisible in that strange cloak of his.

Will shuddered in a sudden frisson of fear and hurried out of the room.

5

IT WAS LONG AFTER MIDNIGHT. THE FLICKERING TORCHES around the castle yard, already replaced once, had begun to burn low again. Will had watched patiently for hours, waiting for this moment—when the light was uncertain and the guards were yawning, in the last hour of their shift.

The day had been one of the worst he could remember. While his yearmates celebrated, enjoying their feast and then spending their time in lighthearted horseplay through the castle and the village, Will had slipped away to the silence of the forest, a kilometer or so from the castle walls. There, in the dim green coolness beneath the trees, he had spent the afternoon reflecting bitterly on the events of the Choosing, nursing the deep pain of disappointment and wondering what the Ranger's paper said.

As the long day wore on, and the shadows began to lengthen in the open fields beside the forest, he came to a decision.

He had to know what was on the paper. And he had to know tonight.

Once night fell, he made his way back to the castle, avoiding villagers and castle folk alike, and secreted himself in the branches of the fig tree again. On the way, he slipped unnoticed into the kitchens and helped himself to bread, cheese and apples. He munched moodily on these, barely tasting them, as the evening passed and the castle began to settle down for the night.

He observed the movements of the guards, getting a feeling for their timing as they went on their regular rounds. In addition to the guard troop, there was a sergeant on duty at the doorway of the tower that led to Baron Arald's quarters. But he was overweight and sleepy and there was little chance that he would pose a risk to Will. After all, he had no intention of using the door or the stairway.

Over the years, his insatiable curiosity, and a penchant for going places where he wasn't supposed to, had developed within him the skill of moving across seemingly open space without being seen.

As the wind stirred the upper branches of the trees, they created moving patterns in the moonlight—patterns that Will now used to great effect. He instinctively matched his movement to the rhythm of the trees, blending easily into the pattern of the yard, becoming part of it and so being concealed by it. In a way, the lack of obvious cover made his task a little easier. The fat sergeant didn't expect anyone to be moving across the open space of the yard. So, not expecting to see anyone, he failed to do so.

Breathless, Will flattened himself against the rough stone of the tower wall. The sergeant was barely five meters away and Will could hear his heavy breathing, but a small buttress in the wall hid him from the man's sight. He studied the wall in front of him, craning back to look up. The Baron's office window was a long way up, and farther around the tower. To reach it, he would have to climb up, then work his way across the face of the wall, to a spot beyond the point where the sergeant stood guard, then up again to the window. He licked his lips nervously. Unlike the smooth inner walls of the tower, the huge blocks of stone that comprised the tower's outer wall had large gaps between them. Climbing would be no problem. He'd have plenty of foot- and handholds all the way up. In some places, the stone would have been worn smooth by the weather over the years, he knew, and he'd have to go carefully. But he'd climbed all the other three towers at some time in the past and he expected no real difficulty with this one.

But this time, if he were seen, he wouldn't be able to pass it off as a prank. He would be climbing in the middle of the night to a part of the castle where he had no right to be. After all, the Baron didn't post guards on this tower for the fun of it. People were supposed to stay away unless they had business here.

He rubbed his hands together nervously. What could they do to him? He had already been passed over in the Choosing. Nobody wanted him. He was condemned to a life in the fields already. What could be worse than that?

But there was a nagging doubt at the back of his mind: He wasn't absolutely sure that he was condemned to that life. A faint spark of hope still remained. Perhaps the Baron would relent. Perhaps, if Will pleaded with him in the morning, and explained about his father and how important it was for him to be accepted for Battleschool, there was a very faint chance that his wish would be granted. And then, once he was accepted, he could show how his eagerness and dedication would make him a worthy student, until his growing spurt happened.

On the other hand, if he were caught in the next few minutes, not even that small chance would remain. He had no idea what they would do to him if he were caught, but he could be reasonably sure that it wouldn't involve being accepted into Battleschool.

He hesitated, needing some slight extra push to get him going. It was the fat sergeant who provided it. Will heard the heavy intake of breath, the shuffling of the man's studded boots against the flagstones as he gathered his equipment together, and he realized that the sergeant was about to make one of his irregular circuits of his beat. Usually, this entailed going a few meters around the tower to either side of the doorway, then returning to his original position. It was more for the purpose of staying awake than anything else, but Will realized that it would bring them face-to-face within the next few seconds if he didn't do something.

Quickly, easily, he began to swarm up the wall. He made the first five meters in a matter of seconds, spread out against the rough stone like a giant, four-legged spider. Then, hearing the heavy footsteps directly below him, he froze, clinging to the wall in case some slight noise might alert the sentry.

In fact, it seemed that the sergeant had heard something. He paused directly below the point where Will clung, peering into the night, trying to see past the dappled, moving shadows cast by the moon and the swaying trees. But, as Will had thought the night before, people seldom look up. The sergeant, eventually satisfied that he had heard nothing significant, continued to march slowly around the tower.

That was the chance Will needed. It also gave him the opportunity to move across the tower face so that he was directly below the window he wanted. Hands and feet finding purchase easily, he moved almost as fast as a man could walk, all the time going higher and higher up the tower wall.

At one point, he looked down and that was a mistake. Despite his good head for heights, his vision swam slightly as he saw how far he had come, and how far below him the hard flagstones of the castle yard were. The sergeant was coming back into view—a tiny figure when seen from this height. Will blinked the moment of vertigo away and continued to climb, perhaps a little more slowly and with a little more care than before.

There was a heart-stopping moment when, stretching his right foot to a new foothold, his left boot slipped on the weather-rounded edge of the massive building blocks, and he was left clinging by his hands alone as he desperately scrabbled for a foothold. Then he recovered and kept moving.

He felt a surge of relief as his hands finally closed over the stone window ledge and he heaved himself up and into the room, swinging his legs over the sill and dropping lightly inside.

The Baron's office was deserted, of course. The three-quarter moon streamed light in through the big window.

And there, on the desk where the Baron had left it, was the single sheet of paper that held the answer to Will's future. Nervously, he glanced around the room. The Baron's huge, high-backed chair stood like a sentry behind the desk. The few other pieces of furniture loomed dark and motionless. On one wall, a portrait of one of the Baron's ancestors glared down at him, accusingly.

He shook off these fanciful thoughts and crossed quickly to the desk, his soft boots making no noise on the bare boards of the floor. The sheet of paper, bright white with the reflected moonlight, was within reach. Just look at it, read it and go, he told himself. That was all he had to do. He stretched out a hand for it.

His fingers touched it.

And a hand shot out of nowhere and seized him by the wrist!

Will shouted aloud in fright. His heart leaped into his mouth and he found himself looking up into the cold eyes of Halt the Ranger.

Where had he come from? Will had been sure there had been nobody else in the room. And there had been no sound of a door opening. Then he remembered how the Ranger could wrap himself in that strange, mottled, gray-green cloak of his and seem to melt into the background, blending with the shadows until he was invisible.

Not that it mattered how Halt had done it. The real problem

was that he had caught Will, here in the Baron's office. And that meant the end to all Will's hopes.

"Thought you might try something like this," said the Ranger in a low voice.

Will, his heart pounding from the shock of the last few moments, said nothing. He hung his head in shame and despair.

"Do you have anything to say?" Halt asked him, and Will shook his head, unwilling to look up and meet that dark, penetrating gaze. Halt's next words confirmed Will's worst fears.

"Well, let's see what the Baron thinks about this," he said.

"Please, Halt! Not . . ." Then Will stopped. There was no excuse for what he had done and the least he could do was face his punishment like a man. Like a warrior. Like his father, he thought.

The Ranger studied him for a moment. Will thought he saw a brief flicker of . . . recognition? Then the eyes darkened once more.

"What?" Halt said curtly. Will shook his head.

"Nothing."

The Ranger's grip was like iron around his wrist as he led Will out the door and onto the wide, curving staircase that led up to the Baron's living quarters. The sentries at the head of the stairs looked up in surprise at the sight of the grim-faced Ranger and the boy beside him. At a brief signal from Halt, they stood aside and opened the doors into the Baron's apartment.

The room was brightly lit and, for a moment, Will looked around in confusion. He was sure he had seen the lights go out on this floor while he waited and watched in the tree. Then he saw the heavy drapes across the window and understood. In contrast to the Baron's sparsely furnished working quarters below, this room was a comfortable clutter of settees, footstools, carpets, tapestries and armchairs. In one of these, Baron Arald sat, reading through a pile of reports.

He looked up from the page he was holding as Halt entered with his captive.

"So you were right," said the Baron, and Halt nodded.

"Just as I said, my lord. Came across the castle yard like a shadow. Dodged the sentry as if he wasn't there and came up the tower wall like a spider."

The Baron set the report down on a side table and leaned forward.

"He climbed the tower, you say?" he asked, a trifle incredulously.

"No rope. No ladder, my lord. Climbed it as easily as you get on your horse in the morning. Easier, in fact," Halt said, with just the ghost of a smile.

The Baron frowned. He was a little overweight and sometimes he needed help getting on his horse after a late night. He obviously wasn't amused by Halt's reminding him of the fact.

"Well now," he said, looking sternly at Will, "this is a serious matter."

Will said nothing. He wasn't sure if he should agree or disagree. Either course had its dangers. But he wished Halt hadn't put the Baron in a bad mood by referring to his weight. It certainly wouldn't make things any better for him.

"So, what shall we do with you, young Will?" the Baron continued. He rose from his chair and began to pace. Will looked up at him, trying to gauge his mood. The strong, bearded face told him nothing. The Baron stopped his pacing and fingered his beard thoughtfully.

"Tell me, young Will," he said, facing away from the miserable boy, "what would you do in my place? What would you do with a boy who broke into your office in the middle of the night and tried to steal an important document?"

"I wasn't stealing, my lord!" The denial burst from Will before he could contain it. The Baron turned to him, one eyebrow raised in apparent disbelief. Will continued weakly, "I just . . . wanted to see it, that's all."

"Perhaps so," said the Baron, that eyebrow still raised. "But you haven't answered my question. What would you do in my place?"

Will hung his head again. He could plead. He could apologize. He could ask for mercy. He could try to explain. But then he squared his shoulders and came to a decision. He had known the consequences of being caught. And he had chosen to take the risk. He had no right now to plead for forgiveness.

"My lord . . . ," he said, hesitantly, knowing that this was a decisive moment in his life. The Baron regarded him, still half turned from the window.

"Yes?" he said, and Will somehow found the resolve to go on.

"My lord, I don't know what I'd do in your place. I do know there is no excuse for my actions and I will accept whatever punishment you decide."

As he spoke, he raised his face to look the Baron in the eye. And in doing so, he caught the Baron's quick glance to Halt. There was something in that glance, he saw. Strangely, it was almost a look of approval, or agreement. Then it was gone.

"Any suggestions, Halt?" the Baron asked, in a carefully neutral tone.

Will looked at the Ranger now. His face was stern, as it always was. The grizzled gray beard and short hair made him seem even more disapproving, more ominous.

"Perhaps we should show him the paper he was so keen to see, my lord," he said, producing the single sheet from inside his sleeve.

The Baron allowed a smile to break through. "Not a bad idea," he said. "I suppose, in a way, it does spell out his punishment, doesn't it?"

Will glanced from one man to the other. There was something

going on here that he didn't understand. The Baron seemed to think that what he had just said was rather amusing. Halt, on the other hand, wasn't sharing in the fun.

"If you say so, my lord," he replied evenly. The Baron waved a hand at him impatiently.

"Take a joke, Halt! Take a joke! Well, go on and show him the paper."

The Ranger crossed the room and handed Will the sheet he had risked so much to see. His hand trembled as he took it. His punishment? But how had the Baron known he would deserve punishment before the actual event?

He realized that the Baron was watching him expectantly. Halt, as ever, was an impassive statue. Will unfolded the sheet and read the words Halt had written there.

> *The boy Will has the potential to be trained as a Ranger.*
> *I will accept him as my apprentice.*

6

WILL STARED AT THE WORDS ON THE PAPER IN UTTER CON-
fusion.

His first reaction was one of relief. He wasn't to be condemned
to a lifetime of farmwork. And he wasn't to be punished for his actions in the Baron's study. Then that initial sense of relief gave way
to a sudden, nagging doubt. He knew nothing about Rangers, beyond myth and superstition. He knew nothing about Halt—apart
from the fact that the grim, gray-cloaked figure had made him feel
nervous whenever he was around.

Now, it seemed, he was being assigned to spend all his time with
him. And he wasn't sure that he liked the idea at all.

He looked up at the two men. The Baron, he could see, was
smiling expectantly. Apparently, he felt that Will should greet his
decision as good news. He couldn't see Halt's face clearly. The deep
cowl of his cloak left his face in shadow.

The Baron's smile faded slightly. He appeared a little puzzled
by Will's reaction to the news—or rather, his lack of any visible reaction.

"Well, what do you say, Will?" he asked, in an encouraging tone.
Will drew a deep breath.

"Thank you, sir . . . my lord," he said uncertainly. What if the Baron's earlier joke about the note containing his punishment was more serious than he thought? Maybe being assigned to be Halt's apprentice was the worst punishment he could have chosen. But the Baron certainly didn't look as if he thought so. He seemed to be very pleased with the idea, and Will knew he wasn't an unkind man. The Baron gave a little sigh of pleasure as he lowered himself into an armchair. He looked up at the Ranger and gestured toward the door.

"Perhaps you might give us a few moments alone, Halt? I'd like to have a word with Will in private," he said. The Ranger bowed gravely.

"Certainly, my lord," he said, the voice coming from deep inside the cowl. He moved, silently as ever, past Will and out through the door that led to the corridor outside. The door closed behind him with barely a sound, and Will shivered. The man was uncanny!

"Sit down, Will." The Baron gestured to one of the low armchairs facing his own. Will sat nervously on the edge of it, as if poised for flight. The Baron noted his body language and sighed.

"You don't seem very pleased with my decision," he said, sounding disappointed. The reaction puzzled Will. He wouldn't have thought a powerful figure like the Baron would care one way or another what an insignificant ward would think about his decisions. He didn't know how to answer, so he sat in silence, until finally the Baron continued.

"Would you prefer to work as a farmhand?" he asked. He couldn't believe that a lively, energetic boy like this could possibly prefer such a dull, uneventful life, but maybe he was wrong. Will hurriedly reassured him on that score.

"No, sir!" he said hastily. The Baron made a small, questioning gesture with his hands.

"Well then, would you prefer that I punished you somehow for what you've done?"

Will started to speak, then realized that his answer might be insulting and stopped. The Baron gestured for him to continue.

"It's just that . . . I'm not sure you haven't, sir," he said. Then, noticing the frown that creased the Baron's forehead as he said the words, he hurried on: "I . . . I don't know much about Rangers, sir. And people say . . ."

He let the words trail off. It was obvious that the Baron held Halt in some esteem and Will didn't think it was politic for him to point out that ordinary people feared Rangers and thought they were warlocks. He saw that the Baron was nodding, and a look of understanding had replaced the perplexed expression he had been wearing.

"Of course. People say they're black magicians, don't they?" he agreed and Will nodded, not even realizing he was doing so. "Tell me, Will, do you find Halt to be a frightening person?"

"No, sir!" Will said hastily, then, as the Baron held his gaze, he reluctantly added, "Well . . . maybe a bit."

The Baron leaned back, steepling his fingers together. Now that he understood the reasons for the boy's reluctance, he berated himself mentally for not foreseeing them. After all, he had a better knowledge of the Ranger Corps than he could expect of a young boy just turned fifteen who was subjected to the usual superstitious mutterings of the castle staff.

"The Rangers are a mysterious group of people," he said. "But there's nothing about them to be frightened of—unless you're an enemy of the kingdom."

He could see that the boy was hanging on his every word, and he added, jokingly, "You're not an enemy of the kingdom, are you, Will?"

"No, sir!" Will said in sudden fright, and the Baron sighed again.

He hated it when people didn't realize he was joking. Unfortunately, as overlord of the castle, his words were treated with great seriousness by most people.

"All right, all right," he said reassuringly. "I know you're not. But believe me, I thought you'd be glad of this appointment—an adventurous lad like you should take to life as a Ranger like a duck to water. It's a big opportunity for you, Will." He paused, studying the boy closely, seeing that he was still uncertain about the whole matter. "Very few boys are chosen to be apprentice Rangers, you know. The opportunity only comes up on rare occasions."

Will nodded. But he still wasn't totally convinced. He thought he owed it to his dream to have one last attempt at Battleschool. After all, the Baron did seem to be in an uncommonly good mood this evening, in spite of the fact that Will had broken into his office.

"I wanted to be a warrior, sir," he said tentatively, but the Baron shook his head immediately.

"I'm afraid your talents lie in other directions. Halt knew that when he first saw you. That's why he asked for you."

"Oh," said Will. There wasn't much else he could say. He felt he should be reassured by all that the Baron had said and, to a certain degree, he was. But there was still so much uncertainty to it all, he thought.

"It's just that Halt seems to be so grim all the time," he said.

"He certainly doesn't have my sparkling sense of humor," the Baron agreed, then, as Will looked blankly at him, he muttered something under his breath.

Will wasn't sure what he'd done to upset him, so he thought it best to change the subject. "But . . . what does a Ranger actually do, my lord?" he asked. Once again, the Baron shook his head.

"That's for Halt to tell you himself. They're a quirky group and they don't like other people talking about them too much. Now, perhaps you should go back to your quarters and try to get some sleep. You're to report to Halt's cottage at six o'clock in the morning."

"Yes, my lord," Will said, rising from his uncomfortable perch on the edge of the chair. He wasn't sure if he was going to enjoy life as a Ranger's apprentice, but it appeared he had no choice in the matter. He bowed to the Baron, who nodded briefly in return, then he turned away for the door. The Baron's voice stopped him.

"Will? This time, use the stairs."

"Yes, my lord," he replied seriously, and was a little puzzled by the way the Baron rolled his eyes to the sky and muttered to himself again. This time, he could make out a few words. It was something about "jokes," he thought.

He let himself out through the door. The sentries were still on duty on the landing by the stairs, but Halt was gone.

Or at least, he appeared to be. With the Ranger, you could never be quite certain.

7

IT FELT STRANGE TO BE LEAVING THE CASTLE AFTER ALL these years. Will turned back at the bottom of the hill, his small bundle of belongings slung over his shoulder, and stared up at the massive walls.

Castle Redmont dominated the landscape. Built on top of a small hill, it was a massive, three-sided structure, facing roughly west and with a tower at each of the three corners. In the center, protected by the three curtain walls, were the castle yard and the Keep, a fourth tower that soared above the others and housed the Baron's official quarters and his private living apartments, along with those of his senior officers. The castle was built in ironstone—a rock that was almost indestructible and, in the low sun of early morning or late afternoon, seemed to glow with an inner red light. It was this characteristic that gave the castle its name—Redmont, or Red Mountain.

At the foot of the hill, and on the other side of the Tarbus River, lay Wensley Village, a cheerfully haphazard cluster of houses, with an inn and those craft shops necessary to meet the demands of day-to-day country life—a cooper, wheelwright, smithy and harness maker. The land around had been cleared for some distance, both to provide farmlands for the villagers to tend and to prevent enemies from being able to approach unseen. In times of danger, the villagers would drive their flocks across the wooden bridge that spanned the Tarbus, removing the center span behind them, and seek shelter behind the massive ironstone walls of the castle, protected by the Baron's soldiers and the knights trained in Redmont's Battleschool.

Halt's cottage lay some distance away from both castle and village, nestling under the shelter of the trees at the edge of the forest. The sun was just rising over the trees as Will made his way to the log cabin. A thin spiral of smoke was rising from the chimney, so Will reasoned that Halt was already up and about. He stepped up onto the verandah that ran the length of one side of the house, hesitated for a moment, then, taking a deep breath, he knocked firmly on the door.

"Come in," said a voice from inside. Will opened the door and went into the cottage.

It was small but surprisingly neat and comfortable-looking inside. He found himself in the main room, a combined living and dining area, with a small kitchen at one end, separated from the main area by a pine bench. There were comfortable chairs ranged around a fire, a well-scrubbed wooden table and pots and pans that gleamed from much polishing. There was even a vase of brightly colored wildflowers on the mantel shelf, and the early morning sun streamed cheerfully through a large window. Two other rooms led off the main room.

Halt sat in one of the chairs, his booted feet resting on the table.

"At least you're on time," he said gruffly. "Have you had your breakfast yet?"

"Yes, sir," said Will, staring in fascination at the Ranger. This was the first time he had ever seen Halt without his gray-green cloak and hood. The Ranger was wearing simple brown and gray woolen clothes and soft-looking leather boots. He was older than Will had realized. His hair and beard were short and dark, but peppered with steel gray flecks. They were both roughly trimmed and Will thought they looked as if Halt had cut them himself with his hunting knife.

The Ranger stood up. He was surprisingly small in build. That was something else that Will had never realized. The gray cloak had concealed a lot about Halt. He was slim and not at all tall. In fact he was considerably shorter than average height. But there was a sense of power and whipcord strength about him so that his lack of height and bulk didn't make him any less daunting a figure.

"Finished staring?" asked the Ranger suddenly.

Will jumped nervously. "Yes, sir! Sorry, sir!" he said.

Halt grunted. He pointed to one of the small rooms Will had noticed as he entered.

"That'll be your room. You can put your things in there."

He moved away to the woodstove in the kitchen area and Will hesitantly entered the room he had indicated. It was small but, like the rest of the cottage, it was also clean and comfortable-looking. A small bed lay alongside one wall. There was a wardrobe for clothes and a rough table with a washing basin and jug on it. There was also, Will noticed, another vase of freshly picked wildflowers adding a bright spot of color to the room. He put his small bundle of clothes and belongings on the bed and went back into the main room.

Halt was still busy by the stove, his back to Will. Will coughed apologetically to attract his attention. Halt continued to stir coffee into a pot on the stove.

Will coughed again.

"Got a cold, boy?" asked the Ranger, without turning around.

"Er . . . no, sir."

"Then why are you coughing?" asked Halt, turning around to face him.

Will hesitated. "Well, sir," he began uncertainly, "I just wanted to ask you . . . what does a Ranger actually *do?*"

"He doesn't ask pointless questions, boy!" said Halt. "He keeps his eyes and ears open and he looks and listens and eventually, if he hasn't got too much cotton wool between his ears, he learns!"

"Oh," said Will. "I see." He didn't, and even though he realized that this was probably no time to ask more questions, he couldn't help himself, repeating, a little rebelliously, "I just wondered what Rangers do, is all."

Halt caught the tone in his voice and turned to him, a strange gleam in his eye.

"Well then, I suppose I'd better tell you," he said. "What Rangers do, or more correctly, what Rangers' *apprentices* do, is the housework."

Will had a sinking feeling as the suspicion struck him that he'd made a tactical error. "The . . . housework?" he repeated. Halt nodded, looking distinctly pleased with himself.

"That's right. Take a look around." He paused, gesturing around the interior of the cabin for Will to do as he suggested, then continued, "See any servants?"

"No, sir," Will said slowly.

"No sir indeed!" Halt said. "Because this isn't a mighty castle with a staff of servants. This is a lowly cabin. And it has water to be fetched and firewood to be chopped and floors to be swept and rugs to be beaten. And who do you suppose might do all those things, boy?"

Will tried to think of some answer other than the one which now seemed inevitable. Nothing came to mind, so he finally said, in a defeated tone, "Would that be me, sir?"

"I believe it would be," the Ranger told him, then rattled off a list of instructions crisply. "Bucket there. Barrel outside the door. Water in the river. Ax in the lean-to, firewood behind the cabin.

Broom by the door and I believe you can probably see where the floor might be?"

"Yes, sir," said Will, beginning to roll up his sleeves. He'd noticed the water barrel as he approached, obviously holding the day's water supply for the cabin. He estimated that it would hold twenty or thirty buckets full. With a sigh, he realized he was going to have a busy morning.

As he walked outside, the empty bucket in one hand, he heard the Ranger say contentedly as he poured himself a mug of coffee and sat down again:

"I'd forgotten how much fun having an apprentice can be."

Will couldn't believe that such a small and seemingly neat cottage could generate so much cleaning and general maintenance. After he had filled the water barrel with fresh river water (thirty-one buckets full), he chopped wood from a stack of logs behind the cabin, piling the split firewood into a neat stack. He swept out the cabin, then, after Halt decided that the rug on the living room floor needed beating, he rolled it up, carried it outside and draped it over a rope slung between two trees, beating it savagely so that clouds of dust flew from it. From time to time, Halt leaned out the window to give him encouragement, which usually consisted of curt comments such as "You've missed a bit on the left side" or "Put some energy into it, boy."

When the rug had been replaced on the floor, Halt decided that several of his cooking pots didn't gleam with sufficient intensity.

"We'll have to give them a bit of a scouring," he said, more or less to himself. Will knew by now that this translated to "*You'll* have to give them a bit of a scouring." So, without a word, he took the pots to the river's edge and half filled them with water and fine sand, scouring and polishing the metal until it gleamed.

Halt, meanwhile, had moved to a canvas chair on the verandah, where he sat reading through a tall pile of what looked to be official communications. Passing by once or twice, Will noticed that several of the papers bore crests and coats of arms, while the vast majority were headed with a simple oakleaf design.

When Will returned from the riverbank, he held the pots up for Halt's inspection. The Ranger grimaced at his distorted reflection in the bright copper surface.

"Hmmm. Not bad. Can see my own face in it," he said, then added, without a hint of a smile, "May not be such a good thing."

Will said nothing. With anyone else he might have suspected it was a joke, but with Halt you simply couldn't tell. Halt studied him for a second or two, then his shoulders lifted slightly in a shrug and he gestured for Will to return the pots to the kitchen. Will was halfway through the door when he heard Halt behind him say:

"Hmmm. That's odd."

Thinking the Ranger might be talking to him, Will paused at the door.

"I beg your pardon?" he said suspiciously. Each time Halt had found a new chore for him to attend to, he had seemed to begin the instruction with a statement like "How unusual. The living room rug is full of dust." Or "I do believe the stove is in dire need of a new supply of firewood."

It was an affectation that Will had found more than a little annoying over the day, although Halt seemed to be quite fond of it. This time, however, it seemed that he had been genuinely musing to himself as he read through a new report—one of the oakleaf-crested ones, Will noted. Now, the Ranger looked up, a little surprised that Will had addressed him.

"What's that?" he said.

Will shrugged. "Sorry. When you said 'that's odd,' I thought you were talking to me."

Halt shook his head several times, still frowning at the report in his hand. "No, no," he said, a trifle distractedly. "I was just reading this . . ." His voice trailed away and he frowned thoughtfully. Will, his curiosity roused, waited expectantly.

"What is it?" he finally ventured to ask. As the Ranger turned those dark eyes on him, he instantly wished he hadn't. Halt regarded him for a second or two.

"Curious, are you?" he said at length, and when Will nodded uncomfortably, he went on in an unexpectedly milder tone. "Well, I suppose that's a good trait for a Ranger's apprentice. After all, that's why we tested you with that paper in the Baron's office."

"You tested me?" Will set the heavy copper kettle down by the door. "You *expected* me to try to see what it said?"

Halt nodded. "Would have been disappointed if you hadn't. Also, I wanted to see how you'd go about it." Then he held up a hand to forestall the torrent of questions that were about to tumble out of Will's mouth. "We'll discuss that later," he said, glancing meaningfully at the kettle and the other pots. Will stooped to retrieve them, and turned back to the house once more. But curiosity still burned in him and he turned to the Ranger again.

"So what does it say?" he asked, nodding toward the report. Again there was a silence as Halt regarded him, perhaps assessing him. Then he said:

"Lord Northolt is dead. Apparently killed by a bear last week while out hunting."

"Lord Northolt?" Will asked. The name was vaguely familiar to him, but he couldn't place it.

"Former supreme commander of the King's army," Halt told him, and Will nodded, as if he had known this. But, since Halt seemed to be answering his questions, he was emboldened to continue.

"What's so odd about it? After all, bears do kill people from time to time."

Halt nodded. "True. But I would have thought Cordom Fief was a little far west for bears. And I would have thought Northolt was too experienced a hunter to go after one alone." He shrugged, as if dismissing the thought. "But then again, life is full of surprises and people do make mistakes." He gestured toward the kitchen again, indicating that the conversation was over. "When you've put those away, you might like to clean out the fireplace," he said.

Will moved to do as he was told. But a few minutes later, as he walked past one of the windows to the large fireplace that took up most of one wall in the living room, he glanced out to see the Ranger tapping the report thoughtfully on his chin, his thoughts obviously a long way away.

8

SOMETIME LATE IN THE AFTERNOON, HALT FINALLY RAN OUT of jobs for Will. He looked around the cabin, noting the gleaming kitchen implements, the spotless fireplace, the thoroughly swept floor and totally dust-free rug. A stack of firewood lay beside the fireplace and another stack, cut and split into shorter lengths, filled the wicker basket beside the kitchen stove.

"Hmmm. Not bad," he said. "Not bad at all."

Will felt a surge of pleasure at the sparing praise, but before he could feel too pleased with himself, Halt added, "Can you cook, boy?"

"Cook, sir?" Will asked uncertainly. Halt raised his eyes to some unseen superior being.

"Why do young people invariably answer a question with another question?" he asked. Then, receiving no reply, he continued, "Yes, cook. Prepare food so that one might eat it. Make meals. I assume you do know what food is—what meals are?"

"Ye-es," Will answered, careful to take any questioning inflection out of the word.

"Well, as I told you this morning, this is no grand castle. If we want to eat food here, we have to cook food here," Halt told him.

There was that word *we* again, Will thought. Every time so far that Halt had said *we must*, it had seemed to translate to mean *you must*.

"I can't cook," Will admitted, and Halt clapped his hands and rubbed them together.

"Of course you can't! Most boys can't. So I'll have to show you how. Come on."

He led the way to the kitchen and introduced Will to the mysteries of cooking: peeling and chopping onions, choosing a piece of beef from the meat safe, trimming it and cutting it into neat cubes, then chopping vegetables, searing the beef in a sizzling pan, and finally adding a generous dash of red wine and some of what Halt called his "secret ingredients." The result was a savory-smelling stew, simmering on the top of the stove.

Now, as they waited for the dinner to be ready, they sat on the verandah in the early evening and talked quietly.

"The Rangers were founded over one hundred and fifty years ago, in King Herbert's reign. Do you know anything about him?" Halt looked sideways at the boy sitting beside him, tossing the question out quickly to see his response.

Will hesitated. He vaguely remembered the name from history lessons in the Ward, but he couldn't remember any details. Still, he decided he'd try to bluff his way through it. He didn't want to look too ignorant on his first day with his new master.

"Oh . . . yes," he said, "King Herbert. We learned about him."

"Really?" said the Ranger expansively. "Perhaps you could tell me a little about him?" He leaned back and crossed his legs, getting himself comfortable. Will cast about desperately in his memory, trying to remember even a shred of detail about King Herbert. He'd done . . . something, but what?

"He was . . ." He hesitated, pretending to gather his thoughts. "The king." That much he was sure of, and he glanced at Halt to see if he could stop now. Halt merely smiled and made a rolling gesture with his hand that meant *go on*.

"He was the king . . . a hundred and fifty years ago," Will said, trying to sound certain of his facts. The Ranger smiled at him, gesturing for him to continue yet again.

"Ummm . . . well, I seem to recall that he was the one who founded the Ranger Corps," he said hopefully, and Halt raised his eyebrows in mock surprise.

"Really? You recall that, do you?" he said, and Will had a horrible moment where he realized that Halt had merely said the Rangers were founded *during* his reign, not necessarily *by* him.

"Ahhh, well, when I say he founded the Rangers, I actually mean he was the king when the Ranger Corps was founded," he said.

"A hundred and fifty years ago?" Halt prompted.

Will nodded emphatically. "That's right."

"Well, that's remarkable, seeing how I just told you those facts a minute or so ago," the Ranger said, his eyebrows coming down like thunderclouds over his eyes. Will thought it might be better if he had said nothing. Finally, the Ranger said, in a milder tone: "Boy, if you don't know something, don't try to bluff your way through it. Simply tell me 'I don't know,' is that clear?"

"Yes, Halt," Will said, eyes downcast. There was a silence, then he said, "Halt?"

"Yes?"

"About King Herbert . . . I don't really know," Will admitted. The Ranger made a small snorting noise.

"Well, I never would have guessed," he said. "But I'm sure you'll remember when I tell you that he was the one who drove the northern clans back over the border into the Highlands?"

And, of course, the moment he mentioned it, Will did remember. King Herbert was known as the "Father of Modern Araluen." He had banded the fifty fiefs together into a powerful union to defeat the northern clans. Will could see a way to regain a little credit in Halt's eyes now. If he mentioned the "Father of Modern Araluen" title, maybe the Ranger would . . .

"He's sometimes known as the Father of Modern Araluen," Halt was saying, and Will realized he'd left it too late. "He created the union between the fifty fiefs that's still our structure today."

"I sort of remember that now," Will put in. He thought the addition of "sort of" helped it sound as if he wasn't just being wise after the event. Halt looked at him, one eyebrow raised, then continued.

"At the time, King Herbert felt that to remain safe, the kingdom needed an effective intelligence force."

"An intelligent force?" said Will.

"Not intelligent. *Intelligence*. Although it does help if your intelligence force is also intelligent. Intelligence is knowledge of what your enemies, or your potential enemies, are up to. What they're planning. What they're thinking. If you know that sort of thing in advance, you can usually come up with a plan to stop them. That's why he founded the Rangers—to keep the kingdom informed. To act as the eyes and ears of the kingdom."

"How do you do that?" Will asked, his interest aroused now. Halt noted the change in tone and a momentary gleam of approval touched his eyes.

"We keep our eyes and ears open. We patrol the kingdom—and beyond. We listen. We observe. We report back."

Will nodded to himself, thinking. Then he asked: "Is that the reason why you can make yourselves invisible?"

Again, the Ranger felt that moment of approval and satisfaction. But he made sure the boy didn't notice it.

"We can't make ourselves invisible," he said. "People just think we can. What we do is make ourselves very hard to see. It takes years of learning and practice to do it properly—but you already have some of the skills required."

Will looked up, surprised. "I do?"

"When you crossed the castle yard last night, you used the shadows and the movement of the wind to conceal yourself, didn't you?"

Will nodded. "Yes." He'd never met anyone before who actually understood his skill for moving without being seen. Halt continued.

"We use the same principles: to blend into the background. To use it to conceal us. To become part of it."

"I see," said Will slowly.

"The trick is to make sure that nobody else does," Halt told him. For a moment, Will thought the Ranger had made a joke. But when he looked up, Halt was as grim-faced as ever.

"How many Rangers are there?" he asked. Halt and the Baron had referred more than once to the Ranger Corps, but Will had only ever seen one—and that was Halt.

"King Herbert established the Corps at fifty. One for each of the fifty fiefdoms. I'm based here. My colleagues are based at the other forty-nine castles throughout the kingdom.

"In addition to providing intelligence about potential enemies, Rangers are the law keepers," said Halt. "We patrol the fiefdom assigned to us and make sure that the laws are being obeyed."

"I thought Baron Arald did that," Will put in. Halt shook his head.

"The Baron is a judge," he said. "People bring their complaints to him so he can settle them. Rangers enforce the law. We take the law out to the people. If a crime has been committed, we look for evidence. We're particularly suited to that role since people often don't realize we're around. We investigate to see who's responsible."

"What happens then?" Will asked. Halt gave a small shrug.

"Sometimes we report back to the baron of the fief and he'll have the person arrested and charged. Sometimes, if it's a matter of urgency, we just . . . deal with it."

"What do we do?" Will asked before he could stop himself. Halt gave him a long, considering look.

"Not too much if we've only been an apprentice for a few hours," he replied. "Those of us who've been Rangers for twenty years or more tend to know what to do without asking."

"Oh," said Will, suitably chastened. Halt continued.

"Then, in times of war, we act as special troops—guiding the armies, scouting before them, going behind enemy lines to cause the enemy grief and so on." He glanced down at the boy. "It's a bit more exciting than working on a farm."

Will nodded. Perhaps life as a Ranger's apprentice was going to have its appeal after all. "What sort of enemies?" he asked. After all, Castle Redmont had been at peace for as long as he could remember.

"Enemies from within and without," Halt told him. "People like the Skandian sea raiders—or Morgarath and his Wargals."

Will shivered, recalling some of the more lurid stories about Morgarath, the Lord of the Mountains of Rain and Night. Halt nodded somberly as he saw Will's reaction.

"Yes," he said, "Morgarath and his Wargals are definitely people to be worried about. That's why the Rangers keep an eye on them. We like to know if they're gathering, if they're getting ready for war."

"Still," said Will, as much to reassure himself as for any other reason, "the last time they attacked, the barons' armies made mincemeat out of them."

"That's true," Halt agreed. "But only because they'd been warned of the attack . . ." He paused and looked meaningfully at Will.

"By a Ranger?" the boy asked.

"Correct. It was a Ranger who brought word that Morgarath's Wargals were on their way . . . then led the cavalry across a secret ford so they could flank the enemy."

"It was a great victory," Will said.

"It certainly was. And all due to a Ranger's alertness and skill, and knowledge of back trails and secret paths."

"My father died in that battle," Will added in a quieter voice, and Halt cast a curious look at him.

"Is that so?" he said.

"He was a hero. A mighty knight," Will continued. The Ranger paused, almost as if he were deciding whether to say something or not. Then he simply replied:

"I wasn't aware of that."

Will was conscious of a sense of disappointment. For a moment, he'd had a feeling that Halt knew something about his father, that he could tell him the story of his heroic death. He shrugged to himself.

"That was why I was so keen to go to Battleschool," he said finally. "To follow in his footsteps."

"You have other talents," Halt told him, and Will remembered the Baron saying much the same thing to him the previous night.

"Halt . . . ," he said. The Ranger nodded for him to continue. "I was sort of wondering . . . the Baron said you chose me?"

Halt nodded again, saying nothing.

"And both of you say I have other qualities—qualities that make me suitable to be a Ranger's apprentice . . ."

"That's right," Halt said.

"Well . . . what are they?"

The Ranger leaned back, linking his hands behind his head.

"You're agile. That's good in a Ranger," he began. "And, as we've discussed, you can move quietly. That's very important. You're fast on your feet. And you're inquisitive . . ."

"Inquisitive? How do you mean?" asked Will. Halt looked at him sternly.

"Always asking questions. Always wanting to know answers," he explained. "That was why I had the Baron test you with that piece of paper."

"But when did you first notice me? I mean, when did you first think of selecting me?" Will wanted to know.

"Oh," said Halt, "I suppose it was when I watched you steal those cakes from Master Chubb's kitchen."

Will's jaw dropped open with amazement.

"You watched me? But that was ages ago!" He had a sudden thought. "Where were you?"

"In the kitchen," said Halt. "You were too busy to notice me when you came in."

Will shook his head in wonder. He had been sure there was nobody in the kitchen. Then he remembered once again how Halt, wrapped in his cloak, could become virtually invisible. There was more to being a Ranger, he realized, than how to cook and clean.

"I was impressed with your skill," said Halt. "But there was one thing that impressed me far more."

"What was that?" asked Will.

"Later, when Master Chubb questioned you, I saw you hesitate. You were going to deny having stolen the cakes. Then I saw you admit it. Remember? He hit you on the head with his wooden spoon."

Will grinned and rubbed his head thoughtfully. He could still hear the CRACK! made by the spoon hitting his head.

"I wondered if I shouldn't have lied," he admitted. Halt shook his head very slowly.

"Oh, no, Will. If you'd lied, you never would have become my apprentice." He stood up and stretched, turning to go indoors to the stew simmering on the stove.

"Now let's eat," he said.

9

HORACE DROPPED HIS PACK ON THE FLOOR OF THE DORMI-
tory and fell across his bed, groaning with relief.

Every muscle in his body ached. He had no idea that he could
feel so sore, so worn-out. He had no idea that there were so many
muscles in the human body that could feel this way. Not for the first
time, he wondered if he was going to get through the three years of
Battleschool training. He'd been a cadet for less than a week and already he was a total physical wreck.

When he'd applied for Battleschool, Horace had a vague notion
of glittering, armor-clad knights doing battle, while lesser folk stood
by and watched in awed admiration. Quite a few of those lesser folk,
in his mental picture, had been attractive girls—Jenny, his yearmate
in the Ward, had been prominent among them. To him, Battleschool
had been a place of glamour and adventure, and Battleschool cadets
were people that others looked up to and envied.

The reality was something else. So far, Battleschool cadets were
people who rose before the dawn and spent the hour before breakfast doing a severe course of physical training: running, lifting
weights, standing in lines of ten or more to lift and hold heavy logs
over their heads. Exhausted by all of this, they were then returned to

their quarters, where they had the opportunity to take a brief shower—the water was cold—before making sure the dormitory and ablutions block were absolutely spotless. Quarters inspection came after that and it was painstaking. Sir Karel, the wiry old knight who carried out the inspection, knew every trick in the book when it came to taking shortcuts in cleaning the dormitory, making your bed and stowing your kit. The slightest infringement on the part of one of the twenty boys in the dormitory would mean all their kit would be scattered across the floor, their beds turned over, the rubbish bins emptied on the floor, and they would have to turn to and start again—in the time when they should have been having breakfast.

As a consequence, new cadets only tried once to pull the wool over Sir Karel's eyes. Breakfast was nothing special. In fact, in Horace's opinion, it was downright basic. But if you missed it, it was a long, hard morning until the lunch hour, which, in keeping with the spartan life in Battleschool, was only twenty minutes long.

After breakfast, there were classes for two hours in military history, the theory of tactics and so on, then the cadets were usually required to run the obstacle course—a series of obstacles designed to test speed, agility, balance and strength. There was a minimum time standard for the course. It had to be completed in under five minutes, and any cadet who failed to do so was immediately sent back to the start to try again. It was rare that anyone completed the course without falling at least once, and the course was littered with mud pools, water hazards and pits filled with nameless but unpleasant matter whose origin Horace didn't want to even think about.

Lunch followed the obstacle course, but if you'd fallen during the run, you had to clean up before entering the mess hall—another of those famous cold showers—and that usually took half the time set aside for the meal break. As a consequence, Horace's overwhelming impressions of the first week of Battleschool were a combination of aching muscles and gnawing hunger.

There were more classes after lunch, then physical jerks in the castle yard under the eye of one of the senior-year cadets. Then the class would form up and perform close-order drill until the end of the school day, when they would have two hours to themselves, to clean and repair gear and prepare lessons for the following day's classes.

Unless, of course, someone had transgressed during the course of the day, or in some way caused displeasure to one of their instructors or observers. In which case, they would all be invited to load their packs with rocks and set out on a twelve-kilometer run along a course mapped out through the surrounding countryside. Invariably, the course was nowhere near any of the level roads or tracks in the area. It meant running through broken, uneven ground, up hills and across streams, through heavily overgrown thickets where hanging vines and thick underbrush would claw at you and try to pull you down.

Horace had just completed one such run. Earlier in the day, one of his classmates had been spotted in Tactics I, passing a note to a friend. Unfortunately, the note was not in the form of text but was an unflattering caricature of the long-nosed instructor who taught the class. Equally unfortunately, the boy possessed considerable skill as a cartoonist and the drawing was instantly recognizable.

As a result, Horace and his class had been invited to fill those packs and start running.

He'd gradually felt himself pulling away from the rest of the boys as they labored up the first hill. Even after a few days, the strict regime of the Battleschool was beginning to show results with Horace. He was fitter than he'd ever been in his life. Added to that was the fact that he had natural ability as an athlete. Though he was unaware of it, he ran with balance and grace, where the others seemed to struggle. As the run progressed, he found himself far in front of the others. He pounded on, head up and breathing evenly through his nostrils. So far, he hadn't had much chance to get to know his new classmates. He'd seen most of them around the castle or the village over the years, of course, but growing up in the Ward had tended to isolate him from the normal, day-to-day life of the castle and village. Ward children couldn't help but feel different from the others. And it was a feeling that the boys and girls with parents still living reciprocated.

The Choosing ceremony was peculiar to Ward members only. Horace was one of twenty new Battleschool recruits that year, the other nineteen coming through what was considered the normal process—parental influence, patronage or recommendation from their teachers. As a result, he was regarded as something of a cu-riosity, and the other boys had so far made no overtures of friendship or even much attempt to get to know him. Still, he thought, smiling with grim satisfaction, he had beaten them all in the run. None of the others were back yet. He'd shown them, all right.

The door at the end of the dormitory crashed back on its hinges and heavy boots sounded on the bare floorboards. Horace raised himself on one elbow and groaned inwardly.

Bryn, Alda and Jerome were marching toward him between the neat rows of perfectly made beds. They were second-year cadets and they seemed to have decided that their life's work was to make Hor-ace's life miserable. Quickly, he swung his legs over the side of the bed and stood up, but not quickly enough.

"What are you doing lying in bed?" Alda yelled at him. "Who told you it was lights out?"

Bryn and Jerome grinned. They enjoyed Alda's verbal sallies. They weren't anywhere near as original. But they made up for their lack of verbal invention with a heavy reliance on the physical side of things.

"Twenty push-ups!" Bryn ordered. "Now!"

Horace hesitated a moment. He was actually bigger than any of them. If it came to a confrontation, he was sure he could beat any one of them. But they were three. And besides, they had the authority of tradition behind them. As far as he knew, it was normal practice for second-year to treat first-year cadets like this, and he could imagine the scorn of his classmates if he were to complain to authority about it. Nobody likes a crybaby, he told himself as he began to drop to the ground. But Bryn had seen the hesitation and perhaps even the fleeting light of rebellion in his eyes.

"Thirty push-ups!" he snapped. "Do it now!"

His muscles protesting, Horace dropped full length to the floor and began the push-ups. Immediately, he felt a foot in the small of his back, bearing down on him as he tried to raise himself from the floor.

"Come on, Baby!" It was Jerome now. "Put a bit of effort into it!"

Horace struggled through a push-up. Jerome had developed the skill of maintaining just the right amount of pressure. Any more and Horace would never have been able to complete the push-up. But the second-year cadet also kept pressing down as Horace started back down again. That made the exercise all the harder. He had to maintain the same amount of upward pressure as he lowered himself, otherwise he would be driven hard against the floor. Groaning, he completed the first, then started another.

"Stop crying, Baby!" Alda yelled at him. Then he moved to Horace's bed.

"Didn't you make this bed this morning?" he yelled. Horace, struggling up again against the pressure of Jerome's foot, could only grunt in reply.

"What? What?" Alda bent so that his face was only centimeters away. "What's that, Baby? Speak up!"

"Yes . . . sir," Horace managed to whisper. Alda shook his head in an exaggerated movement.

"No sir, I think!" he said, standing upright again. "Look at this bed. It"s a pigsty!"

Naturally, the covers were a little rumpled where Horace had dropped across the bed. But it would have taken only a second or two to straighten them. Grinning, Bryn cottoned on to Alda's plan. He stepped forward and kicked the bed over on its side, spilling mattress, blankets and pillows across the floor. Alda joined in, kicking the blankets across the floor.

"Make the bed again!" he yelled. Then a light gleamed in his eye and he turned to the next bed in line, kicking it over as well, scattering the bedclothes and mattresses as he'd done to Horace's.

"Make them all again!" he yelled, delighted with his idea. Bryn joined him, grinning widely, as they tumbled the twenty beds, scattering blankets, pillows and mattresses around the room. Horace, struggling still through the thirty push-ups, gritted his teeth. Perspiration ran into his eyes, stinging them and blurring his vision.

"Crying, are you, Baby?" he heard Jerome yell. "Go home and cry to Mummy then!"

His foot shoved viciously into Horace's back, sending him sprawling on the floor.

"Baby doesn't have a mummy," Alda said. "Baby's a Ward brat. Mummy ran off with a riverboat sailor."

Jerome bent down to him again. "Is that right, Baby?" he hissed. "Did Mummy run away and leave you?"

"My mother is dead," Horace grated at them. Angrily, he began to rise, but Jerome's foot was on the back of his neck, thrusting his face against the hard boards. Horace gave up the attempt.

"Very sad," Alda said, and the other two laughed. "Now clean this mess up, Baby, or we'll have you run the course again."

Horace lay, exhausted, as the three older boys swaggered out of the room, tipping footlockers over as they went, spilling his roommates' belongings onto the floor. He closed his eyes as salt perspiration stung its way into them again.

"I hate this place," he said, his voice muffled by the rough planks of the floor.

10

⟨⟨⟨⟨⟨⟨⟨⟨⟨⟨⟨⟨⟨⟨⟨⟨⟨⟨⟨⟨⟨⟨⟩⟩⟩⟩⟩⟩⟩⟩⟩⟩⟩⟩⟩⟩⟩⟩⟩⟩⟩⟩⟩⟩

"TIME YOU LEARNED ABOUT THE WEAPONS YOU'LL BE USING," said Halt.

They had eaten breakfast well before sunup and Will had followed Halt into the forest. They'd walked for about half an hour, with the Ranger showing Will how to glide from one patch of shade to the next, as silently as possible. Will was a good student in the art of unseen movement, as Halt had already remarked, but he had a lot to learn before he reached Ranger standard. Still, Halt was pleased with his progress. The boy was keen to learn—particularly when it was a matter of field craft like this.

It was a slightly different matter when it came to the less exciting tasks like map reading and chart drawing. Will tended to skip over details that he saw as unimportant until Halt pointed out to him, with some acerbity, "You'd find these skills would become a little more important if you were planning a route for a company of heavy cavalry and forgot to mention that there's a stream in the way."

Now, they stopped in a clearing and Halt dropped a small bundle that had been concealed beneath his cloak.

Will regarded the bundle doubtfully. When he thought of weapons, he thought of swords and battleaxes and war maces—the weapons carried by knights. It was obvious that this small bundle contained none of those.

"What sort of weapons? Do we have swords?" Will asked, his eyes glued to the bundle.

"A Ranger's principal weapons are stealth and silence and his ability to avoid being seen," said Halt. "But if they fail, then you may have to fight."

"So then we have a sword?" Will said hopefully.

Halt knelt and unwrapped the bundle.

"No. Then we have a bow," he said and placed it at Will's feet.

Will's first reaction was one of disappointment. A bow was something people used for hunting, he thought. Everyone had bows. A bow was more a tool than a weapon. As a child, he had made his fair share of them himself, bending a springy tree branch into shape. Then, as Halt said nothing, he looked more closely at the bow. This, he realized, was no bent branch.

It was unlike any bow that Will had seen before. Most of the bow followed one long curve like a normal longbow, but then each tip curved back in the opposite direction. Will, like most of the people of the kingdom, was used to the standard longbow—which was one long piece of wood bent into a continuous curve. This one was a good deal shorter.

"It's called a recurve bow," said Halt, sensing his puzzlement. "You're not strong enough to handle a full longbow yet, so the double curve will give you extra arrow speed and power, with a lower draw weight. I learned how to make one from the Temujai."

"Who are the Temujai?" asked Will, looking up from the strange bow.

"Fierce fighting men from the east," said Halt. "And probably the world's finest archers."

"You fought against them?"

"Against them . . . and with them for a time," said Halt. "Stop asking so many questions."

Will glanced down at the bow in his hand again. Now that he was becoming used to its unusual shape, he could see that it was a beautifully made weapon. Several shaped strips of wood had been glued together, with their grains running in different directions. They were of differing thicknesses and it was this that achieved the double curve of the bow, as the different forces strained against each other, bending the limbs of the bow into a carefully planned pattern. Maybe, he thought, this really was a weapon, after all.

"Can I shoot it?" he asked.

Halt nodded. "If you feel that's a good idea, go ahead," he said.

Quickly, Will chose an arrow from the quiver that had been in the bundle alongside the bow and fitted it to the string. He pulled the arrow back with his thumb and forefinger, aimed at a tree trunk some twenty meters away and fired.

Whack!

The heavy bowstring slapped into the soft flesh on the inside of his arm, stinging like a whip. Will yelled with pain and dropped the bow as if it were red-hot.

Already, a thick red welt was forming on his arm. It throbbed painfully. Will had no idea where the arrow had gone. Nor did he care.

"That hurt!" he said, looking accusingly at the Ranger.

Halt shrugged.

"You're always in a hurry, youngster," he said. "That may teach you to wait a little next time."

He bent to the bundle and pulled out a long cuff made of stiff leather. He slid it onto Will's left arm so that it would protect him from the bowstring. Ruefully, Will noticed that Halt was wearing a similar cuff. Even more ruefully, he realized that he'd noticed this before, but never wondered about the reason for it.

"Now try it again," said Halt.

Will chose another arrow and placed it on the string. As he went to draw it back again, Halt stopped him.

"Not with the thumb and finger," he said. "Let the arrow rest between the first and second fingers on the string . . . like this."

He showed Will how the nock—the notch at the butt end of the arrow—actually clipped to the string and held the arrow in place. Then he demonstrated how to let the string rest on the first joint of the first, second and third fingers, with the first finger above the nock point and the others below it. Finally, he showed him how to allow the string to slip loose so that the arrow was released.

"That's better," he said and, as Will brought the arrow back, continued, "Try to use your back muscles, not just your arms. Feel as if you're pushing your shoulder blades together . . ."

Will tried it and the bow seemed to draw a little easier. He found he could hold it steadier than before.

He fired again. This time, he just missed the tree trunk he'd been aiming for.

"You need to practice," said Halt. "Put it down for now."

Carefully, Will laid the bow down on the ground. He was eager now to see what Halt would produce next from the bundle.

"These are a Ranger's knives," said Halt. He handed Will a double scabbard, like the one he wore on the left-hand side of his own belt.

Will took the double scabbard and examined it. The knives were set one above the other. The top knife was the shorter of the two. It had a thick, heavy grip made of a series of leather discs set one above the other. There was a brass crosspiece between the hilt and the blade and it had a matching brass pommel.

"Take it out," said Halt. "Do it carefully."

Will slid the short knife from the scabbard. It was an unusual shape. Narrow at the hilt, it tapered out sharply, becoming thicker and wider for three quarters of its length to form a broad blade with the weight concentrated toward the tip, then a steep reverse taper created a razor-sharp point. He looked curiously at Halt.

"It's for throwing," said the Ranger. "The extra width at the tip balances the weight of the hilt. And the combined weight of the two helps drive the knife home when you throw it. Watch."

His hand moved smoothly and swiftly to the broad-bladed knife at his own waist. He flicked it free from the scabbard and, in one smooth action, sent it spinning toward a nearby tree.

The knife thudded home into the wood with a satisfying *thock!* Will looked at Halt, impressed with the Ranger's skill and speed.

"How do you learn to do that?" he asked.

Halt looked at him. "Practice."

He gestured for Will to inspect the second knife.

This one was longer. The handle was the same leather disc construction, and there was a short, sturdy crosspiece. The blade was heavy and straight, razor-sharp on one side, thick and heavy on the other.

"This is in case your enemy gets to close quarters," said Halt. "Although if you're any sort of an archer, he never will. It's balanced for throwing, but you can also block a sword stroke with that blade. It's made by the finest steelsmiths in the kingdom. Look after it and keep it sharp."

"I will," the apprentice said softly, admiring the knife in his hands.

"It's similar to what the Skandians call a saxe knife," Halt told him. Will frowned at the unfamiliar name and Halt went on to explain further.

"It's both weapon and tool—a sea ax, originally. But over the years the words sort of slid together to become saxe. Mind you," he added, "the quality of the steel in ours is a long way superior to the Skandian ones."

Will studied the knife more closely, seeing the faint blue tint in the blade, feeling the perfect balance. With its leather and brass hilt, the knife might be plain and functional in appearance. But it was a fine weapon and, Will realized, far superior to the comparatively clumsy swords worn by castle Redmont's warriors.

Halt showed him how to strap the double scabbard to his belt so that his hand fell naturally to the knife hilts. "Now," he said, "all you have to do is learn to use them. And you know what that means, don't you?"

Will nodded his head, grinning.

"A lot of practice," he said.

11

⟨⟨⟨⟨⟨⟨⟨⟨⟨⟨⟨⟨⟨⟨⟨⟨⟨⟨⟨⟩⟩⟩⟩⟩⟩⟩⟩⟩⟩⟩⟩⟩⟩⟩⟩⟩⟩⟩

SIR RODNEY LEANED ON THE TIMBER FENCE SURROUNDING the practice area as he watched the new Battleschool cadets going through their weapons drill. He rubbed his chin thoughtfully, his eyes scanning the twenty new recruits, but always returning to one in particular—the broad-shouldered, tall boy from the Ward, whom Rodney had selected at the Choosing. He thought for a moment, searching for the boy's name.

Horace. That was it.

The drill was a standard format. Each boy, wearing a chain mail shirt and helmet and carrying a shield, stood before a padded hardwood post the height of a man. There was no point practicing sword work unless you were burdened with shield, helmet and armor, as would be the case in a battle, Rodney believed. He thought it was best that the boys became used to the restrictions of the armor and weight of the equipment right from the start.

In addition to shield, helmet and mail, each boy also held a drill sword issued by the armorer. The drill swords were made of wood and bore little resemblance to a real sword, aside from the leather-bound hilt and crosspiece on each. In fact, they were long batons, made of seasoned, hardened hickory. But they weighed much the same as a slender steel blade, and the hilts were weighted to approximate the heft and balance of a real sword.

Eventually, the recruits would progress to drilling with actual swords—albeit with blunted edges and points. But that was still some months away, by which time the less suitable recruits would have been weeded out. It was quite normal for at least a third of the Battleschool applicants to drop out of the harsh training in the first three months. Sometimes it was the boy's choice. For others, it was at the discretion of his instructors or, in extreme cases, Sir Rodney himself. Battleschool was harsh and standards were strict.

The practice yard rang with the thudding of wood against the thick, sun-hardened leather padding on the practice posts. At the head of the yard, drillmaster Sir Karel called the standard strokes that were being practiced.

Five third-year cadets, under the direction of Sir Morton, an assistant drill instructor, moved among the boys, attending to the detail of the basic sword strokes: correcting a wrong movement here, changing the angle of a stroke there, making sure another boy's shield wasn't dropping too far as he struck.

It was boring, repetitive work under the hot afternoon sun. But it was necessary. These were the basic moves by which these boys might well live or die at some later date and it was vital that they should be so totally ingrained as to be instinctive.

It was that thought that had Rodney watching Horace now. As Karel called the basic cadence, Rodney had noticed that Horace was adding an occasional stroke to the sequence, and yet managing to do so without falling behind in his timing.

Karel had just begun another sequence and Sir Rodney leaned forward attentively, his eyes fixed on Horace.

"Thrust! Side cut! Backhand side! Overhand!" called the drillmaster. "Overhead backhand!"

And there it was again! As Karel called for the overhead back-hand cut, Horace delivered it, but then almost instantly switched to a backhanded side cut as well, allowing the first cut to bounce off the post to prepare him instantly for the second. The stroke was delivered with such stunning speed and force that, in real combat, the result would have been devastating. His opponent's shield, raised to block the overhead cut, could never have responded quickly enough to protect uncovered ribs from the rapid side cut that followed. Rodney had become aware over the past few minutes that the trainee was adding these extra strokes to the routine. He had seen it first from the corner of his eye, noticing a slight variation in the strict pattern of the drill, a quick flicker of extra movement that was there and gone almost too quickly to be noticed.

"Rest!" called Karel now, and Rodney noted that, while most of the others let their weapons drop and stood flatfooted, Horace maintained his ready position, the sword tip slightly above waist height, moving on his toes in the break so as not to lose his own natural rhythm.

Apparently, someone else had noticed Horace's extra stroke as well. Sir Morton beckoned over one of the senior cadets and spoke to him, gesturing quickly toward Horace. The first-year trainee, his attention still focused on the training post that was his enemy, didn't see the exchange. He looked up, startled, as the senior cadet approached and called to him.

"You there! At post fourteen. What d'you think you're doing?"

The look on Horace's face was one of bewilderment—and worry. No first-year recruit enjoyed gaining the attention of any of the drillmasters or their assistants. They were all too conscious of that thirty percent attrition rate.

"Sir?" he said anxiously, not understanding the question. The senior cadet continued.

"You're not following the pattern. Follow Sir Karel's call, understand?"

Rodney, watching carefully, was convinced that Horace's bewilderment was genuine. The tall boy made a small movement of the shoulders, almost a shrug but not quite. He was at attention now, the sword resting over his right shoulder and the shield up in the parade position.

"Sir?" he said again, uncertainly. The senior cadet was getting angry now. He hadn't noticed Horace's extra moves himself and obviously assumed the younger boy was simply following a random sequence of his own devising. He leaned forward, his face only a few centimeters away from Horace's, and said, in a voice far too loud for that small amount of separation:

"Sir Karel calls the sequence he wants performed! You perform it! Understand?"

"Sir, I . . . did," Horace replied, very red in the face now. He knew it was a mistake to argue with an instructor, but he also knew that he had performed every one of the strokes Karel had called.

The senior cadet, Rodney saw, was now at a disadvantage. He hadn't actually seen what Horace had done. He covered his uncertainty with bluster. "Oh, you did, did you? Well, perhaps you might just repeat the last sequence for me. What sequence did Sir Karel call?"

Without hesitation, Horace replied. "Sequence five, sir: Thrust. Side cut. Backhand side. Overhand. Overhead backhand."

The senior cadet hesitated. He'd assumed that Horace had simply been in a dream, hacking away at the post any way he chose. But, as far as he could remember, Horace had just repeated the previous sequence perfectly. At least, he thought he had. The senior cadet wasn't altogether sure of the sequence himself by now, but the trainee had replied with no hesitation at all. He was conscious that all the

other trainees were watching with considerable interest. It was a natural reaction. Trainees always enjoyed seeing somebody else being berated for a mistake. It tended to draw attention away from their own
deficiencies.

"What's going on here, Paul?" Sir Morton, the assistant drillmaster, sounded none too pleased with all this discussion. He'd originally ordered the senior cadet to reprimand the trainee for lack of
attention. That reprimand should have been delivered by now and
the matter ended. Instead, the class was being disrupted. Senior
Cadet Paul came to attention.

"Sir, the trainee *says* he performed the sequence," he replied. Horace was about to reply to the implication obvious in the emphasis the
senior cadet placed on the word *says*. Then he thought better of it
and shut his mouth firmly.

"Just a moment." Paul and Sir Morton looked around, a little
surprised. They hadn't seen Sir Rodney approaching. Around them,
the other trainees also came to stiff attention. Sir Rodney was held
in awe by all members of Battleschool, particularly the newer ones.
Morton didn't quite come to attention but he straightened a little,
squaring his shoulders.

Horace bit his lip in an agony of concern. He could see the
prospect of dismissal from Battleschool looming before him. First, he
seemed to have alienated the three second-year cadets who were
making his life a misery. Then he had drawn the unwelcome attention of Senior Cadet Paul and Sir Morton. Now this—the Battlemaster himself. And to make matters worse, he had no idea what he
had done wrong. He searched his memory and he could distinctly remember performing the sequence as it had been called.

"Do you remember the sequence, Cadet Horace?" said the Battlemaster.

The cadet nodded emphatically, then, realizing that this wasn't regarded as an acceptable response to a question from a senior officer, he said:

"Yes, sir. Sequence five, sir."

That was the second time he had identified the sequence, Rodney noted. He would have been willing to bet that not one of the other cadets could have said which sequence from the drill manual they had just completed. He doubted that the senior cadets would have been any better informed. Sir Morton went to say something, but Rodney held up a hand to stop him.

"Perhaps you could repeat it for us now," he said, his stern voice giving no hint of the growing interest he was feeling in this recruit. He gestured to the practice post.

"Take your position. Calling the cadence . . . begin!"

Horace performed the sequence flawlessly, calling the strokes as he went.

"Thrust! Side cut! Backhand side! Overhand! Overhead backhand!"

The drill sword thudded into the leather padding in strict timing. The rhythm was perfect. The execution of the strokes was faultless. But this time, Rodney noticed, there was no additional stroke. The lightning-fast reverse side cut didn't appear. He thought he knew why. Horace was concentrating on getting the sequence correct this time. Previously, he had been acting instinctively.

Sir Karel, attracted by Sir Rodney's intervention into a standard drill session, strolled through the ranks of trainees standing by their practice posts. His eyebrows arched a question at Sir Rodney. As a senior knight, he was entitled to such informality. The Battlemaster held up his hand again. He didn't want anything to break Horace's attention right now. But he was glad Karel was here to witness what he was sure was about to happen.

"Again," he said, in the same stern voice and, once again, Horace went through the sequence. As he finished, Rodney's voice cracked like a whip:

"Again!"

And again Horace performed the fifth sequence. This time, as he finished, Rodney snapped: "Sequence three!"

"Thrust! Thrust! Backstep! Cross parry! Shield block! Side cut!" Horace called as he performed the moves.

Now Rodney could see that the boy was moving lightly on his toes, the sword a flickering tongue that danced out and in and across. And without realizing it, Horace was calling the cadence for the moves nearly half as quickly again as the drillmaster had been.

Karel caught Rodney's eye. He nodded appreciatively. But Rodney wasn't finished yet. Before Horace had time to think, he called the fifth sequence again and the boy responded.

"Thrust! Side cut! Backhand side! Overhand! Overhead backhand!"

"Backhand side!" snapped Sir Rodney instantly and, in response, almost of its own will, Horace's sword flickered in that extra, deadly move. Sir Rodney heard the small sounds of surprise from Morton and Karel. They realized the significance of what they had seen. Senior Cadet Paul, perhaps understandably, wasn't quite so fast to grasp it. As far as he was concerned, the trainee had responded to an extra order from the Battlemaster. He'd done it well, admittedly, and he certainly seemed to know which end of a sword was which. But that was all the cadet had seen.

"Rest!" Sir Rodney ordered, and Horace allowed the sword point to drop to the dust, hand on the pommel, standing feet apart with the sword hilt centered against his belt buckle, in the parade rest position.

"Now, Horace," said the Battlemaster quietly, "do you remember adding that backhand side cut to the sequence the first time?"

Horace frowned, then understanding dawned in his eyes. He wasn't sure, but now that the Battlemaster had prompted his memory, he thought that maybe he had.

"Uh . . . yes, sir. I think so. I'm sorry, sir. I didn't mean to. It just sort of . . . happened."

Rodney glanced quickly at his drillmasters. He could see they understood the significance of what had happened here. He nodded at them, passing a silent message that he wanted nothing made of this—yet.

"Well, no harm done. But pay attention for the rest of the period and just perform the strokes Sir Karel calls for, all right?"

Horace came to attention. "Yes, sir." He snapped his eyes toward the drillmaster. "Sorry, sir!" he added, and Karel dismissed the matter with a wave of his hand.

"Pay closer attention in future." Karel nodded to Sir Rodney, sensing that the Battlemaster wanted to be on his way. "Thank you, sir. Permission to continue?"

Sir Rodney nodded assent. "Carry on, drillmaster." He began to turn away, then, as if he'd remembered something else, he turned back, and added casually, "Oh, by the way, could I see you in my quarters after classes are dismissed this evening?"

"Of course, sir," said Karel, equally casually, knowing that Sir Rodney wanted to discuss this phenomenon, but didn't want Horace to be aware of his interest.

Sir Rodney strolled slowly back to the Battleschool headquarters. Behind him, he heard Karel's preparatory orders, then the repetitive *thud, thud, thud-thud-thud* of wood on leather padding began once more.

12

HALT EXAMINED THE TARGET WILL HAD BEEN SHOOTING AT, and nodded.

"Not bad at all," he said. "Your shooting is definitely improving."

Will couldn't help grinning. That was high praise indeed from Halt. Halt saw the expression and immediately added, "With more practice—a *lot* more practice—you might even achieve mediocrity."

Will wasn't absolutely sure what mediocrity was, but he sensed it wasn't good. The grin faded and Halt dismissed the subject with a wave of his hand.

"That's enough shooting for now. Let's go," he said and set off, striding down a narrow path through the forest.

"Where are we going?" Will asked, half running to keep up with the Ranger's longer strides.

Halt looked up at the trees above him.

"Why does this boy ask so many questions?" he asked the trees.

Naturally, they didn't answer.

They walked for an hour before they came to a small collection of buildings buried deep in the forest.

Will was aching to ask more questions. But he'd learned by now

that Halt wasn't going to answer them, so he held his tongue and
bided his time. Sooner or later, he knew, he'd learn why they'd
come here.

Halt led the way up to the largest of the ramshackle huts, then
stopped, signaling for Will to do likewise.

"Hullo, Old Bob!" he called.

Will heard someone moving inside the hut, then a wrinkled,
bent figure appeared in the doorway. His beard was long and matted and a dirty white color. He was almost completely bald. As he
moved toward them, grinning and nodding a greeting to Halt, Will
caught his breath. Old Bob smelled like a stable. And a none too
clean one at that.

"Morning to you, Ranger!" said Old Bob. "Who's this you've
brung to see me?"

He looked keenly at Will. The eyes were bright and very alert,
despite his dirty, unkempt appearance.

"This is Will, my new apprentice," said Halt. "Will, this is
Old Bob."

"Good morning, sir," said Will politely. The old man cackled.

"Calls me sir! Hear that, Ranger, calls me sir! Make a fine Ranger,
this one will!"

Will smiled at him. Dirty as he might be, there was something
likable about Old Bob—perhaps it was the fact that he seemed to be
in no way overawed by Halt. Will couldn't remember seeing anyone
speaking to the grim-faced Ranger in quite this familiar tone before. Halt grunted impatiently.

"Are they ready?" he asked. The old man cackled again and nodded several times.

"Ready they are indeed!" he said. "Step this way and see them."

He led them to the back of the hut, where a small paddock was fenced off. At the far side, there was a lean-to shed. Just a roof and supporting posts. No walls. Old Bob let out a piercing whistle that made Will jump.

"There they are, see?" he said, pointing to the lean-to.

Will looked and saw two small horses trotting across the yard to greet the old man. As they came closer, he realized that one was a horse, the other was a pony. But both were small, shaggy animals, nothing like the fierce, sleek battlehorses that the Baron and his knights rode to war.

The larger of the two trotted immediately to Halt's side. He patted its neck and handed it an apple from a bin close by the fence. The horse crunched it gratefully. Halt leaned forward and said a few words into its ear. The horse tossed its head and neighed, as if it were sharing some private joke with the Ranger.

The pony waited by Old Bob until he had given it an apple to crunch as well. Then it turned one large, intelligent eye on Will.

"This 'un's called Tug," said the old man. "He looks about your size, don't he?"

He passed the rope bridle to Will, who took it and looked into the horse's eyes. He was a shaggy little beast. His legs were short, but sturdy. His body was barrel shaped. His mane and tail were ragged and unbrushed. All in all, as horses went, he wasn't a very impressive sight, thought Will.

He'd always dreamt of the horse he would one day ride into battle: in those dreams, the horse was tall and majestic. It was fierce and jet black, combed and brushed until it shone like black armor.

This horse almost seemed to sense what he was thinking and butted its head gently against his shoulder.

I may not be very big, its eyes seemed to say, *but I might just surprise you.*

"Well," said Halt. "What do you think of him?" He was fondling the other horse's soft nose. They were obviously old friends. Will hesitated. He didn't want to offend anyone.

"He's sort of . . . small," he said finally.

"So are you," Halt pointed out. Will couldn't think of an answer to that. Old Bob wheezed with laughter.

"He ain't no battlehorse, are he, boy?" he asked.

"Well . . . no, he isn't," Will said awkwardly. He liked Bob and he felt any criticism of the pony might be taken personally. But Old Bob simply laughed again.

"But he'll run any of those fine fancy-looking battlehorses into the ground!" he said proudly. "He's a strong 'un, this 'un. He'll keep going all day, long after them fancy horses have laid down and died."

Will looked at the shaggy little animal doubtfully.

"I'm sure he will," he said politely.

Halt leaned against the paddock fence.

"Why don't you see?" he suggested. "You're fast on your feet. Turn him loose and see if you can capture him again."

Will sensed the challenge in the Ranger's voice. He dropped the rope bridle. The horse, as if realizing that this was some sort of test, skipped lightly away into the center of the small enclosure. Will ducked under the fence rails and walked softly toward the pony. He held out his hand invitingly. "Come on, boy," he said. "Stand still there."

He reached out his hand for the bridle and the little horse suddenly wheeled away. It shied to one side, then the other, then side-stepped neatly around Will and danced backward out of reach.

He tried again.

Again, the horse evaded him easily. Will was beginning to feel foolish. He advanced on the horse and it backed away, moving closer and closer to one of the corners. Then, just when Will thought he had it, it nimbly danced to one side and was away again.

Will lost his temper now and ran after it. The horse whinnied in amusement and romped easily out of his reach. It was enjoying this game.

And so it went. Will would approach, the horse would duck and dodge and escape. Even in the close confines of the small paddock, he couldn't catch it.

He stopped. He was conscious of the fact that Halt was watching him carefully. He thought for a moment or two. There must be a way to do it. He'd never catch a horse as light on its feet and fast-moving as this one. There must be another way . . .

His gaze fell on the bin of apples outside the fence. Quickly, he ducked under the rail and seized an apple. Then he went back into the paddock and stood stock-still, holding the apple out.

"Come on, boy," he said.

Tug's ears shot up. He liked apples. He also thought he liked this boy—he played this game well. Tossing his head approvingly, he trotted forward and took the apple delicately. Will seized hold of the bridle and the pony crunched the apple. If a horse could be said to look blissful, this one did.

Will looked up and saw Halt nodding approval.

"Well thought out," said the Ranger. Old Bob elbowed the gray-cloaked man in the ribs.

"Clever boy, that!" he cackled. "Clever *and* polite! That 'un'll make a good team with Tug, won't he?"

Will patted the shaggy neck and the pricked-up ears. He looked now at the old man.

"Why do you call him Tug?" he asked.

Instantly, Will's arm was nearly torn from its socket as the pony jerked its head back. Will staggered, then regained his balance. Old Bob's braying laugh rang out around the clearing.

"See if you can guess!" he said delightedly.

His laughter was infectious and Will couldn't help smiling himself. Halt glanced up at the sun, which was fast disappearing behind the trees that fringed Old Bob's clearing and the meadows beyond.

"Take him over to the lean-to and Bob can show you how to groom him and look after his tack," he said, then added to the old man, "We'll stay with you tonight, Bob, if that's not inconvenient?"

The old horse handler nodded his head in pleasure. "I'll be glad of the company, Ranger. Sometimes I spend so much time with the horses that I start to think I'm one myself." Unconsciously, he dipped a hand into the apple barrel and selected one, absentmindedly crunching into it—much as Tug had done a few minutes earlier. Halt watched him, one eyebrow raised.

"We might be just in time," he observed dryly. "Then, tomorrow, we'll see if Will can ride Tug as well as catch him," he said, guessing as he said it that his apprentice would get very little sleep that night.

He was right. Old Bob's tiny cabin had only two rooms, so after their supper, Halt stretched out on the floor by the fireplace and Will bedded down in the warm, clean straw of the barn, listening to the gentle whiffling sounds of the two horses. The moon rose and fell as he lay wide awake, wondering and worrying over what the next day might bring. Would he be able to ride Tug? He'd never ridden a horse. Would he fall off the minute he tried?

Would he be hurt? Worse still, would he embarrass himself? He liked Old Bob and he didn't want to look foolish in front of him. Nor in front of Halt, he realized, with a little surprise. He was still wondering when Halt's good opinion had come to mean so much to him when he finally fell asleep.

13

"So, you saw it. What did you think?" Sir Rodney asked. Karel reached across and poured himself another tankard from the jug of beer that was on the table between them. Rodney's quarters were simple enough—even spartan when it was remembered that he was head of the Battleschool. Battlemasters in other fiefs took advantage of the position to surround themselves with the trappings of luxury, but that wasn't Rodney's style. His room was simply furnished, with a pinewood table for a desk and six straight-backed pine chairs around it.

There was a fireplace in the corner, of course. Rodney might have preferred to live in a simple style, but that didn't mean he enjoyed discomfort, and winters in Castle Redmont were cold. Right now it was late summer and the thick stone walls of the castle buildings served to keep the interiors cool. When the cold weather came, those same thick walls would retain the heat of the fire. On one wall, a large bay window looked out over the Battleschool's drill field. Facing the window, on the opposite wall, was a doorway, screened by a thick curtain, leading to Rodney's sleeping quarters—a simple soldier's bed and more wooden furniture. It had been a little more ornate when his wife Antoinette was still alive, but she had died some years previously and the rooms were now unmistakably masculine in character, without any item in them that wasn't functional and with an absolute minimum of decoration.

"I saw it," Karel agreed. "Not sure that I believed it, but I saw it."

"You saw it only once," said Rodney. "He was doing it constantly throughout the session—and I'm convinced that he was doing it unconsciously."

"As fast as the one I saw?" Karel asked. Rodney nodded emphatically.

"If anything, faster. He was adding an extra stroke to the routines but staying in time with the call." He hesitated, then finally said what they were both thinking. "The boy is a natural."

Karel inclined his head thoughtfully. Based on what he'd seen, he wasn't prepared to dispute the fact. And the Battlemaster had been watching the boy for some time during the session, he knew. But naturals were few and far between. They were those unique people for whom the skill of swordplay moved into an entirely different dimension. It became not so much a skill as an instinct to them.

They were the ones who became the champions. The sword masters. Experienced warriors like Sir Rodney and Sir Karel were expert swordsmen, but naturals took the skill to a higher plane. It was as if for them, the sword in their hand became a true extension not just of their bodies, but of their personalities as well. The sword seemed to act in instant communion and harmony with the natural's mind, acting even faster than conscious thought. Naturals were possessed of unique skills in timing and balance and rhythm.

As such, they presented a heavy responsibility to those who were entrusted with their training. For those natural skills and abilities had to be carefully nurtured and developed in a long-term training program to allow the warrior, already highly proficient as a matter of course, to develop his true potential for genius.

"You're sure?" Karel said eventually and Rodney nodded again, his gaze out the window. In his mind he was seeing the boy training, seeing those extra flickers of lightning-fast movement.

"I'm sure," he said simply. "We'll have to let Wallace know that he'll have another pupil next semester."

Wallace was the sword master at the Redmont Battleschool. He was the one who had the responsibility for adding the final polish to the basic skills that Karel and the others taught. In the event of an outstanding trainee—as Horace obviously was—he would give them private instruction in advanced techniques. Karel curled his bottom lip thoughtfully as he thought about the time frame Rodney had suggested.

"Not until then?" he said. The next semester was almost three months away. "Why not get him started straightaway? From what I saw, he's already mastered the basic stuff." But Rodney shook his head.

"We haven't really assessed his personality yet," he said. "He seems a nice enough lad, but you never know. If he turns out to be a misfit of some kind, I don't want to give him the sort of advanced instruction that Wallace can provide."

Once he thought of it, Karel agreed with the Battlemaster. After all, if it should turn out that Horace had to be disqualified from Battleschool because of some other failing, it might be embarrassing, not to mention dangerous, if he were already on the road to being a highly trained swordsman. Disqualified trainees often reacted with resentment.

"And another thing," Rodney added. "Let's keep this to ourselves—and tell Morton the same. I don't want the boy hearing any word of this yet. It might make him cocky and that could be dangerous for him."

"That's true enough," Karel agreed. He finished the last of his beer in two quick drafts, set his tankard down on the table and stood. "Well, I'd better be getting along. I've got reports to finish."

"Who hasn't?" the Battlemaster said with some feeling, and the two old friends exchanged rueful grins. "I never knew there was so much paper involved in running a Battleschool." Karel snorted in derision.

"Sometimes I think we should forget the weapons training and just throw all the paper at the enemy—bury them in it."

He gave an informal salute—just touching one finger to his forehead—that was in keeping with his seniority. Then he turned and headed for the door. He paused as Rodney added one last point to their discussion.

"Keep an eye on the boy, of course," he said. "But don't let him become aware of it."

"Of course," Karel replied. "We don't want him to start thinking there's something special about him."

At that moment, there was no chance that Horace would think there was anything special about him—at least, not in any positive sense. What he did feel was that there was something about him that attracted trouble.

Word had gone around about the strange scene at the training ground. His classmates, not understanding what had happened, all assumed that Horace had somehow annoyed the Battlemaster and now waited for the inevitable retribution. They knew that the rule during the first semester was that, when one member of a class made a mistake, the entire class paid for it. As a result, the atmosphere in their dormitory had been strained, to say the least. Horace had finally made his way out of the room, intending to head for the river to escape the condemnation and blame he could feel from the others.

Unfortunately, when he did so, he walked straight into the waiting arms of Alda, Bryn and Jerome.

The three older boys had heard a garbled version of the scene at the practice yard. They assumed that Horace had been criticized for his sword work and decided to make him suffer for it.

However, they knew that their attentions would not necessarily meet with the approval of the Battleschool staff. Horace, as a newcomer, had no way of knowing that this sort of systematic bullying was totally disapproved of by Sir Rodney and the other instructors. Horace simply assumed that was the way things were supposed to be and, not knowing any better, went along with it, allowing himself to be bullied and insulted.

It was for this reason that the three second-year cadets marched Horace to the riverside, where he had been heading anyway, and away from the sight of instructors. Here, they made him wade thigh-deep into the river, then stand to attention.

"Baby can't use his sword properly," said Alda.

Bryn took up the refrain. "Baby made the Battlemaster angry. Baby doesn't belong in Battleschool. Babies shouldn't be given swords to play with."

"Baby should throw stones instead," Jerome concluded the sarcastic litany. "Pick up a stone, Baby."

Horace hesitated, then glanced around. The riverbed was full of stones and he bent to get one. As he did so, his sleeve and the upper part of his jacket became soaked.

"Not a small stone, Baby," Alda said, smiling evilly at him. "You're a big baby, so you need a big stone."

"A great big stone," Bryn added, indicating with his hands that he wanted Horace to pick up a large rock. Horace looked around him and saw several larger pieces in the crystal-clear water. He bent and retrieved one of them. In doing so, he made a mistake. The rock he chose was easy to lift under the water, but as he brought it above the surface, he grunted with the weight of it.

"Let's see it, Baby," Jerome said. "Hold it up."

Horace braced himself—the swiftly running current of the river made it difficult to keep his balance and hold the heavy rock at the same time—then he lifted it to chest height so his tormentors could see it.

"Right up, Baby," Alda commanded. "Right over your head."

Painfully, Horace obeyed. The rock was feeling heavier by the second, but he held it high above his head and the three boys were satisfied.

"That's good, Baby," Jerome said, and Horace, with a relieved sigh, began to let the rock down again.

"What are you doing?" demanded Jerome angrily. "I said that's good. So that's where I want the rock to stay."

Horace struggled and lifted the rock above his head once more, holding it at arm's length. Alda, Bryn and Jerome nodded their approval.

"Now you can stay there," Alda told him, "while you count to five hundred. Then you can go back to the dormitory."

"Start counting," Bryn ordered him, grinning at the idea.

"One, two, three . . . ," began Horace, but they all shouted at him almost immediately.

"Not so fast, Baby! Nice and slowly. Start again."

"One . . . two . . . three . . . ," Horace counted, and they nodded their approval.

"That's better. Now a nice slow count to five hundred and you can go," Alda told him.

"Don't try to fudge it, because we'll know," threatened Jerome. "And you'll be back here counting to one thousand."

Laughing among themselves, the three students headed back to their quarters. Horace remained in midstream, arms trembling with the weight of the rock, tears of frustration and humiliation filling his eyes. Once, he lost his balance and fell full length in the water. After that, his heavy, sodden clothing made it all the harder to hold the rock above his head, but he kept at it. He couldn't be sure that they weren't concealed somewhere, watching him, and if they were, they'd make him pay for disobeying their instructions.

If this was the way of things, then so be it, he thought. But he promised himself that, first chance he got, he was going to make somebody pay for the humiliation he was undergoing.

Much later, clothes soaked, arms aching and a deep feeling of resentment burning in his heart, he crept back to his quarters. He was too late for the evening meal, but he didn't care. He was too miserable to eat.

14

"WALK HIM AROUND A LITTLE," SAID HALT.

Will glanced back at the shaggy pony, who watched him with intelligent eyes.

"Come on, boy," he said, and pulled on the halter. Instantly, Tug braced his forelegs and refused to move. Will pulled harder on the rope, leaning back in his efforts to make the stubborn little pony move.

Old Bob cackled with laughter.

"He be stronger than you!" he said.

Will felt his ears reddening with embarrassment. He pulled harder. Tug twitched his ears and resisted. It was like trying to pull a house along.

"Don't look at him," Halt said softly. "Just take the rope and walk away from him. He'll follow."

Will tried it that way. He turned his back on Tug, seized the rope firmly and began walking. The pony trotted easily after him. Will looked at Halt and grinned. The Ranger nodded his head toward the far fence of the paddock. Will glanced across and saw a small saddle, placed across the top rail of the fence.

"Saddle him up," said the Ranger.

Tug clip-clopped docilely across to the fence. Will looped the reins around the fence rail and hefted the saddle across the pony's back. He bent down to fasten the girth straps of the saddle.

"Pull them good and tight!" Old Bob advised him.

Finally, the saddle was firmly in position. Will looked eagerly at Halt. "Can I ride him now?" he asked.

The Ranger stroked his uneven beard thoughtfully before he answered. "If you feel that's a good idea, go ahead," he said, finally.

Will hesitated for a moment. The phrase stirred a vague memory with him. But then eagerness overcame caution and he put one foot in the stirrup and swung himself nimbly onto the pony's back. Tug stood, unmoving.

"Get up!" Will said, drumming his heels against the pony's side.

For a moment, nothing happened. Then Will felt a small tremor of movement go through the pony's body.

Suddenly, Tug arched his muscular little back and shot straight into the air, all four feet leaving the ground at the same time. He twisted violently to one side, came down on his front legs and kicked his rear legs high into the sky. Will sailed neatly over the pony's ears, turned a complete somersault in the air and crashed on his back in the dirt. He picked himself up, rubbing his back.

Tug stood nearby, ears up, watching him intently.

Now, why did you go and do a silly thing like that? the eyes seemed to say.

Old Bob leaned against the fence, sides heaving with laughter. Will looked at Halt.

"What did I do wrong?" he asked. Halt ducked under the fence rails and walked across to where Tug stood watching the two of them expectantly. He handed the bridle back to Will, then laid one hand on his shoulder.

"Nothing, if this were an ordinary horse," he said. "But Tug has been trained as a Ranger horse—"

"What's the difference?" Will interrupted angrily, and Halt held his hand up for silence.

"The difference is, each Ranger horse has to be asked before a rider mounts him for the first time," said Halt. "They're trained that way so that they can never be stolen."

Will scratched his head. "I've never heard of such a thing!" he said.

Old Bob smiled as he walked forward. "Not too many folk have," he said. "That's why Ranger horses never get stolen."

"Well," said Will, "what do you say to a Ranger horse before you mount him?"

Halt shrugged. "It varies from horse to horse. Each one responds to a different request." He gestured toward the larger horse. "My horse, for example, responds to the words *permettez moi.*"

"*Permettez moi?*" Will echoed. "What sort of words are they?"

"They're Gallic. They mean, 'Will you allow me?' His parents came from Gallica, you see," Halt explained. Then he turned to Old Bob. "What are the words for Tug here, Bob?"

Bob screwed up his eyes, pretending that he couldn't remember. Then his face cleared.

"Oh, yes, I recall!" he said. "This 'un here, he needs to be asked, 'Do you mind?' afore you get on his back."

"Do you mind?" Will repeated, and Bob shook his head.

"Don't say it to me, youngster! Say it in the horse's ear!"

Feeling a little silly, and not at all sure that the others weren't having a joke at his expense, Will stepped forward and said softly in Tug's ear:

"Do you mind?"

Tug whinnied softly. Will looked doubtfully at the two men, and Bob nodded encouragement.

"Go on! Climb on now! Young Tug won't harm 'ee now."

Very carefully, Will swung himself onto the pony's shaggy back once again. His back still ached from the previous attempt. He sat there a moment. Nothing happened. Then, he tapped his heels gently into Tug's ribs.

"Come on, boy," he said softly.

Tug's ears twitched up and he stepped forward at an easy walk.

Still cautious, Will let him walk around the paddock once or twice, then tapped again with his heels. Tug broke into a gentle trot. Will moved easily to the rhythm of the horse's movement and Halt looked on approvingly. The boy was an instinctive rider.

The Ranger unclipped the short length of rope that held the paddock gate closed and swung the wide gate open.

"Take him out, Will," he called, "and see what he can really do!"

Obediently, Will turned the pony toward the gate and, as they passed through into the open ground beyond, tapped once more with his heels. He felt the muscular little body beneath him bunch momentarily, then Tug broke into a fast gallop.

The wind rushed past Will's ears as he leaned forward over the pony's neck, encouraging him to even greater speed. Tug's ears pricked upward in response and he went even faster than before.

He was like the wind. His short legs were a blur of motion as he carried the boy at full speed toward the edge of the trees. Gently, not sure how the pony would react, Will applied pressure to the left-hand rein.

Instantly, Tug veered to the left, racing away from the trees at an angle. Will kept the gentle pressure on the rein until Tug was headed once again back toward the paddock. Will gasped in amazement as he saw how far they had come. Halt and Old Bob were tiny figures in the distance now. But they grew rapidly larger as Tug flew over the rough grass toward them.

A fallen log loomed in front of them and, before Will could make any effort to avoid it, Tug had gathered himself, steadied and leaped over the obstacle. Will let out a shout of excitement and the pony whinnied briefly in reply.

They were almost back to the paddock now and Will pulled gently on both reins. Instantly, Tug slowed to a canter, then a trot, finally coming down to walking pace as Will maintained the pressure on the reins. He brought the pony to a standstill beside Halt. Tug tossed his shaggy head and whinnied again. Will leaned forward and patted the pony on the neck.

"He's terrific!" he said breathlessly. "He's as fast as the wind!"

Halt nodded gravely. "Perhaps not quite as fast as the wind," he said, "but he can certainly cover ground." He turned to the old man. "You've done well with him, Bob."

Old Bob ducked his head in appreciation and leaned forward to pat the shaggy little pony in his turn. He had spent his life breeding, training and preparing the Ranger Corps' horses and this one ranked among the best he'd seen.

"He'll keep that pace all day," he said fondly. "Run them fat battlehorses into the ground, this 'un will. Youngster rides him well, too, Ranger, don't 'e?"

Halt stroked his beard. "Not too badly," he said. Bob was scandalized.

"Not too badly? You're a hard man, Ranger! Youngster sat him light as a feather through that jump!" The old man looked up at Will, sitting astride the pony, and nodded in appreciation. " 'E don't saw away at them reins like some do, neither. Got a light touch with a horse's soft mouth, 'e 'as."

Will grinned at the old horse trainer's praise. He sneaked a quick look at Halt, but the Ranger was as grave-faced as ever.

He never smiles, Will thought to himself. He went to dismount, then stopped himself hurriedly.

"Is there anything I should say to him before I get off?"

Bob laughed aloud. "No, youngster. Once said and young Tug here will remember—as long as it's you who's riding him." Relieved, Will climbed down. He stood beside the pony and Tug shoved him affectionately with his head. Will glanced at the apple barrel.

"Could I give him another?" he asked.

Halt nodded. "Just one more," he said. "But don't go making a habit of it. He'll be too fat to run if you feed him all the time."

Tug snorted loudly. Apparently he and Halt were at odds over how many apples a pony should have in a day.

Will spent the rest of the day getting tips on riding technique from Old Bob, and learning how to look after and repair Tug's saddle and harness, as well as the finer points of caring for the little horse.

He brushed and curried the shaggy coat until it shone and Tug seemed to appreciate his efforts. Finally, worn-out, his arms aching with the effort, he had slumped to a seat on a hay bale. Which, of course, had to be the exact moment when Halt walked into the stable.

"Come along," he said. "No time to be lolling around doing nothing. We'd best get moving if we're to be home before dark."

And, so saying, he tossed a saddle across the back of his horse. Will didn't bother to protest that he hadn't been "lolling around," as the Ranger put it. For a start, he knew it would be no use. And secondly, he was excited by the fact that they would be riding back to Halt's little cottage by the edge of the forest. It seemed that the two horses were to become a permanent part of their establishment. He realized now that Halt's horse had obviously been so before and that the Ranger had only been waiting until Will had shown his ability to ride and to bond with Tug before reclaiming him from his temporary home in Old Bob's stable.

The horses whinnied to each other from time to time as they trotted back through the dim green forest, for all the world as if they were carrying on their own conversation. Will was bursting with questions he wanted to ask. But, by now, he was wary of chattering too much in the Ranger's presence.

Finally, he could contain himself no longer.

"Halt?" he said, experimentally.

The Ranger grunted. Will took that as a sign that he could continue speaking.

"What's your horse's name?" the boy asked.

Halt looked down at him. His horse was slightly larger than Tug, although nowhere near the size of the giant battlehorses kept in the Baron's stable.

"I believe it's Abelard," he said.

"Abelard?" Will repeated. "What kind of name is that?"

"It's Gallic," said the Ranger, obviously putting an end to the conversation.

They rode a few kilometers farther in silence. The sun was lowering over the trees now and their shadows were long and distorted on the ground in front of them. Will studied Tug's shadow. The pony seemed to have enormously long legs and a ridiculously short body. He wanted to call Halt's attention to it but thought that such a frivolous observation would not impress the Ranger. Instead, he summoned the courage to ask another question that had been occupying his thoughts for some days.

"Halt?" he said again.

The Ranger sighed briefly.

"What now?" he asked. His tone definitely did not encourage further conversation. However, Will pressed on.

"Remember you told me how a Ranger was responsible for Morgarath's defeat?"

"Mmmm," Halt grunted.

"Well, I was just wondering, what was the Ranger's name?" the boy asked.

"Names aren't important," Halt said. "I really can't remember."

"Was it you?" Will continued, sure that it was. Halt turned that level, unsmiling gaze on him again.

"I said, names aren't important," he repeated. There was a silence between them for some seconds, then the Ranger said: "Do you know what *is* important?"

Will shook his head.

"Supper is important!" said the Ranger. "And we'll be late for it if we don't hurry."

He clapped his heels into Abelard's side and the horse shot away like an arrow from Halt's own bow, leaving Will and Tug far behind in a matter of seconds.

Will touched Tug's sides with his own heels and the little pony raced off in pursuit of his bigger friend.

"Come on, Tug!" Will urged. "Let's show them how a real Ranger horse can run."

15

Will rode Tug slowly through the crowded fairground that had been set up outside the castle walls. All the villagers and inhabitants of the castle itself seemed to be out and he had to ride carefully to ensure that Tug didn't step on somebody's foot.

It was Harvest Day, the day when all the crops had been gathered and stored for the winter months ahead. After a hard month of harvesting, the Baron traditionally allowed his people a holiday. Every year, at this time, the traveling fair came to the castle and set up its booths and stalls. There were fire-eaters and jugglers, singers and storytellers. There were stalls where you could attempt to win prizes by throwing soft leather balls at pyramids made from bottle-shaped pieces of wood or by throwing hoops over squares. Will sometimes thought that the squares were perhaps just a little larger than the hoops that one was given to throw and he had never actually seen anyone win one of the prizes. But it was all fun and the Baron paid for it from his own purse.

Right now, however, Will was not concerned with the fair and its attractions. There would be time later in the day for that. At the moment, he was on his way to meet his former wardmates.

By tradition, all the Craftmasters gave their apprentices the day off on Harvest Day, even though they had taken no part in the actual harvest themselves. Will had been wondering for weeks whether or not Halt would conform to the practice. The Ranger seemed to take no notice of tradition and had his own way of doing things. But, two nights before, his anxiety had been settled. Halt had gruffly told him that he could have the holiday, adding that he would probably forget everything that he had learned in the past three months.

Those three months had been a time of constant practice with his bow and the knives that Halt had given him. Three months of stalking through the fields outside the castle, moving from one scant patch of cover to the next, trying to make his way unobserved by Halt's eagle eyes. Three months of riding and caring for Tug, of forming a special bond of friendship with the little pony.

That, he thought, had been the most enjoyable part of it all.

Now, he was ready for a holiday and ready to enjoy himself a little. Even the thought that Horace would be there couldn't dim the pleasure. Maybe, he thought, a few months' hard training in Battleschool had changed Horace's aggressive manner a little.

It was Jenny who had arranged the meeting for the holiday, encouraging the others to join her with the promise of a batch of fresh mince pies that she would bring from the kitchen. She was already one of Master Chubb's prize pupils and he boasted of her artistry to anyone who would listen—giving suitable emphasis to the vital role his training had played in developing her skill, of course.

Will's stomach grumbled with pleasure at the thought of those pies. He was starving, since he had intentionally gone without breakfast so as to leave room for them. Jenny's pies were already legendary in Castle Redmont.

He had arrived at the meeting point early, so he dismounted and led Tug into the shade of an apple tree. The little pony craned his head and looked wistfully at the apples on the branches, well out of his reach. Will grinned at him and scrambled quickly up the tree, picking an apple and handing it to the pony.

"That's all you get," he said. "You know what Halt says about eating too much."

Tug shook his head impatiently. That was still a matter of disagreement between him and the Ranger. Will looked around. There was no sign of the others, so he sat down in the shade of the tree, leaning his back against the knobby trunk to wait.

"Why, it's young Will, isn't it?" said a deep voice close behind him.

Will scrambled hastily to his feet and touched his forehead in a polite salute. It was Baron Arald himself, seated astride his giant battlehorse and accompanied by several of his senior knights.

"Yes, sir," said Will nervously. He wasn't used to being addressed by the Baron. "A happy Harvest Day to you, sir."

The Baron nodded in acknowledgment and leaned forward, slouching comfortably in his saddle. Will had to crane his neck to look up at him.

"I must say, young man, you look quite the part there," the Baron said. "I hardly saw you in that gray Ranger cloak. Has Halt been teaching you all his tricks already?"

Will glanced down at the gray and green mottled cloak that he was wearing. Halt had given it to him some weeks ago. He'd shown Will how the gray and green mottling broke up the shape of the wearer and helped him blend into the landscape. It was one of the reasons, he'd said, why Rangers could move unseen with such ease.

"It's the cloak, sir," Will said. "Halt calls it camouflage." The Baron nodded, obviously familiar with the term, which had been a new concept to Will.

"Just make sure you don't use it to steal more cakes," he said with mock severity, and Will shook his head hurriedly.

"Oh, no, sir!" he said immediately. "Halt told me that if I did anything like that, he'd tan the skin off my backsi—" He stopped awkwardly. He wasn't sure if *backside* was the sort of word you used in the presence of someone as exalted as a Baron.

The Baron nodded again, trying not to let a wide grin break through.

"I'm sure he did," he said. "And how are you getting on with Halt, Will? Are you enjoying learning to be a Ranger?"

Will paused. To be honest, he hadn't had time to think if he was enjoying himself or not. His days were too busy learning new skills, practicing with bow and knives and working with Tug. This was the first time in three months he'd had a moment to actually think about it.

"I suppose so," he said hesitantly. "Only . . ." His voice trailed off and the Baron looked at him more closely.

"Only what?" he prompted.

Will shifted from one foot to the other, wishing that his mouth didn't continually get him into these situations by talking too much. Words had a way of emerging before he'd really had time to consider whether he wanted to say them or not.

"Only . . . Halt never smiles at all," he went on awkwardly. "He's always so serious about things."

He had the impression that the Baron was suppressing another grin.

"Well," said Baron Arald, "being a Ranger is a serious business, you know. I'm sure Halt has impressed that on you."

"All the time," Will said ruefully and, this time, the Baron couldn't help smiling.

"Just pay attention to what he tells you, youngster," he said. "You're learning a very important job there."

"Yes, sir." Will was a little surprised to realize that he *did* agree with the Baron. Baron Arald reached forward to gather up his reins.

On an impulse, before the nobleman could ride away, Will stepped forward.

"Excuse me, sir," he said hesitantly, and the Baron turned back to him.

"Yes, Will?" he asked.

Will shuffled his feet again, then went on. "Sir, remember when our armies fought Morgarath?"

Baron Arald's cheerful face was clouded by a thoughtful frown. "I'll not forget that in a hurry, boy," he said. "What about it?"

"Sir, Halt tells me that a Ranger showed the cavalry a secret way across the Slipsunder, so they were able to attack the enemy's rear . . ."

"That's true," said Arald.

"I've been wondering, sir, what was the Ranger's name?" Will finished, feeling himself flush with his boldness.

"Didn't Halt tell you?" the Baron asked. Will shrugged his shoulders.

"He said names weren't important. He said supper was important, but not names."

"But you think names are important, in spite of what your master has told you?" said the Baron, seeming to frown again. Will gulped and went on.

"I think it was Halt himself, sir," he said. "And I wondered why he hadn't been decorated or honored for his skill."

The Baron thought for a moment, then spoke again.

"Well, you're right, Will," he said. "It was Halt. And I wanted to honor him for it, but he wouldn't allow me. He said that wasn't the Rangers' way."

"But . . . ," Will began in a perplexed tone, but the Baron's up-raised hand stopped him from speaking any further.

"You Rangers have your own ways, Will, as I'm sure you're learning. Sometimes other people don't understand them. Just listen to

Halt and do as he does and I'm sure you'll have an honorable life ahead of you."

"Yes, sir." Will saluted again as the Baron slapped his reins lightly on his horse's neck and turned him away toward the fairground.

"Now, enough of this," said the Baron. "We can't chatter all day. I'm off to the fair. Maybe this year I'll get a hoop over one of those damned squares!"

The Baron started to ride away. Then a thought seemed to strike him and he reined in for a second.

"Will," he called back.

"Yes, sir?"

"Don't tell Halt that I told you he led the cavalry. I don't want him angry at me."

16

JENNY, ALYSS AND GEORGE ARRIVED SHORTLY AFTER. AS SHE
had promised, Jenny was carrying a batch of fresh pies wrapped in a
red cloth. She laid them carefully on the ground under the apple
tree as the others crowded around. Even Alyss, usually so poised
and dignified, seemed anxious to get her hands on one of Jenny's
masterpieces.

"Come on!" George said. "I'm starving!"

Jenny shook her head. "We should wait for Horace," she said,
looking around for him but not seeing him in the passing crowds of
people.

"Oh, come on," George pleaded. "I've been slaving over a hot pe-
tition to the Baron all morning!"

Alyss rolled her eyes to heaven. "Perhaps we should start," she
said. "Otherwise he'll begin a legal argument and we'll be here all
day. We can always put a couple aside for Horace."

Will grinned. George was a different kettle of fish now to the shy,
stammering boy at the Choosing. Scribeschool obviously had caused
him to bloom. Jenny served out two pies each, setting two aside for
Horace.

"That'll do for starters," she said. The others eagerly tucked in and soon began to chorus their praise for the pies. Jenny's reputation was well founded.

"This," said George, standing above them and spreading his arms wide as he addressed an imaginary court, "cannot be described as a mere pie, your honor. To describe this as a pie would be a gross miscarriage of justice, the like of which this court has never seen before!"

Will turned to Alyss. "How long has he been like this?" he asked.

She smiled. "They all get this way with a few months' legal training. These days, the main problem with George is getting him to shut up."

"Oh, sit down, George," said Jenny, blushing at his praise but delighted nonetheless. "You are a complete idiot."

"Perhaps, my fair miss. But it is the sheer magic of these works of art that has turned my brain. These are not pies, these are symphonies!" He raised his remaining half pie to the others in a mock toast.

"I give you . . . Miss Jenny's symphony of pies!"

Alyss and Will, grinning at each other and at George, raised their own pies in response, and echoed the toast. Then all four apprentices burst out laughing.

It was a pity that Horace chose that precise moment to arrive. Alone among them, he was miserable in his new situation. The work was hard and unremitting and the discipline was unwavering. He had expected that, of course, and under normal circumstances he could have handled it. But being the focus for Bryn, Alda and Jerome's spite was making his life a nightmare—literally. The three second-year cadets would rouse him from his bed at all hours of the night, dragging him out to perform the most humiliating and exhausting tasks.

The lack of sleep and the worry of never knowing when they might appear to torment him further was causing him to fall behind in his classroom work. His roommates, sensing that if they showed any sympathy for him they might become targets along with him, had cast him adrift, so that he felt totally alone in his misery. The one thing he had always aspired to was rapidly becoming ashes in his mouth. He hated Battleschool, but he could see no way out of his predicament without embarrassing and humiliating himself even further.

Now, on the one day when he could escape from the restrictions and the tensions of Battleschool, he arrived to find his former ward-mates already busy at their feast, and he was angry and hurt that they hadn't bothered to wait for him. He had no idea that Jenny had set some of the pies aside for him. He assumed that she had divided them up already and that hurt more than anything. Of all of his for-mer wardmates, she was the one he felt closest to. Jenny was always cheerful, always friendly, always willing to listen to another's troubles. He realized that he had been looking forward to seeing her again today and now he felt that she had let him down.

He was predisposed to think badly of the others. Alyss had al-ways seemed to hold herself aloof from him, as if he weren't good enough for her, and Will had spent his time playing tricks on him, then running away and climbing into that immense tree where Hor-ace couldn't follow. At least, that was how Horace saw things in his current vulnerable state. He conveniently forgot the times he had cuffed Will over the ear, or held him in a headlock until the smaller boy was forced to cry, "Yield!"

As for George, Horace had never taken much notice of him. The thin boy was studious and devoted to his books and Horace had always considered him a pallid, uninteresting person. Now here he was performing for them while they laughed and ate the pies and left nothing for him and suddenly he hated them all.

"Well, this is very nice, isn't it?" he said bitterly, and they turned to him, the laughter dying on their faces. As was inevitable, Jenny was the first one to recover.

"Horace! You're here at last!" she said. She started toward him, but the cold look on his face stopped her.

"At last?" he said. "I'm a few minutes late and suddenly I'm here 'at last'? And just too late because you've already pigged out on all the pies."

Which was hardly fair to poor Jenny. Like most cooks, once she had prepared a meal, she had little interest in eating it. Her real pleasure lay in watching others enjoy the results of her work—and listening to their praise. Consequently, she hadn't had any of the pies. She turned back now to the two that she had covered in a napkin to keep for him.

"No, no," she said quickly. "There are still some left! Look!"

But Horace's pent-up anger prevented him from acting or speaking rationally. "Well," he said, in a voice heavy with sarcasm, "maybe I ought to come back later and give you time to finish them as well."

"Horace!" Tears sprang to Jenny's eyes. She had no idea what was wrong with Horace. All she knew was that her plan for a pleasant reunion with her old wardmates was falling in ruins.

George stepped forward now, peering curiously at Horace. The tall, thin boy cocked his head to one side, to study the apprentice warrior more closely—as if he were an exhibit or a piece of evidence in a law court.

"There's no call to be so unpleasant," he said reasonably. But reason wasn't what Horace wanted to hear. He shoved the other boy aside angrily.

"Get away from me," he said. "And mind how you talk to a warrior."

"You're not a warrior yet," Will told him scornfully. "You're still only an apprentice like the rest of us."

Jenny made a small gesture with her hands, urging Will to drop the matter. Horace, who was in the act of helping himself to the remaining pies, looked up slowly. He measured Will up and down for a second or two.

"Oho!" he said. "I see the apprentice spy is with us today!" He looked to see if the others were laughing at his wit. They weren't and it only served to make him more unpleasant.

"I suppose Halt is teaching you to slink around, spying on everyone, is he?" Horace stepped forward, without waiting for an answer, and fingered Will's mottled cloak sarcastically.

"What's this? Didn't you have enough dye to make it all one color?"

"It's a Ranger cloak," Will said quietly, holding down the anger that was building inside him.

Horace snorted scornfully, cramming half of one of the pies into his mouth and spraying crumbs as he did so.

"Don't be so unpleasant," George said. Horace rounded on the apprentice scribe, his face red.

"Watch your tongue, boy!" he snapped. "You're talking to a warrior, you know!"

"An apprentice warrior," Will repeated firmly, laying stress on the word *apprentice*.

Horace went redder and looked angrily between the two of them. Will tensed himself, sensing that the bigger boy was about to launch an attack. But there was something in Will's eyes and his ready stance that made Horace think twice about it. He had never seen that look of defiance before. In the past, if he'd threatened Will, he had always seen fear. This newfound confidence unsettled him a little.

Instead, he turned back to George and gave him a heavy shove in the chest.

"How's that for unpleasant?" he said as the tall, thin boy staggered back. George's arms windmilled as he tried to save himself from falling. Accidentally, he struck Tug a glancing blow on the side. The little pony, grazing peacefully, reared suddenly against his bridle.

"Steady, Tug," Will said, and Tug quieted immediately. But now Horace had noticed him for the first time. He stepped forward and looked more closely at the shaggy pony.

"What's this?" he asked in mock disbelief. "Has someone brought a big ugly dog to the party?"

Will clenched his fists. "He's my horse," he said quietly. He could put up with Horace sneering at him, but he wasn't going to stand by and see his horse insulted.

Horace let out a braying laugh.

"A horse?" he said. "That's not a horse! In the Battleschool we ride real horses! Not shaggy dogs! Looks like he needs a good bath to me too!" He wrinkled his nose and pretended to sniff closer to Tug.

The pony glanced sideways at Will. *Who is this unpleasant clod?* his eyes seemed to say. Then Will, carefully hiding the wicked grin that was trying to show on his face, said casually:

"He's a Ranger horse. Only a Ranger can ride him."

Horace laughed again. "My grandmother could ride that shaggy dog!"

"Maybe she could," said Will, "but I'll bet you can't."

Before he'd even finished the challenge, Horace was untying the bridle. Tug looked at Will and the boy could have sworn the horse nodded slightly.

Horace swung himself easily up onto Tug's back. The pony stood, unmoving.

"Nothing to it!" Horace crowed. Then he dug his heels into Tug's sides. "Come on, doggy! Let's have a run."

Will saw the familiar, preparatory bunching of muscles in Tug's legs and body. Then the pony sprang into the air off all four feet, twisted violently, came down on his front legs and shot his hindquarters high into the air.

Horace flew like a bird for several seconds. Then he crashed flat on his back in the dust. George and Alyss looked on in delighted disbelief as the bully lay there for a second or two, stunned and winded. Jenny went to step forward to see if he was all right. Then her mouth set in a determined line and she stopped. Horace had asked for it, she thought.

There was a chance then, just a chance, that the whole incident might end there. But Will couldn't resist the temptation to have one last word.

"Maybe you'd better ask your grandmother if she'll teach you to ride," he said, straight-faced. George and Alyss managed to hide their smiles but, unfortunately, it was Jenny who couldn't stop the small giggle that escaped her.

In an instant, Horace scrambled to his feet, his face dark with rage. He looked around, saw a fallen branch from the apple tree and grabbed it, brandishing it over his head as he rushed at Tug.

"I'll show you, and your damned horse!" he yelled furiously, swinging the stick wildly at Tug. The pony danced sideways out of harm's way and, before Horace could strike again, Will was on him.

He landed on Horace's back and his weight and the force of his leap drove them both to the ground. They rolled there, grappling with each other, each trying to gain an advantage. Tug, alarmed to see his master in danger, whinnied nervously and reared.

One of Horace's wildly flailing arms caught Will a ringing blow across the ear. Then Will managed to get his right arm free and punched Horace hard in the nose.

Blood ran down the bigger boy's face. Will's arms were hard and well muscled after his three months' training with Halt. But Horace was being taught in a hard school too. He drove a fist into Will's stomach and Will gasped as the air was driven out of him.

Horace scrambled to his feet but Will, in a move that Halt had shown him, swung his own legs in a wide arc, cutting Horace's feet from under him and sending him tumbling again.

Always strike first, Halt had dinned into his brain in the hours they'd spent practicing unarmed combat. Now, as the other boy crashed to the ground again, Will dived upon him, trying to pin his arms beneath his knees.

Then Will felt an iron grip on the back of his collar and he was being hauled in the air, like a fish upon a hook, wriggling and protesting.

"What's going on here, you two hooligans?" said a loud, angry voice in his ear.

Will twisted around and realized that he was being held by Sir Rodney, the Battlemaster. And the big warrior looked extremely angry. Horace scrambled to his feet and stood at attention. Sir Rodney released Will's collar and the Ranger's apprentice dropped to the ground like a sack of potatoes. Then he too stood to attention.

"Two apprentices," said Sir Rodney angrily, "brawling like hooligans and spoiling the holiday! And, to make things worse, one of them is my *own* apprentice!"

Will and Horace shuffled their feet, eyes down, unable to meet the Battlemaster's furious gaze.

"All right, Horace, what's going on here?"

Horace shuffled his feet again and went red. He didn't answer. Sir Rodney looked at Will.

"All right, you, the Ranger's boy! What's this all about?"

Will hesitated. "Just a fight, sir," he mumbled.

"I can see that!" the Battlemaster shouted. "I'm not an idiot, you know!" He paused for a moment, waiting to see if either boy had anything further to add. They were both silent. Sir Rodney sighed in ex-asperation. Boys! If they weren't getting under your feet, they were fighting. And if they weren't fighting, they were stealing or breaking something.

"All right," he said finally. "The fight's over. Now shake hands and be done with it." He paused and, as neither boy made a move to shake hands, roared in his parade-ground voice:

"*Get on with it!*"

Galvanized into action, Will and Horace reluctantly shook hands. But as Will looked into Horace's eyes, he saw that the matter was far from settled.

We'll finish this another time, the angry look in Horace's eyes said.

Any time you like, the apprentice Ranger's eyes replied.

17

SNOW LAY THICK ON THE GROUND AS WILL AND HALT rode slowly home from the forest.

The situation between Will and Horace remained unresolved as time had passed. There had been little chance for the two boys to resume the argument, as their respective masters kept them busy and their paths seldom crossed.

Will had seen the apprentice warrior occasionally, but always at a distance. They hadn't spoken or even had the chance to acknowledge each other's presence. But the ill feeling was still there, Will knew, and one day it would come to a head.

Strangely, he found that the prospect didn't disturb him nearly as much as it might have a few months ago. It was not that he looked forward to renewing the fight with Horace, but he found he could face the idea with a certain amount of equanimity. He felt a deep satisfaction when he recalled that good, solid punch he had landed on Horace's nose. He also realized, with a slight sense of surprise, that the memory of the incident was made more enjoyable by the fact that it had happened in the presence of Jenny and—this was where the surprise lay—Alyss. Inconclusive as the event might have been, there was still a lot about it to set Will thinking and re-membering.

But not right now, he realized, as Halt's angry tone dragged him back to the present.

"Could we possibly continue with our tracking, or did you have something more important to do?" he inquired. Instantly, Will cast around, trying to see what Halt had pointed out. As they rode through the crisp, white snow, their horses' hooves making only the smallest of sounds, Halt had been pointing to disturbances in the even white cover. They were tracks left by animals and it was Will's task to identify them. He had sharp eyes and a good mind for the task. He normally enjoyed these tracking lessons, but now his at-tention had wandered and he had no idea where he was supposed to be looking.

"There," Halt said, his tone leaving no doubt that he didn't expect to have to repeat such things, as he pointed to the left. Will stood in his stirrups to see the disturbed snow more clearly.

"Rabbit," he said promptly. Halt turned to look sidelong at him.

"Rabbit?" he asked, and Will looked again, correcting himself al-most immediately.

"Rabbits," he said, stressing the plural ending. Halt insisted on accuracy.

"I should think so," Halt muttered at him. "After all, if they were Skandian tracks there, you'd need to be sure you knew how many there were."

"I suppose so," said Will, meekly.

"You suppose so!" Halt replied sarcastically. "Believe me, Will, there's a big difference between knowing there's one Skandian about and knowing that there are half a dozen."

Will nodded apologetically. One of the changes that had come over their relationship lately was the fact that Halt almost never referred to him as "boy" anymore. These days, it was always "Will." Will liked that. It made him feel that somehow he'd been accepted by the grim-faced Ranger. All the same, he did wish that Halt would smile once or twice when he said it.

Or even once.

Halt's low voice snapped him out of his daydreaming.

"So . . . rabbits. Is that all?"

Will looked again. In the disturbed snow, difficult to see, but there now that Halt had pointed it out to him, was another set of tracks.

"A stoat!" he said triumphantly and Halt nodded again.

"A stoat," he agreed. "But you should have known there was something else there, Will. Look at how deep those rabbit tracks are. It's obvious that something had frightened them. When you see a sign like that, it's a hint to look for something extra."

"I see," said Will. But Halt shook his head.

"No. All too often, you don't see, because you don't maintain your concentration. You'll have to work on that."

Will said nothing. He merely accepted the criticism. He'd learned by now that Halt didn't criticize without reason. And when there was reason, no amount of excuses could save him.

They rode on in silence. Will strained his eyes at the ground around them, looking for more tracks, more animal signs. They went another kilometer or so and were starting to see some of the familiar landmarks that told him he was close to their cottage when he saw something.

"Look!" he cried, pointing to a tumbled section of snow just off the path. "What's that?"

Halt turned to look. The tracks, if they were tracks, were like no

others that Will had seen so far. The Ranger urged his horse nearer
to the edge of the path and looked more closely.

"Hmmm," he said thoughtfully. "That's one I haven't shown you
yet. Don't see too many of them these days, so take a good look,
Will."

He swung easily down from the saddle and walked through the
knee-deep snow toward the disturbance. Will followed him.

"What is it?" the boy asked.

"Wild boar," said Halt briefly. "And a big one."

Will glanced nervously around them. He mightn't know what a
wild boar's tracks looked like in the snow, but he knew enough about
the creatures to know they were very, very dangerous.

Halt noticed the look and made a reassuring movement with
his hand.

"Relax," he said. "He's nowhere near us."

"Can you tell that from the tracks?" Will asked. He stared, fascinated, at the snow. The deep ruts and furrows had obviously been
made by a very large animal. And it looked as if it were a very large,
very *angry* animal.

"No," said Halt evenly. "I can tell it from our horses. If a boar that
size were anywhere in the district, those two would be snuffing and
pawing and whinnying so hard, we wouldn't be able to hear ourselves think."

"Oh," said Will, feeling a little foolish. He relaxed the grip that
he'd taken on his bow. However, in spite of the Ranger's assurances,
he couldn't resist taking just one more look around behind them.
And as he did so, his heart began pounding faster and faster.

The thick undergrowth on the other side of the track was moving, ever so slightly. Normally, he might have passed the movement
off as due to the breeze, but his training with Halt had heightened

his reasoning and his observation. At the moment, there was no breeze. Not the slightest breath.

But still, the bushes continued to move.

Will's hand went slowly to his quiver. Moving deliberately, so as to avoid startling the creature in the bushes, he drew an arrow and placed it on the string of his bow.

"Halt?" He tried to keep his voice down, but couldn't prevent it from quaking just a little. He wondered if his bow would stop a charging boar. He didn't think so.

Halt looked around, his gaze taking in the arrow nocked to Will's bowstring and noting the direction in which Will was looking.

"I hope you're not thinking of shooting the poor old farmer who's hiding behind those bushes," he said seriously. Yet he pitched his voice so that it carried clearly across the track to the thick clump of bushes on the other side.

Instantly, there was a scuffle of movement from the bush and Will heard a nervous voice crying out:

"Don't shoot, good sir! Please, don't shoot! It's only me!"

The bushes parted as a disheveled and frightened-looking old man stood up and hurried forward. His haste was his undoing, however, as his foot caught in a tangle of underbrush and he sprawled forward onto the snow. He scrambled awkwardly to his feet, hands held out, palms first, to show that he carried no weapons. As he came, he continued a nonstop babble of words:

"Only me, sir! No need for shootin', sir! Only me, I swear, and I'm no danger to the likes of you!"

He hurried forward into the center of the track, his eyes fixed on the bow in Will's hands and the gleaming, razor-sharp tip of the arrow. Slowly, Will released the tension on the string and lowered the bow as he took a closer look at the interloper. He was skinny in the extreme. Dressed in a ragged and dirty farmer's smock, he had long, awkward arms and legs and knobby elbows and knees. His beard was gray and matted and he was going bald on top of his head.

The man stopped a few meters from them and smiled nervously at the two cloaked figures.

"Only me," he repeated, one last time.

18

WILL COULDN'T HELP SMILING TO HIMSELF. ANYTHING LESS
like a ferocious, charging wild boar, he couldn't imagine.

"How did you know he was there?" he asked Halt in a soft voice.
The Ranger shrugged.

"Saw him a few minutes ago. You'll learn eventually to sense
when someone's watching you. Then you know to look for them."

Will shook his head in admiration. Halt's powers of observation were uncanny. No wonder people at the castle held him in such
awe!

"Now then," Halt said sternly, "why are you skulking there? Who
told you to spy on us?"

The old man rubbed his hands nervously together, his eyes flicking from Halt's forbidding expression to the arrow tip, lowered now
but still nocked to the string on Will's bow.

"Not spying, sir! No, no! Not spying. I heard you coming and
thought you was that monster porker coming back!"

Halt's eyebrows drew together. "You thought I was a wild boar?"
he asked. Again, the farmer shook his head.

"No. No. No. No," he gabbled. "Leastways, not once I'd saw you!
But then I wasn't sure who you might be. Could be bandits, like."

"What are you doing here?" Halt asked. "You're not a local, are you?"

The farmer, anxious to please, shook his head once again.

"Come from over Willowtree Creek, I do!" he said. "Been trailing that porker and hoping to find someone as could turn him into bacon."

Halt was suddenly vitally interested. He dropped the mock severe tone in which he had been talking.

"You've seen the boar, then?" he asked, and the farmer rubbed his hands again and looked fearfully around, as if nervous that the "porker" would appear from the trees any minute.

"Seen him. Heard him. Don't want to see him no more. He's a bad 'un, sir, mark my words."

Halt glanced back at the tracks again.

"He's certainly a big one, anyway," he mused.

"And evil, sir!" the farmer went on. "That 'un has a real devil of a temper in him. Why, he'd as soon tear up a man or a horse as have his breakfast, he would!"

"So what did you have in mind for him?" Halt asked, then added, "What's your name, by the way?"

The farmer bobbed his head and knuckled his forehead in salute.

"Peter, sir. Salt Peter, they calls me, on account of I likes a little salt on my meat, I do."

Halt nodded. "I'm sure you do," he said patiently. "But what were you hoping to do about this boar?"

Salt Peter scratched his head and looked a little lost. "Don't rightly know. Hoped maybe I'd find a soldier or a warrior or a knight to get rid of him. Or maybe a Ranger," he added as an afterthought.

Will grinned. Halt stood up from where he'd gone down on one knee to examine the tracks in the snow. He dusted a little snow from his knee and walked back to where Salt Peter stood, nervously shifting from one foot to another.

"Has he been causing a lot of trouble?" the Ranger asked, and the old farmer nodded rapidly, several times.

"That he has, sir! That he has! Killed three dogs. Tore up fields and fences, he has. And as near as anything killed my son-in-law when he tried to stop him. Like I said, sir, he's a bad 'un!"

Halt rubbed his chin thoughtfully.

"Hmmm," he said. "Well, there's no question that we'd better do something about it." He looked up at the sun, sitting low to the horizon in the western sky, then turned to Will. "How much daylight would you say is left, Will?"

Will studied the position of the sun. These days, Halt never missed an opportunity to teach him or question him or test his knowledge and developing skills. He knew it was best to consider carefully before making an answer. Halt preferred accurate replies, not fast ones.

"A little over an hour?" Will said. He saw Halt's eyebrows draw together in a frown and remembered that the Ranger also disliked being answered with a question.

"Are you asking me, or telling me?" Halt said. Will shook his head, annoyed at himself.

"A little over an hour," he replied more confidently and, this time, the Ranger nodded agreement.

"Correct." He turned to the old farmer again. "Very well, Salt Peter, I want you to take a message to Baron Arald."

"Baron Arald?" the farmer asked nervously. Halt frowned again.

"See what you've done?" he said to Will. "You've got him answering questions with questions now!"

"Sorry," Will mumbled, grinning in spite of himself. Halt shook his head and continued speaking to Salt Peter.

"That's right, Baron Arald. You'll find his castle a couple of kilometers along this track."

Salt Peter peered under one hand, looking along the track as if he could see the castle already. "A castle, you say?" he said, in a wondering voice. "I've never seen a castle!"

Halt sighed impatiently. Keeping this old chatterbox's mind on the subject was beginning to make him short-tempered. "That's right, a castle. Now, go to the guard at the gate . . ."

"Is it a big castle?" asked the old fellow.

"It's a *huge* castle!" Halt roared at him. Salt Peter bounded back in fright. He had a hurt look on his face.

"No need to bellow, young man," he said huffily. "I were only asking, is all."

"Well then, stop interrupting me," said the Ranger, "We're wasting time here. Now, are you listening?"

Salt Peter nodded.

"Good," Halt continued. "Go to the guard on the gate and say you have a message from Halt for Baron Arald."

A look of recognition spread across the old man's face. "Halt?" he asked. "Not the Ranger Halt?"

"Yes," replied Halt wearily. "The Ranger Halt."

"The one who led the ambush on Morgarath's Wargals?" asked Salt Peter.

"The same," said Halt, in a dangerously low voice. Salt Peter looked around him.

"Well," he said. "Where is he?"

"*I'm Halt!*" The Ranger thundered at him, placing his face a few centimeters from Salt Peter's as he did so. Again, the old farmer recoiled a few steps. Then he gathered his courage and shook his head in disbelief.

"No, no, no," he said definitely. "You can't be him. Why, the Ranger Halt is as tall as two men—and as broad. A giant of a man, he is! Brave, fierce in battle, he is. You couldn't be him."

Halt turned away, trying to regain his temper. Will couldn't help the smile breaking out on his face again.

"I . . . am . . . Halt," said the Ranger, spacing his words out so that Salt Peter couldn't make any mistake. "I was taller when I was young, and a lot broader. But now I'm this size." He thrust his glittering eyes close to the farmer's and glared at him. "Do you understand?"

"Well, if you say so . . . ," said Salt Peter. He still didn't believe the Ranger, but there was a very dangerous gleam in Halt's eyes that warned him it would not be wise to disagree any further.

"Good," said Halt icily. "Now, tell the Baron that Halt and Will . . ."

Salt Peter opened his mouth to ask another question. Halt clamped his hand over the old man's mouth immediately and pointed to where Will stood beside Tug.

"That's Will there." Salt Peter nodded, his eyes wide over the hand that was clamped firmly over his mouth, stopping any further questions or interruptions. The Ranger continued:

"Tell him Halt and Will are tracking a wild boar. When we find its lair, we'll return to the castle. In the meantime, the Baron should gather his men for a hunt tomorrow morning."

He slowly took his hand down from the farmer's mouth. "Have you got all that?" the Ranger asked. Salt Peter nodded carefully. "Then repeat it back to me," Halt prompted.

"Go to the castle, tell the gate guard I have a message from you . . . Halt . . . for the Baron. Tell the Baron that you . . . Halt . . . and him . . . Will . . . are tracking a wild boar to find its lair. Tell him to have his men ready for a hunt tomorrow."

"Good," said Halt. He gestured to Will and the two of them swung back into their saddles. Salt Peter stood uncertainly on the track, looking up at them.

"Off you go," said Halt, pointing in the direction of the castle. The old farmer went a few paces, then, when he judged he was at a safe distance, he turned around and called back at the grim-faced Ranger:

"I don't believes you, you know! Nobody grows shorter and thinner!"

Halt sighed and turned his horse away into the forest.

19

THEY RODE SLOWLY THROUGH THE FAILING LIGHT, LEANING sideways in their saddles to follow the trail left by the boar.

They had no trouble tracking him. The huge body had left a deep trench in the thick snow. Even without the snow, Will thought, it would have been easy. The boar was obviously in a very bad temper. It had slashed at the surrounding trees and shrubs with its tusks as it went, leaving a clear-cut path of destruction through the forest.

"Halt?" he said tentatively when they had gone a kilometer or so into the dense trees.

"Mmmm?" said Halt, a little absently.

"Why bother the Baron? Couldn't we simply kill the boar with our bows?"

Halt shook his head.

"He's a big one, Will. You can see the size of the trail he's left. We could take half a dozen arrows to kill him, and even then he'd take time to die. With a brute like this, it's better to make sure."

"How do we do that?"

Halt looked up for a second. "I suppose you've never seen a boar hunt?"

Will shook his head. Halt reined in for a few seconds to explain and Will brought Tug to a stop beside him.

"Well, first," said the Ranger, "we'll need dogs. That's another reason why we can't simply finish him off with our bows. When we find him, he'll have most likely gone to ground in a thicket or in dense bushes where we can't get at him. The dogs will drive him out and we'll have a ring of men around the lair with boar spears."

"And they throw them at him?" Will asked. Halt shook his head.

"Not if they have any brains," he said. "The boar spear is more than two meters long, with a double-sided blade and a crosspiece set behind the blade. The idea is to make the boar charge at the spearman. Then he sets the butt of the spear in the ground and lets the boar run onto it. The crosspiece stops the boar running right down the shaft and getting the spearman."

Will looked doubtful. "That sounds dangerous."

The Ranger nodded. "It is. But men like the Baron and Sir Rodney and the other knights love it. They wouldn't miss the chance of a boar hunt for worlds."

"What about you?" asked Will. "Will you have a boar spear?"

Halt shook his head. "I'll be sitting right here on Abelard," he said. "And you'll be on Tug, in case the boar breaks through the ring of men around him. Or in case he's just wounded and gets away."

"What do we do if that happens?" Will asked.

"We run him down before he can go to ground again," said Halt grimly. "And *then* we kill him with our bows."

The following day was a Saturday and, after breakfast, the Battleschool students were free to spend the day as they pleased. In Horace's case, this usually meant trying to stay out of sight whenever Alda, Bryn and Jerome came looking for him. But lately they'd realized he was avoiding them and had taken to waiting for him outside the mess hall. As he came out onto the parade ground this morning, he saw them waiting, smiling at him. He hesitated. It was too late to turn back. With a sinking heart, he continued on toward them.

"Horace!" He was startled by a voice coming from right behind him. He turned and saw Sir Rodney watching him, a curious look in his eyes as he glanced at the three second-year cadets waiting in the yard. Horace wondered if the Battlemaster knew about the treatment he was getting. He assumed he did. Horace guessed it was part of the toughening process of Battleschool.

"Sir!" he replied, wondering what he'd done wrong. Rodney's features softened and he smiled at the young man. He seemed extraordinarily pleased about something.

"Relax, Horace. It's Saturday, after all. Ever been on a boar hunt?"

"Um . . . no, sir." In spite of Sir Rodney's invitation to relax, he remained stiffly at attention.

"Time you did then. Draw a boar spear and hunting knife from the armory, have Ulf assign you a horse and report back here in twenty minutes."

"Yes, sir," Horace replied. Sir Rodney rubbed his hands together with evident pleasure.

"Seems Halt and his apprentice have scared us up a wild boar. Time we all had a bit of fun." He grinned encouragingly at the apprentice, then strode away eagerly to get his own equipment ready. When Horace turned back to the yard, he noticed that Alda, Bryn and Jerome were nowhere to be seen. He might have thought more about why the three bullies would disappear when Sir Rodney was around, but he had too much on his mind, wondering what he'd be expected to do in a boar hunt.

It was midmorning by the time Halt led the hunting party to the boar's lair.

The huge animal had gone to ground in a dense clump of undergrowth deep inside the forest. Halt and Will had found the hiding place just before dark the previous evening.

Now, as they approached, Halt made a signal and the Baron and his hunters dismounted, leaving their horses in the care of one of the stable hands who had accompanied them. They covered the last few hundred meters on foot. Halt and Will were the only two who remained on horseback.

There were fifteen hunters in all, each one armed with a boar spear of the type Halt had described. They spread out in a wide circle as they came closer to the boar's lair. Will was a little surprised to recognize Horace as one of the hunting group. He was the only apprentice warrior in the party. All the others were knights.

With a hundred meters to go, Halt held up his hand, signaling the hunters to stop. He urged Abelard into a gentle trot and crossed to where Will sat nervously astride Tug. The little horse was moving restlessly as he scented the presence of the boar.

"Remember," the Ranger said quietly to Will, "if you have to shoot, aim for a spot just behind the left shoulder. A clean shot to the heart will be your only chance to stop him if he's charging."

Will nodded, licking his dry lips nervously. He reached forward and comforted Tug with a quick pat on the neck. The little horse tossed his head in response to his master's touch.

"And stay close to the Baron," Halt reminded him, before moving to resume his position on the opposite side of the circle of hunters.

Halt was in the position of most danger, accompanying the hunters who were least experienced—and therefore most likely to make a mistake. If the boar broke through the ring on his side, he would be responsible for chasing it down and killing it. He had assigned Will to stay with the Baron and the more experienced of the hunters, where there was less likely to be trouble. This placed him close to Horace as well. Sir Rodney had positioned the apprentice between himself and the Baron. After all, this was the boy's first hunt and the Battlemaster didn't want to take any undue risks. Horace was there to watch and learn. If the boar charged in their direction, he was to let the Baron or Sir Rodney take care of it.

Horace glanced up once, making eye contact with Will. There was no animosity in the look. In fact, he gave the Ranger's apprentice a strained half smile. Will realized, watching Horace lick his lips over and over again, that the other boy was every bit as nervous as he was himself.

Halt signaled again and the circle began closing in on the thicket. As the circle became smaller, Will lost sight of his teacher and the other men on the far side of the boar's lair. He knew, from Tug's continued nervousness, that the boar must be inside the bushes still. But Tug was well trained and continued to move in as his rider urged him gently forward.

A deep roaring sound came from inside the thicket and Will's hair stood on end. He'd never heard the cry of an angry wild boar before. The noise was halfway between a grunt and a scream and, for a moment, the hunters hesitated.

"He's in there all right!" called the Baron, grinning at Will with excitement. "Let's hope he comes out on our side, eh, boys?"

Will wasn't at all sure that he wanted the boar to come charging out on their side of the thicket. He thought that he'd like it very well if it went the other way.

But the Baron and Sir Rodney were both grinning like schoolboys as they readied their boar spears. They were enjoying this, just as Halt had said they would. Quickly, Will unslung his bow from across his shoulders and fitted an arrow to the string. He fingered the tip for a moment, making sure it was still razor-sharp. His throat was dry. He wasn't sure that he would be able to talk if anyone spoke to him.

The dogs plunged against their restraining leashes, setting the echoes awake in the forest with their excited baying. It was their noise that had aroused the boar. Now, as they continued to give voice, Will could hear the huge animal slashing and cutting at the trees and shrubs in its lair with its long tusks.

The Baron turned to Bert, his dog handler, and made a hand signal for the hounds to be released.

The big, powerful animals were gone almost instantly, flashing across the cleared space to the thicket and disappearing inside. They were savage, heavily built beasts, bred specifically for the purpose of hunting boar.

The noise from the thicket was indescribable. The furious baying of the dogs was joined by the blood-chilling screams of the angry boar. There was a crashing and snapping of bushes and young saplings. The very thicket seemed to shake.

Then, suddenly, the boar was in the clear.

He came out halfway around the circle, between the points where Will and Halt were stationed. With an infuriated scream, he threw off one of the dogs that still clung to him, paused a moment, then charged at the hunters with blinding speed.

The young knight directly in front of the boar's charge didn't hesitate. He dropped to one knee, bracing the butt end of his spear into the ground and presenting the gleaming point to the charging animal.

The boar had no chance to turn. His own rush carried him onto the spear head. He plunged upward, screaming in pain and fury, trying to dislodge the killing piece of steel. But the young knight held grimly to the spear, holding it firmly against the ground and giving the enraged animal no chance to throw it free.

Will watched with wide-eyed alarm as the stout ash shaft of the spear bent like a bow under the weight of the boar's rush, then the carefully sharpened tip penetrated to the animal's heart and it was all over.

With one last screaming roar, the huge boar toppled sideways and lay dead.

The matted body was almost as large as a horse's and every inch was solid muscle. The tusks, harmless now in death, curved back over his ferocious snout. They were stained with the earth that he'd ripped up in his fury, and with the blood of at least one of the dogs.

Will looked at the massive body and shuddered. If this was a wild boar, he thought, he wasn't in any hurry to see another one.

20

The other hunters crowded around the young knight who had made the kill, congratulating him and patting his back. Baron Arald started across toward him, but paused beside Tug, looking up to Will as he spoke.

"You won't see another that size in a long time, Will," he said gruffly. "Pity he didn't come our way. I would have liked a trophy like that for myself." He continued on his way toward Sir Rodney, who was already with the group of warriors around the dead boar.

Consequently, Will found himself, for the first time in some weeks, face-to-face with Horace. There was an awkward pause, with neither boy willing to make the first move. Horace, excited by the events of the morning, his heart still pounding with the thrill of fear he'd felt when the boar first appeared, wanted to share the moment with Will. In the light of what they had just seen, their childish squabble seemed unimportant, and now he felt badly about his behavior on that day six weeks ago. But he couldn't find the words to express his feelings and he saw no encouragement to do so in Will's set features, so with a slight shrug, he started to step past Tug to go and congratulate the young hunter. As he did so, the pony stiffened and pricked his ears, giving a warning neigh.

Will looked back at the thicket and his blood seemed to freeze in his veins.

There, standing just outside the shelter of the bushes, was another boar—even larger than the one which now lay dead in the snow.

"Look out!" he cried as the huge beast slashed at the earth with its tusks.

It was a bad situation. The line of hunters had broken up, most of them having moved over to marvel at the size of the dead boar and to praise its killer. Only Will and Horace remained in the path of the second boar—mainly, Will realized, because Horace had hesitated for those few vital seconds.

Horace spun around at Will's shout. He looked at Will, then swung to look at the new danger. The boar lowered his head, tore at the ground again and charged. It all happened with terrifying speed. One moment the huge animal was ripping the ground with its tusks. The next, it was hurtling toward them. Placing himself between Will and the boar, Horace turned without hesitation to face it, setting his spear as Sir Rodney and the Baron had showed him.

But, as he did so, his foot slipped on an icy patch in the snow and he sprawled helplessly onto his side, the long spear falling from his grasp.

There was not a second to lose. Horace lay helpless before those murderous tusks. Will kicked his feet clear of the stirrups and dropped to the ground, sighting and drawing back the bowstring even as he did so. He knew his small bow would have no chance of stopping the boar's maddened rush. All he could hope to do was to distract the maddened animal, to turn it away from the helpless boy on the ground.

He fired and instantly ran to one side, away from the fallen apprentice. He yelled at the top of his lungs and fired again.

The arrows stuck out of the boar's thick hide like needles in a pin cushion. They did it no serious harm, but the pain of them burned through the animal like a hot knife. Its red, angry eyes fastened on the small, capering figure to one side and, furiously, it swung after Will.

There was no time to fire again. Horace was safe for the moment. Now Will himself was in danger. He sprinted for the shelter of a tree and ducked behind it, just in time!

The boar's enraged charge carried it straight into the trunk of the tree. Its huge body crashed against the trunk, shaking it to its roots, sending showers of snow cascading out of its upper branches.

Amazingly, the boar seemed unaffected by the crash. It backed up a few paces and charged at Will again. The boy darted around the tree trunk again, narrowly avoiding the slashing tusks as the boar thundered by.

Screaming in fury, the huge animal spun in its tracks, skidding in the snow, and came at him again. This time, it came more slowly, giving Will no chance to dart to one side at the last moment. The boar came at a trot, fury in its red eyes, tusks slashing from side to side, its hot breath steaming in the freezing winter air.

Behind him, Will could hear the shouts of the hunters, but he knew they'd arrive too late to help him. He nocked another arrow, knowing that he had no chance of hitting a vital spot as the pig came at him head-on.

Then there was a thud of muffled hooves on the snow and a small, shaggy shape was driving toward the furious monster.

"No, Tug!" Will screamed, in an agony of fear for his horse. But the pony charged at the huge boar, spinning in his tracks and lashing out with his rear hooves as he came within range. Tug's rear hooves caught the pig in the ribs and, with all the force of the pony's upper legs behind it, sent the boar rolling sideways in the snow.

The boar was up in an instant, even more furious than before.

The pony had caught him off balance, but the kick had done no serious damage. Now, the boar slashed and cut at Tug as the little pony neighed in fear and danced sideways out of the reach of those razor-sharp tusks.

"Tug! Get clear!" Will screamed again. His heart was in his throat. If those tusks caught the vulnerable tendons in the horse's lower legs, Tug would be crippled for life. He couldn't stand by and watch his horse put himself in such peril for his master. He drew and fired again and, dragging the long Ranger knife from his belt, charged across the snow at the huge, furious beast.

The third arrow struck the pig in the side. Again, he had missed a vulnerable spot and only wounded the monster. He yelled at it as he ran, screaming for Tug to get clear. The boar saw him coming, recognizing the small figure that had first driven it to such fury. Its red, hate-filled eyes fastened upon him and its head lowered for a final, killing charge.

Will saw the muscles bunch in the massive hindquarters. He was too far from cover to run. He'd have to face the charge here in the open. He dropped to one knee and, hopelessly, held out the keen-bladed Ranger knife in front of him as the boar charged. Dimly, he heard Horace's hoarse cry as the apprentice warrior charged forward to help him, his spear at the ready.

Then a deep, whistling hiss cut across the sound of the boar's hooves, followed by a solid, meaty SMACK! The boar reared up in midstride, twisting in sudden agony, and fell, dead as a stone, in the snow.

Halt's heavy-shafted, long arrow was almost buried in its side, driven there by the full power of the Ranger's mighty longbow. He'd struck the charging monster right behind the left shoulder, driving the head of the arrow into and through the pig's massive heart.

A perfect shot.

Halt reined in Abelard in a shower of snow and hurled himself to the ground, throwing his arms around the shaking boy. Will, overcome with relief, buried his face into the rough cloth of the Ranger's cloak. He didn't want anyone to see the tears of relief that were streaming down his face.

Gently, Halt took the knife from Will's hand.

"What on earth were you hoping to do with this?" he asked.

Will simply shook his head. He couldn't speak. He felt Tug's soft muzzle butting gently against him and looked up into the big, intelligent eyes.

Then it was all noise and confusion as the hunters gathered around, marveling at the size of the second boar and slapping Will on the back for his courage. He stood among them, a small figure, ashamed still of the tears that slid down his cheeks, no matter how hard he tried to stop them.

He felt a hand on his shoulder and turned to find he was looking into Horace's eyes—and the apprentice warrior was shaking his head slowly in admiration and disbelief.

"You saved my life," he said. "That was the bravest thing I've ever seen."

Will tried to shrug the other boy's thanks aside, but Horace pressed on. He remembered all the times in the past when he'd teased Will, when he'd bullied him. Now, acting instinctively, the smaller boy had saved him from those murderous, slashing tusks. It said something for Horace's growing maturity that he had forgotten his own instinctive action, when he had placed himself between the charging boar and the apprentice Ranger.

"But why, Will? After all, we . . ." He couldn't bring himself to finish the statement, but Will somehow knew what was in his mind.

"Horace, we may have fought in the past," he said. "But I don't hate you. I never hated you."

Horace nodded once, a look of understanding coming over his face. Then he seemed to come to a decision. "I owe you my life, Will," he said in a determined voice. "I'll never forget that debt. If ever you need a friend, if ever you need help, you can call on me."

The two boys faced each other for a moment, then Horace thrust out his hand and Will took it. The circle of knights around them was silent, witnessing, but not wanting to interrupt, this important moment for the two boys. Then Baron Arald stepped forward and put his arms around them both.

"Well said, both of you!" he said heartily and the knights chorused their assent.

The Baron grinned delightedly. It had been a perfect morning, all told. A bit of excitement. Two huge boars killed. And now two of his wards forging the sort of special bond that only came from shared danger.

"We've got two fine young men here!" he said to the group at large, and again there was that hearty chorus of assent. "Halt, Rodney, you can both be proud of your apprentices!"

"Indeed we are, my lord," Sir Rodney replied. He nodded approvingly at Horace. He'd seen the way the boy had turned without hesitation to face the charge. And he approved of Horace's open offer of friendship to Will. He remembered all too well seeing them fighting on Harvest Day. It seemed such childish squabbles were behind them now and he felt a deep satisfaction that he had chosen Horace for Battleschool.

Halt, for his part, said nothing. But when Will turned to look at his mentor, the grizzled Ranger met his eye, and simply nodded.

And that, Will knew, was the equivalent of three hearty cheers from Halt.

21

IN THE DAYS FOLLOWING THE BOAR HUNT, WILL NOTICED A change in the way he was treated. There was a certain deference, even respect, in the way people spoke to him and looked at him as he passed. It was most noticeable among the people of the village. Being simple folk, with rather limited boundaries to their day-to-day lives, they tended to glamorize and exaggerate any event that was in any way out of the ordinary.

By the end of the first week, the events of the hunt had been so blown out of proportion that they had Will single-handedly killing both boars as they charged out of the thicket. A couple of days after that, to hear the story related, you could almost believe that he had accomplished the feat with one arrow, firing it clean through the first boar and into the heart of the second.

"I really didn't do too much at all," he said to Halt one evening, as they sat by the fire in the warm little cottage they shared on the edge of the forest. "I mean, it's not as if I thought it through and decided to do it. It just sort of happened. And after all, you killed the boar, not me."

Halt merely nodded, staring fixedly at the leaping yellow flames in the grate.

"People will think what they want to," he said quietly. "Never take too much notice of it."

Nevertheless, Will was troubled by the adulation. He felt people were making an altogether too big thing out of it all. He would have enjoyed the respect if it had been based on what had actually happened. In his heart, he felt he had done something worthwhile, and perhaps even honorable. But he was being lionized for a totally fictional account of events and, being an essentially honest person, he couldn't really take any pride in that.

He also felt a little embarrassed because he was one of the few people who had noticed Horace's original, instinctively courageous action, placing himself between the charging boar and Will and Tug. Will had mentioned this last fact to Halt. He felt that perhaps the Ranger might have an opportunity to appraise Sir Rodney of Horace's unselfish action, but his teacher had merely nodded and said briefly:

"Sir Rodney knows. He doesn't miss much. He's got a little more up top than the average bash and whacker."

And with that, Will had to be content.

Around the castle, with the knights from the Battleschool and the various Craftmasters and apprentices, the attitudes were different. There, Will enjoyed a simple acceptance, and the recognition of the fact that he had done well. He noticed that people tended to know his name now, so that they greeted him as well as Halt when the two of them had business in the castle grounds. The Baron himself was friendlier than ever. It was a source of pride to him to see one of his castle wards acquit himself well.

The one person Will would have liked to discuss it all with was Horace himself. But as their paths seldom crossed, the opportunity hadn't arisen. He wanted to make sure that the warrior apprentice knew that Will set no store by the ridiculous stories that had swept the village, and he hoped that his former wardmate knew he had done nothing to spread the rumors.

In the meantime, Will's lessons and training proceeded at an accelerated pace. In a month's time, Halt had told him, they would be leaving for the Gathering—an annual event in the Rangers' calendar.

This was the time when all fifty Rangers came together to exchange news, to discuss any problems that might have arisen throughout the kingdom and to make plans. Of greater importance to Will, it was also the time when apprentices were assessed, to see if they were fit to progress to the next year of their training. It was bad luck for Will that he had been in training for only seven months. If he didn't pass the assessment at this year's Gathering, he would have to wait another year, until the next opportunity arose. As a result, he practiced and practiced from dawn till dusk each day. The idea of a Saturday holiday was a long forgotten luxury to him. He fired arrow after arrow into targets of different sizes, in different conditions, from standing, kneeling, sitting positions. He even fired from hidden positions in trees.

And he practiced with his knives. Standing to throw, kneeling, sitting, diving to the left, diving to the right. He practiced throwing the larger of the two knives so that it struck its target hilt first. After all, as Halt said, sometimes you only needed to stun the person you were throwing at, so it was a good idea to know how to do it.

He practiced his stealth skills, learning to stay stock-still even when he was sure that he had been discovered and learning that, all too often, people simply didn't notice him until he actually did move and gave the game away. He learned the trick that searchers would use, letting their gaze pass over a spot and then flicking back to it instantly to catch any slight movement. He learned about sweepers— the rear scouts who would follow silently behind a party on the move to catch out anyone who might have remained unseen, then broken cover when the party had gone past.

He worked with Tug, strengthening the bond and affection that had taken root so quickly between the two of them. He learned to use the little horse's extra senses of smell and hearing to give him warning of any danger and he learned the signals that the horse was trained to send to its rider.

So it was little wonder that, at the end of the day, Will had no inclination to walk up the winding path that led to Castle Redmont and find Horace so that he could discuss things with him. He accepted that, sooner or later, the chance would come. In the meantime, he could only hope that Horace was being given credit for his actions by Sir Rodney and the other members of the Battleschool.

Unfortunately for Horace, it seemed that nothing could be further from the truth.

Sir Rodney was puzzled by the muscular young apprentice. He seemed to have all the qualities that the Battleschool was looking for. He was brave. He followed orders immediately and he was still showing extraordinary skill in his weapons training. But his class work was below standard. Assignments were handed in late or sloppily finished. He seemed to have trouble paying attention to his instructors—as if he were distracted all the time. On top of that, it was suspected that he had a predilection for fighting. None of the staff had ever witnessed him fighting, but he was often seen to be sporting bruises and minor contusions, and he seemed to have made no close friends among his classmates. On the contrary, they took pains to steer clear of him. It all served to create a picture of an argumentative, antisocial, lazy recruit who had a certain amount of skill at arms.

All things considered, and with a great deal of reluctance, the Battlemaster was beginning to feel that he would have to expel Horace from Battleschool. All the evidence seemed to point in that direction. Yet his instincts told him he was wrong. That there was some other factor he wasn't aware of.

In point of fact, there were three other factors: Alda, Bryn and Jerome. And even as the Battlemaster was considering the future of his newest recruit, they had Horace surrounded once more.

It seemed that each time Horace managed to find a place where he could escape their attentions, the three older students tracked him down. Of course, this wasn't difficult for them, as they had a network of spies and informants among the other younger boys who were afraid of them, both in and outside the Battleschool. This time, they had cornered Horace behind the armory, in a quiet spot that he had discovered a few days before. He was hemmed in against the stone wall of the armory building, the three bullies standing in a half circle before him. Each of them carried a thick cane and Alda had a piece of heavy sacking folded over one arm.

"We've been looking for you, Baby," said Alda. Horace said nothing. His eyes shifted from one to the other as he wondered which of them would be the first to make a move.

"Baby's made a fool of us," Bryn said.

"Made a fool of the entire Battleschool." That was Jerome. Horace frowned, puzzled by their words. He had no idea what they were talking about. Alda's next statement made it clear.

"Baby had to be rescued from the big, bad boar," he said.

"By a little, creeping apprentice sneaker," Bryn added, the sneer heavy in his tone.

"And that makes us all look bad." Jerome shoved him against the shoulder as he spoke, pushing him back against the rough stone of the wall. His face was red and angry and Horace knew he was building himself up for something. Horace's hands bunched into fists at his side. Jerome saw the action.

"Don't threaten me, Baby! Time you learned a lesson." He stepped forward threateningly. Horace turned to face him and, in the same instant, knew he had made a mistake. Jerome's move was a feint. The real attack came from Alda, who whipped a heavy hessian sack over Horace's head before he could resist, pulling a drawcord tight so that he was contained from the waist up, blinded and helpless.

He felt several loops of the drawcord falling over his shoulders to fasten it, then the blows began.

He staggered blindly, helpless to defend himself as the three boys rained blows down on him from the heavy canes they had been carrying. He blundered into the wall and fell, unable to break his fall with his arms immobilized by his side. The blows continued, falling on his unprotected head, his arms and his legs as the three boys continued their mindless litany of hate.

"Call for the sneaker to save you now, Baby."

"This is for making us all look like fools."

"Learn respect for your Battleschool, Baby."

On and on it went as he writhed on the ground, trying in vain to escape the blows. It was the worst beating they had ever given him and they continued until, gradually, mercifully, he fell still, semiconscious. They each hit him a few more times, then Alda dragged the sack clear. Horace drew in one giant shuddering breath of fresh air. He ached and hurt viciously in every part of his body. From a long distance away, he heard Bryn's voice.

"Now let's teach the sneaker the same lesson." The others laughed and he heard them moving away. He groaned softly, longing for the release of unconsciousness, wanting to let himself sink into its dark, welcoming arms so that the pain would go away, at least for a while.

Then the full import of Bryn's words struck him. They were going to give the same treatment to Will—for the ridiculous reason that they felt his action in saving Horace had somehow belittled them and their Battleschool. With a gigantic effort, he pushed the welcoming folds of darkness back and struggled to his feet, moaning with the pain, chest heaving, head spinning, as he supported himself against the wall. He remembered his promise to Will: *If you ever need a friend, you can call on me.*

It was time to make good on the promise.

22

WILL WAS IN THE OPEN MEADOW BEHIND HALT'S COTTAGE, practicing. He had four targets set up at different ranges and was alternating his shots at random between the four of them, never firing at the same one twice in a row. Halt had set the exercise for him before he had gone to the Baron's office to discuss a dispatch that had come in from the King.

"If you fire twice at the same target," he had said, "you'll begin to rely on the first shot to determine your direction and elevation. That way, you'll never learn to shoot instinctively. You'll always need to fire a sighting shot first."

Will knew his teacher was right. But that didn't make the exercise any easier. To add to the difficulty, Halt had stipulated that he should let no more than five seconds elapse between each shot.

Frowning in concentration, he let the last five arrows of a set go. One after the other, in rapid succession, they flashed across the meadow, thudding into the targets. Will, his quiver empty for the tenth time that morning, stopped to survey the results. He nodded in satisfaction. Every arrow had hit a target, and most of them were clustered in the inner ring or the bull's-eye itself. It was shooting of an exceptionally high quality and it proved to him the value of constant practice. He wasn't to know it, of course, but there were already few archers in the kingdom, outside of the Ranger Corps, who could have matched him. Even the archers in the King's army weren't trained to shoot with such individual speed and accuracy. They were trained to fire as a group, sending a mass of arrows against an attacking force. As a result, their training concentrated more on coordinated actions, so that all arrows were fired simultaneously.

He had just set the bow down, preparatory to recovering his arrows, when the sound of a footstep behind him made him turn. He was a little surprised to see three Battleschool apprentices watching him, their red surcoats marking them as second-year trainees. He didn't recognize any of them, but he nodded a friendly greeting.

"Good morning," he said. "What brings you down here?"

It was unusual to find Battleschool apprentices this far from the castle. He noted the thick canes that they all carried and decided they must have set out for a walk. The closest of them, a handsome, blond-haired boy, smiled and said:

"We're looking for the Ranger's apprentice."

Will couldn't help smiling in return. After all, the Ranger cloak that he wore marked him unmistakably as an apprentice Ranger. But perhaps the Battleschool apprentice was only being polite.

"Well, you've found him," he said. "What can I do for you?"

"We've brought a message from the Battleschool for you," the boy replied.

Like all Battleschool trainees, he was tall and well muscled, as were his companions. They moved closer to him now and Will instinctively backed off a pace. They were a little too close, he felt. Closer than they needed to be to pass on a message.

"It's about what happened at the boar hunt," said one of the others. This one was red-haired, with a heavy dusting of freckles, and a nose that showed distinct signs of having been broken—probably in one of the training combats that Battleschool students were always practicing. Will shrugged uncomfortably. There was something in the air he didn't like. The blond boy was smiling still. But neither the redhead nor their third companion, an olive-skinned boy who was the tallest of the three, looked as if they thought there was anything to smile about.

"You know," Will said, "people are talking a lot of nonsense about that. I didn't do much."

"We know," the red-haired boy snapped angrily and again, Will took a pace back as they all moved a little closer. Halt's training was ringing alarm bells in his mind now. *Never let people get too close to you*, he'd been told. *If they try to, be on your guard, no matter who they are or how friendly you think they are.*

"But when you go swanking around telling everyone you saved a big, clumsy Battleschool apprentice, you make us look foolish," the tall boy accused. Will looked at him, frowning.

"I never said that!" he protested. "I . . ."

And at that moment, while he was distracted by Bryn, Alda made his move, stepping quickly forward with the sack held open to throw it over Will's head. It was the same tactic they had used so successfully with Horace, but Will was already on his guard and, as the other boy moved, he sensed the attack and reacted.

Unexpectedly, he dived forward toward Alda, rolling in a somersault that took him under the sack, then letting his legs sweep around, scything Alda's legs from under him so that the bigger boy was sent sprawling. But there were three of them and that was too many for him to keep track of. He'd evaded Alda and Bryn but as he rolled to his feet, completing the movement, Jerome brought his cane around in a ringing crack across the back of his shoulders.

With a cry of pain and shock, Will staggered forward, as Bryn now brought his cane around and hit him across the side. By then,

Alda had regained his feet, furious with the way Will had evaded him, and he struck Will across the point of the shoulder.

The pain was excruciating and, with a sob of agony, Will dropped to his knees.

Instantly, the three Battleschool apprentices crowded forward, ringing him, trapping him between them, the heavy canes raised to continue the beating.

"That's enough!"

The unexpected voice stopped them. Will, crouched on the ground, waiting for the beating to begin, arms over his head, looked up and saw Horace, bruised and battered, standing a few meters away. He held one of the wooden Battleschool drill swords in his right hand. One eye was blackened and there was a trickle of blood running from his lip. But in his eyes there was a look of hatred and sheer determination that, for a moment, made the three older boys hesitate. Then they realized that there were three of them and Horace's sword was, after all, no more of a weapon than the canes they carried. Forgetting Will for the moment, they fanned out and moved to encircle Horace, the heavy canes raised to strike.

"Baby followed us," said Alda.

"Baby wants another beating," Jerome agreed.

"And Baby's going to get it," said Bryn, smiling confidently. But then a yell of fright was torn from his lips as a sudden, jarring force slammed against the cane, whipping it from his grasp and sending it spinning to land several meters away.

A similar yell to his right told him that the same thing had happened to Jerome.

Confused, Bryn looked around to where the two canes lay. With a sinking feeling, he saw that each one was transfixed by a black-shafted arrow.

"I think one at a time is fairer, don't you?" said Halt.

Bryn and Jerome felt a surge of terror as they looked up to see the grim-faced Ranger standing in the shadows ten meters away, another arrow already nocked to the string of his massive longbow.

Only Alda showed any sign of rebellion. "This is Battleschool business, Ranger," he said, trying to bluster his way through the situation. "You'd best stay out of it."

Will, slowly regaining his feet, saw the dark anger that burned deep in Halt's eyes at the arrogant words. For a moment, he almost felt sorry for Alda, then he felt the throbbing pain in his back and shoulders and any thoughts of sympathy were instantly blotted out.

"Battleschool business, is it, sonny?" Halt said in a dangerously low voice. He moved forward, covering the ground between him and Alda in a few deceptively swift, gliding steps. Before Alda knew it, Halt was barely a meter away. Still, the apprentice remained defiant. The dark look on Halt's face was unsettling, but seen close-up, Alda realized that he was a good head taller than the Ranger and his confidence flowed back. All these years he had been nervous of the mysterious man who now stood before him. He had never realized what a puny figure he really was.

Which was Alda's second mistake of the day. Halt was small. But *puny* was not a word that entered into it. In addition, Halt had spent a lifetime fighting far more dangerous adversaries than a second-year Battleschool apprentice.

"I seem to notice that there was a Ranger apprentice being attacked," Halt was saying softly. "I think that makes it Ranger's business as well, don't you?"

Alda shrugged, confident now that, whatever the Ranger might do, he could more than handle it.

"Make it your business if you like," he said, a sneer entering his voice. "I really don't care one way or the other."

Halt nodded several times as he digested that speech. Then he replied. "Well then, I think I *will* make it my business—but I won't be needing this."

As he said it, he replaced the arrow in his quiver and lightly tossed the bow to one side, turning away as he did so. Inadvertently, Alda's eyes followed the action and instantly he felt a searing pain as Halt stamped backward with the edge of his boot, catching the apprentice's foot between arch and ankle and driving into it. As Alda doubled over to clasp his injured foot, the Ranger pivoted on his left heel and his right elbow slammed upward into Alda's nose, jerking him upright again and sending him staggering back, eyes streaming with the pain. For a second or two, Alda's sight was blurred by the reflex tears and he felt a slight pricking sensation under his chin. As his eyes cleared, he found the Ranger's eyes were only a few centimeters from his own. There was no anger there. Instead, there was a look of utter contempt and disregard that was somehow far more frightening.

The pricking sensation became a little more pronounced and, as he tried to look down, Alda gave a gasp of fear. Halt's larger knife, razor edged and needle pointed, was just under his chin, pressing lightly into the soft flesh of his throat.

"Don't *ever* talk to me like that again, boy," the Ranger said, so softly that Alda had to strain to hear the words. "And don't ever lay a hand on my apprentice again. Understand?"

Alda, all his arrogance gone, his heart pounding in terror, could say nothing. The knife pricked a little harder against his throat and he felt a warm trickle of blood sliding down under his collar. Halt's eyes blazed suddenly, like the coals of a fire in a sudden draft.

"Understand?" he repeated, and Alda croaked a reply.

"Yes . . . sir."

Halt stepped back, re-sheathing the knife in one fluid movement. Alda sank to the ground, massaging his injured ankle. He was sure there was damage to the tendons. Ignoring him, Halt turned to face the other two second-year apprentices. Instinctively, they had moved closer together and were watching him fearfully, uncertain as to what he was going to do next. Halt pointed to Bryn.

"You," he said, his words edged with contempt, "pick up your cane."

Fearfully, Bryn moved to where his cane lay on the ground, Halt's arrow still embedded halfway along its length. Without taking his eyes off the Ranger, fearing some trick, he stooped at the knees, his hand scrabbling awkwardly until it touched the cane. Then he stood again, holding it uncertainly in his left hand.

"Now give me back my arrow," the Ranger ordered, and the tall, swarthy boy struggled to remove the arrow, stepping close enough to hand it to Halt, tensed in every muscle as he waited for some unexpected move from the Ranger. Halt, however, merely took the arrow and replaced it in his quiver. Bryn stepped hurriedly back out of reach. Halt gave a small, contemptuous laugh. Then he turned to Horace.

"I take it these are the three who gave you those bruises?" he asked. Horace said nothing for a moment, then realized that his continued silence was ridiculous. There was no reason why he should shield the three bullies any further. There never had been a reason.

"Yes, sir," he said decisively. Halt nodded, rubbing his chin.

"I rather thought so," he said. "Well then, I've heard rumors that you're pretty good with a sword. How about a practice bout with this hero in front of me?"

A slow grin spread over Horace's face as he understood what the Ranger was suggesting. He started forward. "I think I'd like that."

Bryn backed away a pace. "Just a moment!" he cried. "You can't expect me to . . ."

He got no further. The Ranger's eyes glittered with that danger-

ous light once more and he took a half step forward, his hand dropping to the hilt of the saxe knife again.

"You've got a cane. I suggest you use it. Now get on with it," he
ordered, his voice very low and dangerous.

Realizing he was trapped, Bryn turned to face Horace. Now that
it was a matter of one-on-one, he felt far less confident about deal-
ing with the younger boy. Everyone had heard of Horace's almost uncanny natural swordsmanship.

Deciding that attack might be the best defense, Bryn stepped forward and aimed an overhead slash at Horace. Horace parried it easily. He parried Bryn's next two strokes with equal ease. Then, as he
blocked Bryn's fourth stroke, he flicked his wooden blade down the
length of the other boy's cane in the instant before the two weapons
disengaged. There was no crosspiece to protect Bryn's hand from
the movement and the hardwood drill sword slammed painfully into
his fingers. With a cry of agony, he dropped the heavy stick, leaping
back and wringing his injured hand painfully under his arm. Horace stood, ready to resume.

"I didn't hear anybody call stop," Halt said mildly.

"But . . . he's disarmed me!" Bryn whined.

Halt smiled at him. "So he has. But I'm sure he'll let you pick up
your cane and start again. Go ahead."

Bryn looked from Halt to Horace and back again. He saw no
pity in either face.

"I don't want to," he said in a very small voice. Horace found it
hard to reconcile this cringing figure with the sneering bully who had
been making his life hell for the past few months. Halt appeared to
consider Bryn's statement.

"We'll note your protest," he said cheerfully. "Now continue,
please."

Bryn's hand throbbed painfully. But even worse than the pain was

the fear of what was to come, the certainty that Horace would punish him without mercy. He bent down and reached fearfully for the
cane, his eyes fixed on Horace. The younger boy waited patiently
until Bryn was ready, then made a sudden feint forward.

Bryn yelped in fear and threw the cane aside. Horace shook his
head in disgust.

"Who's the baby now?" he asked. Bryn wouldn't meet his gaze.
He shrank away, his eyes cast down.

"If he's going to be a baby," Halt suggested, "I suppose you'll just
have to paddle him."

A grin spread over Horace's face. He sprang forward and grabbed
Bryn by the scruff of his neck, spinning him around. Then he proceeded to whack the older boy's backside with the flat of the drill
sword, over and over again, following him around the clearing as
Bryn tried to pull away from the remorseless punishment. Bryn
howled and hopped and sobbed but Horace's grip was firm on his
collar and there was no escape. Finally, when Horace felt he had re-
paid all the bullying, the insults and the pain that he had suffered, he
let go.

Bryn staggered away and dropped to his hands and knees, sobbing with pain and fear.

Jerome had watched the proceedings in horror, knowing his turn
was coming. He began to edge away, hoping to escape while the
Ranger's attention was distracted.

"Take one more step and I'll put an arrow through you."

Will tried to model his voice on the quiet, threatening tone Halt
had used. He had retrieved several of his arrows from the nearest target and now he had one of them ready, laid on the bowstring. Halt
glanced around approvingly.

"Good idea," he said. "Aim for the left calf. It's a very painful
wound." He glanced over to where Bryn lay, sobbing, on the ground

at Horace's feet. "I think he's had enough," he said. Then he jerked a thumb at Jerome.

"Your turn," he said briefly. Horace retrieved the cane that Bryn had dropped and moved toward Jerome, holding it out to him. Jerome backed away.

"No!" Jerome yelled, wide-eyed. "It's not fair! He . . ."

"Well, of course it's not *fair*," Halt agreed in a reasonable tone. "I gather you think three against one is fair. Now get on with it."

Will had often heard the saying that a cornered rat will eventually show fight. Jerome proved it now. He went onto the attack and to his own surprise, Horace gave ground before the rain of blows aimed at him. The bully's confidence began to grow as he advanced. He failed to notice that Horace was blocking every stroke with consummate ease, almost with contempt. Jerome's best strokes never even looked like they were breaking through Horace's defense. The second-year apprentice might as well have been hitting a stone wall.

Then, Horace stopped retreating. He stood fast, blocking Jerome's latest stroke with an iron wrist. They stood chest to chest for a few seconds, and then Horace began to push Jerome back. His left hand gripped Jerome's right wrist, keeping their weapons locked together. Jerome's feet skidded on the snow as Horace forced him backward, farther and farther. Then he gave a final heave and sent Jerome sprawling on the ground.

Jerome had seen what happened to Bryn. He knew that surrender wasn't an option. He scrambled to his feet and defended himself desperately as Horace began his own attack. Jerome was driven back by a whirlwind of forehands, backhands, side and overhead cuts. He managed to block some of the strokes, but the blistering speed of Horace's attack defeated him. Blows rained on his shins, elbows and shoulders almost at will. Horace seemed to concentrate on the bony spots that would hurt most. Occasionally, he used the rounded point of the sword to thrust into Jerome's ribs—just hard enough to bruise, without breaking bones.

Finally, Jerome had had enough. He wheeled away from the onslaught, dropped the cane and fell to the ground, hands clasped protectively over his head. His backside was raised invitingly in the air and Horace paused and looked a question at Halt. The Ranger made a little gesture toward Jerome.

"Why not?" he said. "An opportunity like that doesn't come every day."

But even he winced at the thundering kick in the backside that Horace delivered. Jerome, nose down in the wet snow, skidded at least a meter from the force of it.

Halt retrieved the cane that Jerome had dropped. He studied it for a moment, testing its weight and balance.

"Really not much of a weapon," he said. "You have to wonder why they chose it." Then he tossed the cane to Alda. "Get busy," he ordered.

The blond boy, still crouched, nursing his injured ankle, looked at the cane in disbelief. Blood streamed down his face from his shattered nose. He'd never be quite so good looking again, Will thought.

"But . . . but . . . I'm injured!" he protested, hobbling awkwardly to his feet. He couldn't believe that Halt would require him to go through the punishment he'd just witnessed.

Halt paused, studying him as if that fact hadn't occurred to him. For a moment, a ray of hope shone in Alda's mind.

"So you are," the Ranger said. "So you are." He looked a little disappointed, and Alda began to believe that Halt's sense of fair play would spare him the sort of punishment that had been handed out to his friends. Then the Ranger's face cleared.

"But just a minute," he said, "so is Horace. Isn't that right, Will?"

Will grinned. "Definitely, Halt," he said, and Alda's brief hope vanished without a trace.

Halt now turned to Horace, asking with mock concern, "Are you sure you're not too badly injured to continue, Horace?"

Horace smiled. It was a smile that never reached his eyes. "Oh, I think I can manage," he said.

"Well, that's settled then!" Halt said cheerfully. "Let's continue, shall we?"

And Alda knew there was to be no escape for him either. He faced up to Horace and the final duel began.

Alda was the best swordsman of the three bullies, and at least he gave Horace some competition for a few minutes. But as they felt each other out with stroke and counterstroke, thrust and parry, he quickly realized that Horace was his master. His only chance, he felt, was to try something unexpected.

He disengaged, then changed his grip on the cane, holding it in both hands like a quarterstaff and launching a series of rapid left and right hooking blows with it.

For a second, Horace was caught by surprise and he fell back. But he recovered with catlike speed and aimed an overhead blow at Alda. The second-year student attempted the standard quarterstaff parry, holding the staff at either end, to block the sword stroke with the middle section. In theory, it was the right tactic. In practice, the hardened hickory drill sword simply sheared through the cane, leaving Alda holding two useless, shortened sticks. Totally unnerved, he let them drop and stood defenseless before Horace.

Horace looked at his long-time tormentor, then at the sword in his hand.

"I don't need this," he muttered, and let the sword drop.

The right-hand punch that he threw traveled no more than

twenty centimeters to the point of Alda's jaw. But it had his shoulder and body weight and months of suffering and loneliness behind it—the loneliness that only a victim of bullying can know.

Will's eyes widened slightly as Alda came off his feet and hurtled backward, to come crashing down in the cold snow beside his two friends. He thought about the times in the past when he had fought with Horace. If he'd known the other boy was capable of throwing a punch like that, he never would have done so.

Alda didn't move. Odds were, he wouldn't move for some time, Will thought. Horace stepped back, shaking his bruised knuckles and heaving a sigh of satisfaction.

"You have no idea how good that felt," he said. "Thank you, Ranger."

Halt nodded acknowledgment. "Thank you for taking a hand when they attacked Will. And by the way, my friends call me Halt."

23

IN THE WEEKS FOLLOWING HIS FINAL ENCOUNTER WITH THE three bullies, Horace noticed a definite change in life at the Battleschool.

The most important factor in the change was that Alda, Bryn and Jerome were all expelled from the school—and from the castle and its neighboring village. Sir Rodney had been suspicious for some time that there had been a problem among the ranks of his junior students. A quiet visit from Halt alerted him as to where it lay and the resultant investigation soon brought to light the full story of the way Horace had been victimized. Sir Rodney's judgment was swift and uncompromising. The three second-year students were given a half day to prepare and pack. They were supplied with a small amount of money and a week's supplies and were transported to the fief's boundaries, where they were told, in no uncertain terms, not to return.

Once they were gone, Horace's lot improved considerably. The daily routine of the Battleschool was still as harsh and challenging as ever. But without the added burden that Alda, Bryn and Jerome had laid upon him, Horace found he could easily cope with the drills, the discipline and the studies. He rapidly began to achieve the potential that Sir Rodney had seen in him. In addition, his roommates, without the fear of incurring the bullies' vengeance, began to be more welcoming and friendly.

In short, Horace felt that things were definitely looking up.

His only regret was that he hadn't been able to thank Halt properly for the improvement in his life. After the events in the meadow, Horace had been placed in the infirmary for several days while his bruises and contusions were attended to. By the time he was released, he found that Halt and Will had already left for the Rangers' Gathering.

"Are we nearly there?" Will asked, for perhaps the tenth time that morning.

Halt gave vent to a small sigh of exasperation. Other than that, he made no reply. They had been on the road now for three days and it seemed to Will that they must be close to the Gathering Ground. Several times in the past hour, he had noticed an unfamiliar scent on the air. He mentioned it to Halt, who said briefly, "It's salt. We're getting close to the sea," then refused to elaborate any further. Will glanced sidelong at his teacher, hoping that perhaps Halt might deign to share a little more information with him, but the Ranger's keen eyes were scanning the ground in front of them. From time to time, Will noticed, he looked up into the trees that flanked the road.

"Are you looking for something?" Will asked, and Halt turned in his saddle.

"Finally, a useful question," he said. "Yes, as a matter of fact, I am. The Chief Ranger will have sentries out around the Gathering Ground. I always like to try to fool them as I'm approaching."

"Why?" asked Will, and Halt allowed himself a tight little grin.

"It keeps them on their toes," he explained. "They'll try to slip be-hind us and follow us in, just so they can say they've ambushed me. It's a silly game they like to play."

"Why is it silly?" asked Will. It sounded exactly like the sort of skill exercises that he and Halt practiced regularly. The grizzled Ranger turned in his saddle and fixed Will with an unblinking stare.

"Because they never succeed," he said. "And this year they'll be trying even harder because they know I'm bringing an apprentice. They'll want to see how good you are."

"Is this part of the testing?" Will asked, and Halt nodded.

"It's the start of it. Do you remember what I told you last night?"

Will nodded. For the past two nights, around the campfire, Halt's soft voice had given Will advice and instructions on how to conduct himself at the Gathering. Last night, they'd devised tactics for use in case of an ambush—just the sort of thing that Halt had mentioned now.

"When will we . . . ," he began, but suddenly Halt was alert. He held up a warning finger for silence and Will stopped speaking in-stantly. The Ranger's head was turned slightly to listen. The two horses continued without hesitation.

"Hear it?" Halt asked.

Will craned his head too. He thought that, just maybe, he could hear soft hoofbeats behind them. But he wasn't sure. The gait of their own horses masked any real sound from the trail behind. If there was someone there, his horse was moving in step with their own.

"Change gait," Halt whispered. "On three. One, two, three."

Simultaneously, they both nudged their left toes into the horses' shoulders. It was just one of many signals to which Tug and Abelard were trained to respond.

Instantly, both horses hesitated in their stride. They seemed to skip a pace, then continued in their even gait.

But the hesitation had changed the pattern of their hoofbeats, and for an instant, Will could hear another set of horse's hooves behind them, like a slightly delayed echo. Then the other horse changed gait as well to match their own and the sound was gone.

"Ranger horse," Halt said softly. "It'll be Gilan, for sure."

"How can you tell?" Will asked.

"Only a Ranger horse could change his pace as quickly as that. And it'll be Gilan because it's always Gilan. He loves trying to catch me out."

"Why?" asked Will, and Halt looked sternly at him.

"Because he was my last apprentice," he explained. "And for some reason, former apprentices just love to catch their former masters with their breeches down." He looked accusingly at his current apprentice. Will was about to protest that he would never behave in such a fashion after he graduated, then realized that he probably would, and at the very first opportunity. The protest died unspoken.

Halt signaled for silence, and scanned the trail ahead of them. Then he pointed. "That's the spot there," he said. "Ready?"

There was a large tree close to the side of the trail, with branches hanging out just above head height. Will studied it for a moment, then nodded. Tug and Abelard continued their even pacing toward the tree. As they came closer, Will kicked his feet from the stirrups and rose to stand, crouching, on Tug's back. The horse didn't vary his pace as his master shifted position.

As they passed under the branches, Will reached up and seized the lowest one, swinging himself up onto it. The instant his weight left Tug's back, the little horse began to pace more vigorously, forcing his hooves into the ground with each step so that there would be no sign to a tracker behind them that his load had suddenly lightened.

Silently, Will climbed higher into the tree until he found a spot where he had a solid perch and a clear view. He could see Halt and the two horses moving slowly down the trail.

As they reached the next bend, Halt urged Tug to keep going, then halted Abelard and swung down from the saddle. He dropped to his knees, seeming to study the ground for signs of tracks.

Now Will could hear the other horse behind them. He looked back the way they had come, but another bend hid their follower from sight.

Then, the soft hoofbeats ceased.

Will's mouth was dry and his heart beat faster and faster inside his ribcage. He was sure the sound must be audible to anyone within fifty meters or so. But his training asserted itself and he stood motionless on the tree branch, among the leaves and dappled shadows, watching the trail behind them.

A movement!

He saw it from the corner of his eye, then it was gone. He peered closely at the spot for a second or two, then remembered Halt's lessons.

Don't focus your attention on one spot. Keep a wide focus all the time and keep scanning. You'll see him as a movement, not as a figure. Remember, he's a Ranger too and he's been trained in the art of not being seen.

Will widened his focus and scanned the forest behind them. Within seconds, he was rewarded by another sign of movement. A branch swung back into place as an unseen figure passed silently by.

Then, ten meters farther on, a bush swayed slightly. Then he saw a clump of tall grass springing slowly back into position from where a passing foot had crushed it momentarily.

Will stayed stock-still. He marveled at the fact that their pursuer could move through the forest without his seeing him. Obviously, the other Ranger had left his horse behind and was stalking Halt on foot. Will's eyes swiveled for a quick glance at Halt. His teacher still seemed to be preoccupied with some sign on the ground.

Another movement came from the forest. The unseen Ranger had passed Will's hiding place now and was moving back toward the trail, intent on surprising Halt from behind.

Suddenly, a tall figure in a gray-green cloak seemed to rise out of the ground in the middle of the trail, some twenty meters behind the kneeling figure of Halt. Will blinked. One moment the figure hadn't been there. Next, he seemed to materialize out of thin air. Will's hand began to move toward the quiver of arrows slung over his back, then he halted the movement. Halt had told him the night before:

Wait until we're talking. If he's not talking, he'll hear the slightest movement you make.

Will gulped, hoping that the tall figure hadn't heard the movement of his hand toward the quiver. But it seemed that he'd stopped in time. Below him, he heard a cheerful voice call out.

"Halt, Halt!"

Halt turned and rose slowly to his feet, brushing the dirt from his knees as he rose. He put his head on one side and studied the figure in the middle of the trail, who was leaning easily on a longbow identical to Halt's own.

"Well, Gilan," he called, "I see you're still making that old joke."

The tall Ranger shrugged and replied cheerfully, "The joke appears to be on you this year, Halt."

As Gilan spoke, Will's hand moved quickly but quietly to his quiver and selected an arrow, laying it ready on the bowstring. Halt was speaking again now.

"Really, Gilan? And what joke would that be, I wonder?"

The amusement was evident in Gilan's voice as he replied to his old master.

"Come now, Halt. Admit it. For once I've got the best of you—and you know how many years I've been trying."

Halt rubbed one hand over his grizzled beard thoughtfully.

"It beats me why you keep on trying, Gilan, as a matter of fact."

Gilan laughed. "You should know how much pleasure it gives an ex-apprentice to get the better of his master, Halt. Now come on. Admit it. This year, I've won."

As the tall figure spoke, Will carefully drew back the arrow, sighting on a tree trunk some two meters to Gilan's left. Halt's instructions echoed in his ears: *Choose a target close enough to startle him when you shoot. But for pity's sake not too close. If he moves, I don't want you putting an arrow through him!*

Halt hadn't moved from his position in the center of the trail. Gilan was now shifting his weight uneasily from one foot to another. Halt's unperturbed manner was beginning to bother him. It appeared that, all of a sudden, he wasn't totally sure that Halt was merely trying to bluff his way out of the trap.

Halt's next words added to his suspicions.

"Ah, yes . . . apprentices and masters. They're a strange combination, all right. But tell me, Gilan, my old apprentice, aren't you forgetting something this year?"

Perhaps it was the way Halt laid a little extra stress on the word "apprentice," but suddenly Gilan became aware that he had made a mistake. His head began to turn, searching for the apprentice that he'd forgotten.

As he began the movement, Will released his arrow.

The shaft hissed through the air past the tall Ranger and thudded, quivering, into the tree that Will had selected. Gilan jerked back with shock, then his eyes swung into the branches of the tree where Will stood concealed. Will marveled that, even caught by surprise as he was, Gilan was still able to react so quickly in identifying the direction from which his attacker had shot.

Gilan shook his head ruefully. His keen eyes could make out the small gray and green clad figure concealed in the shadows of the tree's foliage.

"Come down, Will," Halt called. "And meet Gilan, one of our more careless Rangers." He shook his head at Gilan. "I told you when you were a boy, didn't I? Never be too hasty. Don't rush into things."

Gilan nodded, somewhat crestfallen. He looked even more so when Will dropped to the ground from the lowest branch and the tall Ranger saw how small and young the apprentice was.

"It appears," he said, "that I was so intent on catching myself an old gray fox that I overlooked the small monkey hiding in the trees." He grinned at his own mistake.

"Monkey, is it?" Halt said gruffly. "I'd say he's made a monkey out of you today. Will, this is Gilan, my former apprentice and now Ranger of Meric Fief—although what they did to deserve him is beyond me."

Gilan's grin widened and he held out his hand to Will.

"And just as I was thinking I'd finally got the better of you, Halt," he said cheerfully. "So you're Will," he continued, shaking hands firmly. "I'm pleased to meet you. That was a neat piece of work, young fellow."

Will grinned at Halt and the older Ranger made a slight, meaningful movement of his head. Will remembered the final instructions that Halt had given him the night before: *Once you best a man, never gloat. Be generous and find something in his actions to praise. He won't enjoy being bested, but he'll make a good face of it. Show him you appreciate it. Praise can win you a friend. Gloating will only ever make enemies.*

"Yes, I'm Will," he said. Then he added, "Could you perhaps teach me how you move like that? It was brilliant."

Gilan laughed ruefully. "Not too brilliant, I think. You obviously saw me coming from a long way away."

Will shook his head, remembering how hard he'd tried to spot Gilan. Now that he thought of it, his praise and his request were more genuine than he'd realized.

"I saw you when you arrived," he said. "And I saw where you'd been. But I never once saw you from the time you rounded that bend. I wish I could move like that."

Gilan's face showed his pleasure at Will's obvious sincerity.

"Well, Halt," he said, "I see this young fellow doesn't merely have talent. He has excellent manners as well."

Halt regarded the two of them: his current apprentice and his former student. He nodded to Will, approving his tactful words.

"Unseen movement was always Gilan's best skill," he said. "You'd do well if he agreed to tutor you." He moved toward his ex-apprentice and placed his arm around the taller man's shoulders. "It's good to see you again."

They embraced each other warmly. Then Halt held the other man at arm's length, studying him carefully.

"You get lankier every year," he said finally. "When are you going to put some meat on those bones?"

Gilan smiled. It was obviously an old joke between them.

"You appear to have enough for both of us," he said. He poked Halt in the ribs, none too gently. "Is that the beginnings of a potbelly I see there?" He grinned at Will. "I'll wager he's sitting around the cabin letting you do all the housework these days?"

Before Halt or Will could reply, he turned away and let out a whistle. A few seconds later, his horse trotted around the bend in the road. As the tall young Ranger moved toward his horse and mounted, Will noticed a sword hanging in a scabbard from the saddle. He turned to Halt, puzzled.

"I thought we weren't allowed to have swords," he said quietly. Halt frowned for a moment, not understanding, then followed Will's gaze and realized what had prompted the question.

"It's not that we're not allowed," he explained, as they both mounted. "It's a matter of priorities. It takes years to become a good swordsman and we don't have the time. We have other skills to develop."

He saw the next question forming on Will's lips and went on. "Gilan's father is a knight, so Gilan had already been training with the sword for some years before he joined the Rangers. He was considered a special case and he was allowed to continue that training when he was apprenticed to me."

"But I thought . . . ," Will began and then hesitated. Gilan was trotting his horse toward them and he wasn't sure if it would be polite to ask his next question in front of him.

"Never say that in front of Halt," Gilan said, overhearing Will's last words. "He'll simply reply, 'You're an apprentice. You're not ready to think,' or 'If you thought about it, you wouldn't ask.' "

Will had to smile. Halt had used those exact words to him on more than one occasion, and Gilan's impersonation of the older Ranger was uncanny. Now, however, both men were looking expectantly at him, waiting to hear the question he had been about to ask, so he plunged ahead.

"If Gilan's father was a knight, wasn't he automatically eligible for Battleschool? Or did they think he was too small as well?"

Halt and Gilan exchanged a look. Halt raised one eyebrow, then gestured for Gilan to reply.

"I could have gone to Battleschool," he said. "But I chose to join the Rangers."

"Some of us do, you know," Halt put in mildly. Will thought this over. He had always assumed that the Rangers did not come from the ranks of the Kingdom's nobles. Apparently he was wrong.

"But I thought . . . ," he began and instantly realized his mistake. Halt and Gilan looked at him, then looked at each other, and said in chorus:

"You're an apprentice. You're not ready to think."

Then they wheeled their horses and trotted off. Will hurriedly retrieved Tug and cantered after them. As he caught up, the two Rangers edged their horses to either side, allowing him space to ride between them. Gilan grinned once at him. Halt was as grim as ever. But as they continued in a companionable silence, Will became aware of the comforting realization that he was now a part of an exclusive, tightly knit group.

It was a warm sense of belonging, as if, somehow, he had arrived home for the first time in his life.

24

"SOMETHING'S HAPPENED," HALT SAID QUIETLY, SIGNALING for his two companions to rein in their horses.

The three riders had cantered the last half a kilometer to the Gathering Ground. Now, as they crested a slight rise, the open space among the trees lay just below them, a hundred meters away. Small, one-man tents stretched in ordered ranks, and the smoke of cooking fires scented the air. An archery range had been set up to one side of the open space, and several dozen horses, all small and shaggy Ranger horses, were grazing close to the trees.

Even from where they sat on their horses, they could make out an air of urgency and activity throughout the camp. In the center of the tent lines was a larger pavilion, easily four meters by four meters and with enough headroom for a tall man to stand. The sides were currently rolled up and Will could see a group of green and gray clad men standing around a table, apparently deep in conversation. As they watched, one of the group detached himself, running to a horse waiting just outside the entrance. He mounted and spun the horse on its back legs, setting out through the camp at a gallop, heading for the narrow track through the trees at the far side.

He had barely disappeared into the deep shadows under the trees when another rider appeared from the opposite direction, galloping through the lines and reining in outside the large tent. His horse had barely stopped before he swung down and headed in to join the group inside.

"What is it?" Will asked. Frowning, he realized that several of the small tents were being struck and rolled up by their owners.

"Not sure," Halt replied. He gestured to the tent lines. "See if you can find us a decent campsite. I'll see what's going on."

He urged Abelard forward, then turned and called back: "Don't pitch the tents yet. From the looks of things, we may not be needing them." Then Abelard's hooves were drumming on the turf as he galloped toward the center of the camp.

Will and Gilan found a campsite under a large tree, reasonably close to the central gathering area. Then, uncertain as to what they should do next, they sat on a log, waiting for Halt's return. As a senior Ranger in the Corps, Halt had access to the larger pavilion, which Gilan explained was the command tent. The Corps Commandant, a Ranger named Crowley, would meet with his staff there each day to organize activities and to collate and evaluate the reports and information that individual Rangers brought to the Gathering.

Most of the tents near the two younger Rangers were unoccupied, but there was a thin gangly Ranger outside one, pacing impatiently back and forth, looking every bit as confused as Gilan and Will. Seeing them on the log, he moved over to join them.

"Any news?" he said immediately, and his face fell when Gilan answered.

"We were just about to ask you the same question." He held out his hand in greeting. "It's Merron, isn't it?" he said and they shook hands.

"That's right. And you're Gilan if I remember correctly." Gilan introduced Will, and the newcomer, who appeared to be in his early thirties, looked at him speculatively.

"So you're Halt's new apprentice," he said. "We wondered what you'd be like. I was going to be one of your assessors, you know."

"Going to be?" Gilan asked quickly, and Merron looked at him.

"Yes. I doubt we'll continue with the Gathering now." He hesitated, then added, "You mean you haven't heard?" The two newcomers shook their heads.

"Morgarath is up to something again," he said quietly, and Will felt a shiver of fear up his spine at the mention of that evil name.

"What's happened?" Gilan asked, his eyes narrowing. Merron shook his head, stirring the dirt in front of him with the toe of his boot in a frustrated gesture.

"There's no clear news so far. Only garbled reports. But it looks as if a force of Wargals broke out of Three Step Pass some days ago. They overran the sentries there and headed north."

"Was Morgarath with them?" Gilan asked. Will remained wide-eyed and silent. He couldn't bring himself to ask any questions, couldn't bring himself to actually mention Morgarath's name.

Merron shrugged in reply. "We don't know. Don't think so at this stage, but Crowley has been sending scouts out for the past two days. Could be it's just a raid. But if it's more than that, it could mean the start of another war. If so, it's a bad time to lose Lord Lorriac."

Gilan looked up, concern in his voice. "Lorriac is dead?" he asked, and Merron nodded.

"A stroke apparently. Or his heart. He was found dead a few days ago, with not a mark on him. Staring straight ahead. Stone cold dead."

"But he was in his prime!" Gilan said. "I saw him only a month ago and he was as healthy as a bull."

Merron shrugged. He had no explanation. He only knew the facts of the matter. "I suppose it can happen to anyone," he said. "You just never know."

"Who's Lord Lorriac?" Will asked Gilan quietly. The young Ranger shook his head thoughtfully as he answered.

"Lorriac of Steden. He was the leader of the King's heavy cavalry. Probably our best cavalry commander. As Merron said, if there's war, he'll be sorely missed."

A cold hand of fear closed around Will's heart. All his life people had spoken in whispers of Morgarath, if they had spoken of him at all. The Great Enemy had assumed the proportions almost of a myth—a legend from the old, dark days. Now the myth was becoming reality once more—a confronting, terrifying reality. He looked at Gilan for reassurance, but the young Ranger's handsome face showed nothing but doubt and concern for the future.

It was almost an hour before Halt rejoined them. As it was after midday, Will and Gilan had prepared a meal of bread, cold meat and dried fruit. The gray-haired Ranger slid down from Abelard's saddle and accepted a plate from Will, eating the food in quick bites.

"The Gathering's over," he said shortly, between mouthfuls. Seeing the senior Ranger's arrival, Merron had drifted back to join their group. He and Halt greeted each other briefly, then Merron posed the question that was on all their minds.

"Is it war?" he asked anxiously, and Halt shook his head.

"We don't know for certain. Latest reports show that Morgarath is still in the mountains."

"Then why did the Wargals break out?" Will asked. Everyone knew that Wargals only did the will of Morgarath. They never would have performed such a radical act without his direction. Halt's face was grim as he answered.

"They're only a small party—perhaps fifty of them. They were intended to act as a diversion. While our guards were busy chasing the Wargals, Crowley thinks that the two Kalkara slipped out of the Mountains and are holed up somewhere on the Solitary Plain."

Gilan gave a low whistle. Merron actually took a step back in surprise. Both the younger Rangers' faces showed their utter horror at the news. Will had no idea what the Kalkara might be, but judging from Halt's expression and the reactions of Gilan and Merron, they were obviously not good news.

"You mean they still exist?" Merron said. "I thought they died out years ago."

"Oh, they still exist all right," Halt said. "There are only two of them left, but that's enough to worry about."

There was a long silence between them. Finally, hesitantly, Will had to ask:

"What are they?"

Halt shook his head sadly. It was not a subject that he wanted to discuss with someone as young as Will. But, knowing what lay ahead of them all, he had no choice. The boy had to know.

"When Morgarath was planning his rebellion, he wanted more than an ordinary army. He knew that if he could terrify his enemies, his task would be far easier. So over the years, he made several expeditions into the Mountains of Rain and Night, searching."

"Searching for what?" Will asked, although he had the uncomfortable feeling that he knew what the answer would be.

"For allies he could use against the kingdom. The Mountains are an ancient, undisturbed part of the world. They've remained unchanged for centuries and there were rumors that strange beasts and ancient monsters still lived there. The rumors turned out to be all too true."

"Like the Wargals," Will put in, and Halt nodded.

"Yes. Like the Wargals. And he very quickly enslaved them and bent them to his will," he said with a touch of bitterness in his voice. "But then he found the Kalkara. And they're worse than Wargals. Much, much worse."

Will said nothing. The thought of beasts that were worse than Wargals was a disturbing one, to say the least.

"There were three of them. But one was killed about eight years ago, so we know a little more about them. Think of a creature somewhere between an ape and a bear, that walks upright, and you'll have an idea of what a Kalkara looks like."

"So does Morgarath control them with his mind, like the Wargals?" Will asked. Halt shook his head.

"No. They're more intelligent than Wargals. But they are totally obsessed with silver. They worship it and hoard it and Morgarath apparently gives it to them in large amounts so they'll do his bidding. And they do it well. They can be incredibly cunning while they stalk their prey."

"Prey?" Will asked. "What sort of prey?"

Halt and Gilan exchanged a glance and Will could see that his mentor was reluctant to talk about the subject. For a moment, he thought Halt was going to begin another of his dissertations on Will's endless questions. But then he realized this was a far more serious matter than idle curiosity as the grizzled Ranger replied quietly, "The Kalkara are assassins. Once they've been given a specific victim, they will do anything in their power to reach that person and kill them."

"Can't we stop them?" Will asked, his gaze shifting briefly to Halt's massive longbow and the bristling quiver of black arrows.

"They're very difficult to kill. They have a thick hair covering that's matted and bonded together so that it's almost like scales. An arrow will hardly penetrate. A battleax or a broadsword is best against them. Or a good thrust with a heavy spear might do the job."

Will felt a moment of relief. These Kalkara had started to sound almost invincible. But there were plenty of accomplished knights in the kingdom who would doubtless be able to account for them.

"So was it a knight who killed the one eight years ago?" he asked. Halt shook his head.

"Not *a* knight. Three. It took three fully armed knights to kill it, and only one of them survived the battle. What's more, he was crippled for life," Halt finished grimly.

"Three men? All of them knights?" Will said incredulously. "But how—"

Gilan interrupted him before he could finish. "The problem is, if you get close enough to use a sword or spear, the Kalkara can usually stop you before you have a chance."

As he spoke, his fingers drummed lightly on the hilt of the sword that he wore at his waist.

"How does it stop you?" Will asked, the momentary feeling of relief instantly dispelled by Gilan's words. This time it was Merron who answered.

"Its eyes," the gangly Ranger said. "If you look into its eyes, you are frozen helpless—the way a snake freezes a bird with its gaze before it kills it."

Will looked from one to the other of the three men, uncomprehending. What Merron was saying seemed too far-fetched to be true. Yet Halt wasn't contradicting him.

"Freezes you . . . how can it do that? Are you talking about magic here?"

Halt shrugged. Merron looked away uncomfortably. None of them liked discussing this subject.

"Some people call it magic," Halt finally said. "I think it's more likely a form of hypnotism. Either way, Merron is right. If a Kalkara can make you look into its eyes, you become paralyzed by sheer terror, unable to do anything to save yourself."

Will glanced around anxiously, as if expecting any moment to see an ape-bear creature charging out of the silent trees. He could feel panic growing in his chest. Somehow, he'd come to think of Halt as invincible. Yet here he was, seeming to admit that there was no defense against these vile monsters.

"Isn't there anything you can do?" he asked in a hopeless voice. Halt shrugged.

"Legend has it that they are particularly vulnerable to fire. Problem is, as before, getting close enough to do any damage. Carrying a naked flame makes it a little difficult to stalk a Kalkara. They tend to hunt at night and they can see you coming."

Will found it difficult to believe what he was hearing. Halt seemed so matter-of-fact about it all, and Gilan and Merron were obviously disturbed by his news.

There was an awkward silence, which Gilan broke by asking, "What makes Crowley think that Morgarath is using them?"

Halt hesitated. He'd been told Crowley's thoughts in private council. Then he shrugged. They'd all need to know about it sooner or later and they *were* all members of the Ranger Corps, even Will.

"He's already used them twice in the past year—to kill Lord Northolt and Lord Lorriac." The three younger men all exchanged puzzled glances, so he went on. "Northolt was thought to be killed by a bear, remember?" Will nodded slowly. He remembered now. On his first day as Halt's apprentice, the Ranger had received news of the supreme commander's death. "I thought at the time that Northolt was too skilled a hunter to be killed that way. Crowley evidently agrees."

"But what about Lorriac? Everyone said it was a stroke." It was Merron who asked this question. Halt glanced at him briefly, then answered.

"You'd heard that, had you? Well, his physician was most surprised. Said he'd never seen a healthier man. On the other hand . . ." He paused, and Gilan finished the thought.

"It could have been the work of the Kalkara."

Halt nodded. "Exactly. We don't know the full effects of the freezing stare they've developed. Maintained over a long enough time, the terror could well be enough to stop a man's heart. And there were vague reports that a large, dark animal was seen in the area."

Again, silence settled over the small group under the trees. Around them, Rangers bustled to and fro, striking camp and saddling their horses. Halt finally roused them all from their thoughts.

"We'd best be moving. Merron, you'll need to return to your fief. Crowley wants the army alerted and mobilized. Orders will be distributed in a few minutes."

Merron nodded and turned away toward his campsite. He paused and turned back. Something in Halt's voice, the way he had said "you'll need to return to your fief," had made him think.

"What about you three?" he said. "Where are you going?"

Even before Halt answered, Will knew what he was going to say. But that didn't make it any less terrifying or blood-chilling when the words were said.

"We're going after the Kalkara."

25

THE CAMP BUZZED WITH ACTIVITY AS TENTS CAME DOWN and Rangers repacked their equipment and tied on their saddle bags. Already, the first few riders had departed, heading back to their own fiefs.

Will was fastening the ties on their saddle packs, having replaced the few items they had taken out. Halt sat a few meters away, frowning thoughtfully as he studied a map of the area surrounding the Solitary Plain. The Plain itself was a vast, unmapped area, with no roads and few features indicated. A shadow fell across him and he looked up. Gilan stood there, a worried look on his face.

"Halt," he said in a low, concerned voice. "Are you sure about this?"

Halt met his gaze steadily. "Very sure, Gilan. It simply has to be done."

"But he's only a boy!" Gilan protested, looking quickly to where Will was tying a pack roll back in place behind Tug's saddle. Halt let go a long breath, his eyes dropping from Gilan's as he spoke.

"I know that. But he's a Ranger. Apprentice or not, he's a member of the Corps, like all of us." He saw that Gilan was about to protest further, out of concern for Will, and he felt a surge of affection for his old apprentice.

"Gilan, in an ideal world, I wouldn't put him at risk like this. But this isn't an ideal world. Everyone's going to have to play his part in this campaign, even boys like Will. Morgarath is preparing for something big. Crowley's agents have got wind that, on top of everything else, he's been in touch with the Skandians."

"The Skandians? What for?"

Halt shrugged. "We don't know the details, but my bet is he's hoping to form an alliance with them. They'll fight anyone for money. And apparently, they'll fight *for* anyone as well," he added, his distaste for mercenaries obvious in his voice. "The point is, we're shorthanded enough while Crowley tries to raise the army. Normally, I wouldn't go after the Kalkara with a force of less than five senior Rangers. But he simply can't spare them for me. So I've had to settle for the two I trust most—you and Will."

Gilan grinned crookedly. "Well, thanks for that, anyway." He was touched by Halt's confidence. He still looked up to his old mentor. Most of the Ranger Corps did.

"Besides, I thought that rusty old sword of yours might come in handy if we run into those horrors," Halt said. The Ranger Corps had chosen wisely when they allowed Gilan to continue his training with the weapon. Although very few people knew it, Gilan was one of the finest swordsmen in Araluen.

"As for Will," Halt continued, "don't sell him short. He's very resourceful. He's quick and brave and a damn good shot already. Best of all, he thinks quickly. My real thinking is that if we get on the trail of the Kalkara, we can send him for reinforcements. That'll help us and keep him out of harm's way."

Gilan scratched his chin thoughtfully. Now that Halt had explained it, it seemed the only logical course for them to take. He met the older man's eyes and nodded his understanding of the situation. Then he turned to organize his own kit, only to find that

Will had already repacked it and tied it to his saddle. He smiled at Halt.

"You're right," he said. "He does think for himself."

The three of them rode out a little while later, while the other Rangers were still receiving their orders. Mobilizing the Araluen army would be no small task, and it would be the Rangers' job to coordinate it, then be ready to guide the individual forces from the fifty fiefs to their assembly point at the Plains of Uthal. With both Gilan and Halt assigned to searching for the Kalkara, other Rangers had to be tasked with coordinating the forces from their fiefs as well.

There was little said between the three companions as Halt led the way to the southwest. Even Will's natural curiosity was subdued by the magnitude of the task ahead of them. As they rode in silence, his mind's eye kept conjuring images of savage bearlike creatures with the features of apes—creatures that might well prove to be invincible, even for someone of Halt's skill.

Eventually, however, as monotony set in, the horrific images receded and he began to wonder what plan, if any, Halt had in mind.

"Halt," he said, a little breathlessly, "where do you hope to find the Kalkara?"

Halt looked at the serious young face beside him. They were traveling at the Rangers' forced march pace—forty minutes in the saddle, riding at a steady canter, then twenty minutes on foot, leading the horses and allowing them to travel unburdened, while the men ran at a steady trot.

Every four hours, they would pause for one hour's rest, when they ate a quick meal of dried meat, hard bread and fruit, then rolled into their cloaks to sleep.

They had been leading the horses for some time now and Halt judged that it was time to rest. He led Abelard off the road and into the shelter of a grove of trees. Will and Gilan followed, dropping the reins and allowing their horses to graze.

"The best way I can think of," Halt said, in answer to Will's question, "is to start at their lair and see if they're in the vicinity."

"Do we know where that is?" Gilan asked.

"Best intelligence we have is that it's somewhere on the Solitary Plain, beyond the Stone Flutes. We'll scout around that area and see what we can find. If they're in the area, we should find that the odd sheep or goat is going missing from villages nearby. Although getting the villagers themselves to talk will be another matter. Plainspeople are a closemouthed bunch at the best of times."

"What's this Plain you're talking about?" Will asked, through a mouthful of hard bread. "And what on earth is a Stone Flute?"

"The Solitary Plain is a vast flat area—very few trees, mainly covered in rock outcrops and long grass," Halt told him. "The wind seems to always be blowing, no matter what time of year you go there. It's a dismal, depressing place and the Stone Flutes are the most dismal part of it."

"But what are . . . ," Will began, but Halt had only paused briefly.

"The Stone Flutes? Nobody really knows. They're a circle of standing stones built by the ancients, smack in the middle of the windiest part of the Plain.

"Nobody has ever worked out their original purpose but they're arranged in such a way that the wind is deflected around the circle, and through a series of holes in the stones themselves. They create a constant keening sound, although why anyone thought they sounded like flutes is beyond me. The sound is eerie and discordant and you can hear it from kilometers away. After a few minutes, it sets your teeth on edge—and it goes on and on for hours."

Will was silent. The thought of a dismal, windswept plain and stones that emitted a nonstop, keening wail seemed to take the last vestige of warmth from the late afternoon sun. He shivered involuntarily. Halt saw the movement and leaned forward to clap him on the shoulder encouragingly.

"Cheer up," he said. "Nothing's ever as bad as it sounds. Now let's get some rest."

They reached the outskirts of the Solitary Plain by noon the second day. Halt was right, Will thought, it was a vast, depressing place. The featureless ground stretched out before them for kilometer after kilometer, covered in tall, gray grass, made rank and dry by the constant wind.

The wind itself almost seemed to be a living presence. It rubbed on their nerves, blowing constantly and unvaryingly from the west, bending the tall grass before it as it swept across the flat ground of the Solitary Plain.

"Now you can see why they call it the Solitary Plain," Halt said to the two of them, reining Abelard in so they could come abreast of him. "When you ride out into this damned wind, you feel as if you're the only person left alive on earth."

It was true, Will thought. He felt small and insignificant against the emptiness of the Plain. And with the feeling of insignificance came an accompanying feeling of impotence. The wasteland they were riding across seemed to hint at the presence of arcane forces—forces far greater than his own capabilities. Even Gilan, normally cheerful and ebullient, seemed affected by the heavy, depressing atmosphere of the place. Only Halt seemed unchanged, remaining grim and taciturn as ever.

Gradually, as they rode, Will became aware of a disquieting sensation. Something was lurking, just outside the range of his conscious perception. Something that made him feel uneasy. He couldn't isolate it, couldn't even tell where it was coming from or what form

it took. It was just there, ever present. He shifted in his saddle, standing in the stirrups to scan the featureless horizon in the hopes that
he might see the source of it all. Halt noticed the movement.

"You've noticed them," he said. "It's the Stones."

And now that Halt said it, Will realized that it had been a
sound—so faint and so continuous that he couldn't isolate it as
such—that had been creating the sense of unease in his mind, and
the tight cramping of fear in the pit of his stomach. Or perhaps it was
just that as Halt said it, they came into proper earshot of the Stone
Flutes. Because now he could isolate it. It was an unmelodic series of
musical notes, all being played at once but creating a harsh, discordant sound that jangled the nerves and unsettled the mind. His left
hand crept unobtrusively to the hilt of his saxe knife as he rode, and
he drew comfort from the solid, dependable touch of the weapon.

They rode on through the afternoon, never seeming to advance
across the empty, featureless Plain. With each pace their horses took,
the horizons behind and before them seemed to neither recede nor
draw closer. It was as if they were marking time in an empty world.
The constant keening sound of the Stone Flutes was with them all
day, growing gradually stronger as they traveled. It was the only sign
that they were making progress. The hours passed and the sound
continued and Will found it no easier to bear. It wore at his nerves,
keeping him constantly on edge. As the sun began to sink at the
western rim, Halt reined Abelard in.

"We'll rest for the night," he announced. "It's almost impossible to
maintain a constant course in the dark. Without any significant land
features to set a course by, we could easily wind up going around in
circles."

Gratefully, the others dismounted. Fit as they were, the hours
spent at forced march pace had left them bone weary. Will began
scouting around the few stunted bushes that grew on the Plain,

searching for firewood. Halt, realizing what was in his mind, shook his head.

"No fire," he said. "We'd be visible for miles and we have no idea who might be watching."

Will paused, letting the small bundle he had gathered fall to the ground. "You mean the Kalkara?" he said. Halt shrugged.

"Them, or Plainspeople. We can't be sure that some of them aren't in league with the Kalkara. After all, living cheek by jowl with creatures like that, you might well end up cooperating with them, just to ensure your own safety. And we don't want them getting word that there are strangers on the Plain."

Gilan was unsaddling Blaze, his bay horse. He dropped the saddle to the ground and rubbed the horse down with a handful of the ever-present dry grass.

"You don't think we've been seen already?" he asked. Halt considered the question for a few seconds before answering.

"We might have been. There are just too many unknowns here—like where the Kalkara actually have their lair, whether or not the Plainspeople are their allies, whether or not any of them have seen us and reported our presence. But until I *know* we have been seen, we'll assume we haven't. So, no fire."

Gilan nodded reluctantly. "You're right, of course," he said. "It's just I'd happily kill someone for a cup of coffee."

"Light a fire to brew it," Halt told him, "and you might end up having to do just that."

26

It was a cold, cheerless camp. Tired from the hard pace they had been keeping up, the Rangers ate a cold meal—bread, dried fruit and cold meat once more, washed down with cold water from their canteens. Will was beginning to hate the sight of the virtually tasteless hard rations they carried. Then Halt took the first watch as Will and Gilan rolled themselves into their cloaks and slept.

It wasn't the first rough camp that Will had endured since his training period began. But this was the first time there wasn't the slight comfort of a crackling fire, or at least a bed of warm coals, to sleep by. He slept fitfully, uncomfortable dreams chasing through his subconscious—dreams of fearful creatures, strange and terrifying things that stayed just outside his consciousness, but close enough to the surface that he felt their presence, and was unsettled by them.

He was almost glad when Halt shook him gently awake for his watch.

The wind was scudding clouds across the moon. The moaning song of the Stones was stronger than ever. Will felt a weariness of spirit and wondered if the Stones had been designed to wear people down like this. The long grass around them hissed a counterpoint to the far-off keening. Halt pointed to a spot in the heavens, indicating an angle of elevation for Will to remember.

"When the moon reaches that angle," he told the apprentice, "turn over the watch to Gilan."

Will nodded, rousing himself and standing to stretch his stiff muscles. He picked up his bow and quiver and walked to the bush Halt had selected as a vantage point. Rangers on watch never stayed in the open by the campsite but always moved away ten or twenty meters, and found a place of concealment. That way, strangers coming upon the campsite would be less likely to see them. It was one of the many skills Will had learned in his months of training.

He took two arrows from the quiver and held them between the fingers of his bow hand. He would hold them thus for the four hours of his watch. If he needed them, there would be no excessive movement as he took an arrow from his quiver—movement that might alert an attacker. Then he flipped the cowl of his cloak over his head so he would merge with the irregular shape of the bush. His head and eyes scanned from side to side as Halt had taught him, changing focus constantly, from close to the campsite and out to the dim horizon around them. That way, his vision would not become fixated on one distance and one area and he'd stand a better chance of seeing movement. From time to time, he turned slowly through a complete circle, scanning the entire ground around them, moving slowly to keep his own movement as imperceptible as possible.

The keening of the Stones and the hissing of wind through the grass formed a constant background. But he began to hear other noises as well—the rustling of small animals in the grass, and other, less explicable, sounds. With each one, his heart raced a little faster, wondering if this might be the Kalkara, creeping in on the sleeping figures of his friends. Once, he was convinced that he could hear the breath of a heavy animal. Fear rose up in him, clutching at his throat, until he realized that, with his senses tuned to the utmost degree, he could actually hear his companions breathing quietly in their sleep.

He knew that, from any more than five meters away, he would be virtually invisible to the human eye, thanks to the cloak, the shadows and the shape of the bush around him. But he wondered if the Kalkara depended on sight alone. Perhaps they had other senses that would tell them that there was an enemy concealed in the bush. Perhaps, even now, they were moving closer, concealed by the long shifting grass, ready to strike . . .

His nerves, already stretched beyond endurance by the Stone Flutes' dismal song, urged him to spin around and identify the source of each new sound as he heard it. But he knew that to do so would be to reveal himself. He forced himself to move slowly, turning carefully until he faced the direction from which he thought the sound had come, assessing each new risk before discarding it.

In the long hours of tense watching, he saw nothing but the racing clouds, the fleeting moon and the undulating sea of grass that surrounded them. By the time the moon reached the preordained elevation, he was physically and mentally drained. He woke Gilan to take over the watch, then rolled back into his cloak again.

This time there were no dreams. Exhausted, he slept soundly until the gray light of dawn.

They saw the Stone Flutes by midmorning—a gray and surprisingly small circle of granite monoliths that stood at the top of a rise in the Plain. Their elected course took the riders a kilometer or so to one side of the Stones and Will was content to go no closer. The depressing song was now louder than ever, ebbing and flowing on the tide of the wind.

"Next flute player I meet," said Gilan with grim humor, "I'm going to split his lip for him."

They rode on, the kilometers passing beneath their horses' hooves, hour after hour, one the same as the next, with nothing new to see and always with the faint howl of the Stones at their back, keeping their nerves on edge.

The Plainsman rose suddenly from the grass some fifty meters away from them. Small, dressed in gray rags and with long hair hanging unkempt to his shoulders, he glared at them through mad eyes for several seconds.

Will's heart had barely recovered from the shock of his sudden appearance when he was off, bent double and running through the grass, seeming to sink into it. Within seconds, he had disappeared, swallowed by the grass. Halt was about to urge Abelard in pursuit, but he stopped. The arrow he had selected instantly and laid on the bowstring remained undrawn. Gilan was also ready to shoot, his reactions every bit as sharp as Halt's. He too held his shot, looking curiously at his senior.

Halt shrugged. "May mean nothing," he said. "Or maybe he's off to tell the Kalkara. But we can hardly kill him on suspicion."

Gilan let out a short bark of laughter, more to release the tension he felt as a result of the man's unexpected appearance.

"I suppose there's no difference," he said, "whether we find the Kalkara or they find us." Halt's eyes fixed on him for a moment, without any sign of answering humor.

"Believe me, Gilan," he said, "there's a big difference."

They had abandoned the forced march pace now and walked

their horses slowly through the tall grass. Behind them, the sound of the Stones began to fade a little, much to Will's relief. Now, he realized, the wind was carrying it away from them.

Some time passed following the sudden appearance of the Plain dweller, with no further sign of life. A question had been nagging at Will all through the afternoon.

"Halt?" he said experimentally, not sure if Halt would order him to silence. The Ranger looked at him, eyebrows raised in a sign that he was prepared to answer questions, so Will continued. "Why do you think Morgarath has enlisted the Kalkara? What does he stand to gain?"

Halt realized that Gilan was waiting for his answer as well. He marshaled his thoughts before he replied. He was a little reluctant to verbalize his thoughts, as so much of the answer depended on guesswork and intuition.

"Who knows why Morgarath ever does anything?" he answered slowly. "I can't give you a definite answer. All I can tell you is what I assume—and what Crowley thinks as well."

He glanced quickly at his two companions. It was obvious from their expectant expressions that they were prepared to accept his assumptions as ironclad fact. Sometimes, he thought wryly, a reputation for being right all the time could be a heavy burden.

"There's a war coming," he went on. "That much is already obvious. The Wargals are on the move and we've heard that Morgarath has been in contact with Ragnak." He saw the puzzled expression flit across Will's face. Gilan, he knew, understood who Ragnak was. "Ragnak is the Oberjarl, or supreme lord, if you like, of the Skandians—the sea wolves." He saw the quick flash of comprehension and went on.

"This is obviously going to be a bigger war than we've fought before and we're going to need all our resources—and our best commanders to lead us. I think that's what Morgarath has in mind. He's seeking to weaken us by having the Kalkara kill our leaders. Northolt, the supreme army commander, and Lorriac, our best cavalry commander, have gone already. Certainly there will be other men who will step into those positions but there will inevitably be some confusion in the changeover period, some loss of cohesion. I think that's what's behind Morgarath's plan."

Gilan said thoughtfully, "There's another aspect as well. Both those men were instrumental in his defeat last time. He's destroying our command structure and getting revenge at the same time."

Halt nodded. "That's true, of course. And to a twisted mind like Morgarath's, revenge is a powerful motive."

"So you think there'll be more killings?" Will asked, and Halt met his gaze steadily.

"I think there'll be more attempts. Morgarath has sent them out twice with targets and they've succeeded. I don't see any reason why they won't go after others. Morgarath has reason to hate a lot of people in the kingdom. The King himself, perhaps. Or maybe Baron Arald—he caused Morgarath some grief in the last war."

And so did you, Will thought, with a sudden flash of fear for his teacher. He was about to voice the thought that Halt might be a target, then realized that Halt was probably well aware of the fact himself. Gilan was asking the older Ranger another question.

"One thing I don't understand. Why do the Kalkara keep returning to their hideout? Why not just move from one victim to the next?"

"I suppose that's one of the few advantages we do have," Halt told them. "They're savage and merciless and more intelligent than Wargals. But they're not human. They are totally single-minded. Show them a victim and they'll hunt him down and kill him or die themselves in the attempt. But they can only keep track of one victim at a time. Between killings, they'll return to their lair. Then Morgarath—or one of his underlings—will prime them for their next victim and they'll head out again. Our best hope is to intercept them on the way if they've been given a new target. Or kill them in their lair if they haven't."

Will looked for the thousandth time at the featureless grass plain that lay before them. Somewhere out there, the two fearsome creatures were waiting, perhaps with a new victim already in mind. Halt's voice interrupted his train of thought.

"Sun's going down," he said. "We may as well camp here."

They swung down stiffly from their saddles, easing the girths to make their horses more comfortable.

"That's one thing about this blasted place," Gilan said, looking around them. "One spot is as good as another to camp. Or as bad."

Will woke from a dreamless sleep to the touch of Halt's hand on his shoulder. He tossed back the cloak, glanced at the scudding moon overhead and frowned. He couldn't have been asleep for more than an hour. He started to say so, but Halt stopped him, placing a finger to his lips for silence. Will looked around and realized Gilan was already awake, standing above him, his head turned to the northeast, back the way they had come, listening.

Will came to his feet, moving carefully to avoid making any undue noise. His hands had automatically gone to his weapons, but he relaxed as he realized there was no immediate threat. The other two were listening intently. Then Halt raised a hand and pointed to the north.

"There it is again," he said softly.

Then Will heard it, above the moaning of the Stone Flutes and the soughing of the wind through the grass, and the blood froze in his veins. It was a high-pitched, bestial howl that ululated and climbed in pitch. An inhuman sound carried to them on the wind from the throat of a monster.

Seconds later, another howl answered the first. Slightly deeper in pitch, it seemed to come from a position a little to the left of the first. Without needing to be told, Will knew what the sounds meant.

"It's the Kalkara," Halt said grimly. "They have a new target and they're hunting."

27

THE THREE COMPANIONS SPENT A SLEEPLESS NIGHT AS THE hunting cries of the Kalkara dwindled to the north. When they first heard the sounds, Gilan had moved to saddle Blaze, the bay horse snorting nervously at the fearsome howling of the two beasts. Halt, however, gestured for him to stop.

"I'm not going after those things in the dark," he said briefly. "We'll wait till first light, then look for their tracks."

The tracks were easy enough to find, as the Kalkara obviously made no attempt to conceal their passing. The long grass had been crushed by the two heavy bodies, leaving a clear trail pointing east-northeast. Halt found the trail left by the first of the two monsters, then a few minutes later, Gilan found the second, about a quarter-kilometer to the left and traveling parallel—close enough to provide support in case of an attack, but distant enough to avoid any trap set for its brother.

Halt considered the situation for a few moments, then came to a decision.

"You stay with the second one," he told Gilan. "Will and I will follow this one. I want to make sure they both keep heading in the same direction. I don't want one of them doubling back to come be-hind us."

"You think they know we're here?" Will asked, working hard to keep his voice sounding steady and disinterested.

"They could. There's been time for that Plainsman we saw to have warned them. Or maybe it's just coincidence and they're head-ing out on their next mission." He glanced at the trail of crushed grass, moving irrevocably in one constant direction. "They certainly seem to have a purpose." He turned to Gilan again. "In any event, keep your eyes peeled and pay close attention to Blaze. The horses will sense these beasts before we will. We don't want to run into an ambush."

Gilan nodded and swung Blaze away to return to the second trail. At a hand signal from Halt, the three Rangers began riding for-ward, following the direction the Kalkara had taken.

"I'll watch the trail," Halt told Will. "You keep an eye on Gilan, just in case."

Will turned his attention to the tall Ranger, some two hundred meters away and keeping pace with them. Blaze was only visible from the shoulders up, his lower half masked by the long grass. From time to time, undulations in the intervening ground took both rider and horse out of sight, and the first time this happened, Will re-acted with a cry of alarm as Gilan simply seemed to disappear into the ground. Halt turned quickly, an arrow already at half draw, but at that moment, Gilan and Blaze reappeared, seemingly unconscious of the moment of panic they'd caused.

"Sorry," Will muttered, annoyed that he'd allowed his nerves to get the better of him. Halt regarded him shrewdly.

"That's all right," he said steadily. "I'd rather you let me know any time you even think there's a problem." Halt knew only too well that, having called a false alarm once, Will might be reluctant to react next time—and that could be fatal for all of them.

"Tell me every time you lose sight of Gilan. And tell me again when he reappears," he said. Will nodded, understanding his teacher's reasoning.

And so they rode on, the keening cry of the Flutes swelling in their ears again as they approached the stone circle. This time, they would pass much closer, Will realized, as the Kalkara seemed to be heading straight for the site. As they rode, their passage was marked by intermittent reports from Will.

"He's gone . . . still gone . . . All right. I see him again." The dips and rises in the ground were virtually invisible under the waving cover of tall grass. In fact, Will was never sure whether it was Gilan passing through a depression or he and Halt. Often it was a combination of both.

There was one bad time Gilan and Blaze sank from sight and didn't reappear within the customary few seconds.

"I can't see him . . . ," Will reported. Then: "Still gone . . . still gone . . . no sign of him . . ." His voice began to rise in pitch as the tension grew within him. "No sign of them . . . *still* no sign . . ."

Halt brought Abelard to a stop, his bow ready once again, his eyes searching the ground to their left as they waited for Gilan to reappear. He let go a piercing whistle, three ascending notes. There was a pause, then an answering whistle, this time the same three notes in descending order, came clearly to them. Will heaved a sigh of relief and just at that moment Gilan reappeared, large as life. He faced them and made a large gesture with both arms raised in an obvious question: *What's the problem?*

Halt made a negative gesture and they moved on.

As they approached the Stone Flutes, Halt became more and more watchful. The Kalkara that he and Will were trailing was heading straight toward the circle. He reined in Abelard and shaded his eyes, studying the dismal gray rocks intently, looking for movement or any sign that the Kalkara might be lying in wait to ambush them.

"It's the only decent cover for miles around," he said. "Let's not take the chance that the damn thing could be lurking in there waiting for us. We'll go a little carefully, I think."

He signaled for Gilan to join them and explained the situation. Then they split up to form a wide perimeter around the Stones, riding in slowly from three different directions, checking their horses for any possible sign of reaction as they came closer. But the site was empty, although close-up, the jangling moan of the wind through the flute holes was close to unbearable. Halt chewed his lip reflectively, staring out across the sea of grass at the two undeviating trails left by the Kalkara.

"This is taking us too long," he said finally. "As long as we can see their trails for a couple of hundred meters ahead, we'll move faster. Slow down when you come to a rise or any time when the trail isn't visible for more than fifty meters."

Gilan nodded his understanding and resumed his wide position. They urged their horses on now in a canter, the easy lope of the Ranger horse that would eat the kilometers ahead of them. Will maintained his watch on Gilan and whenever the visible trail diminished, either Halt or Gilan would whistle and they would slow to a walk until the ground opened up again before them.

As night fell, they camped once again. Halt still refused to follow the two killers in the dark, even though the moon meant their trail was easily visible.

"Too easy for them to double back in the dark," he said. "I want plenty of warning when they finally come at us."

"You think they will?" asked Will, noticing that Halt had said *when*, not *if*. The Ranger smiled reassuringly at his young pupil.

"Always assume an enemy knows you're there and that he will attack you," he said. "That way, you tend to avoid unpleasant surprises." He smiled grimly to reassure the boy. "It can still be unpleasant, but at least it's not a surprise."

In the morning, they resumed the trail once more, moving at the same brisk pace, slowing only when they had no clear sight of the lie of the land ahead of them. By early afternoon, they had reached the edge of the Plain and rode once again into the wooded country to the north of the Mountains of Rain and Night.

Here, they found, the two Kalkara had joined company, no longer keeping the wide separation they had maintained on the open ground of the Plain. But their chosen path remained the same, east of northeast. The three Rangers followed this course for another hour before Halt reined in Abelard and signaled the others to dismount for a conference. They grouped around a map of the kingdom that he unrolled out on the grass, using arrows as weights to stop the edges from rerolling.

"Judging from their tracks, we've made up some time on them," he said. "But they're still a good half day ahead of us. Now, this is the direction they're following . . ."

He took another arrow and laid it on the map, orientating it so that it pointed to the direction the Kalkara had been following for the past two days and nights.

"As you can see, if they keep going in this direction, there are only two places of any significance that they could be heading for." He pointed to a place on the map. "Here—the Gorlan Ruins. Or farther north, Castle Araluen itself."

Gilan drew in breath sharply. "Castle Araluen?" he said. "You don't think they'd dare try for King Duncan?"

Halt looked at him and shook his head. "I simply don't know," he replied. "We don't know nearly enough about these beasts and half of what we think we know is probably myth and legend. But you've got to admit, it would be a bold stroke—a masterstroke—and Morgarath has never been averse to that sort of thing."

He let the others digest the thought for a few moments, then traced a line from their current position to the northwest. "Now, I've been thinking. Look, here's Castle Redmont. Perhaps a day's ride away—and then another day to here."

From Redmont, he traced a line northeast, to the Gorlan Ruins marked on the map.

"One person, riding hard, and using two horses, could make it in less than a day to Redmont, and then lead the Baron and Sir Rodney here, to the Ruins. If the Kalkara keep moving at the pace they are, we might just be able to intercept them there. It'll be close, but it's possible. And with two warriors like Arald and Rodney on hand, we'll stand a far better chance of stopping the damn things once and for all."

"One moment, Halt," Gilan interrupted. "You said *one* person, riding *two* horses?"

Halt met Gilan's gaze with his own. He could see that the young Ranger had already divined what he had in mind.

"That's right, Gilan," he said. "And the lightest one among us will travel fastest. I want you to turn Blaze over to Will. If he alternates between Tug and your horse, he can do it in the time."

He saw the reluctance on Gilan's face and understood it perfectly. No Ranger would like the idea of handing his horse over to someone else—even another Ranger. But at the same time Gilan understood the logic behind the suggestion. Halt waited for the younger man to break the silence, while Will watched the two of them, eyes wide with alarm at the thought of the responsibility that was about to be loaded onto him.

Finally, reluctantly, Gilan broke the silence.

"I suppose it makes sense," he said. "So what do you want me to do?"

"Follow behind me on foot," Halt said briskly, rolling the chart up and replacing it in his saddlebag. "If you can get hold of a horse anywhere, do so and catch up with me. Otherwise, we'll rendezvous at Gorlan. If we miss the Kalkara there, Will can wait for you—with Blaze. I'll keep following the Kalkara until you all catch up with me."

Gilan nodded his acquiescence and Halt felt a surge of fondness for him as he did. Once Gilan saw the sense of his proposal, he wasn't the kind to raise arguments or objections. He did say, rather ruefully:

"I thought you said my sword might come in handy?"

"I did," replied Halt, "but this gives me a chance to bring in two fully armored knights, with axes and lances. And you know that's the best way to fight the Kalkara."

"True," said Gilan, then, taking Blaze's bridle, he knotted the reins together and threw them over the bay's neck. "You may as well start out on Tug," he said to Will. "That'll give Blaze a chance to rest. He'll follow behind you without a lead rein and so will Tug when you're riding Blaze. Tie the reins up like this on Tug's neck so they don't dangle down and snag anything."

He began to turn back to Halt, then remembered something. "Oh yes, before you mount him the first time, remember to say *Brown Eyes*."

"*Brown Eyes*," Will repeated, and Gilan couldn't help grinning.

"Not to me. To the horse." It was an old Ranger joke and they all smiled. Then Halt brought them back to the business at hand.

"Will? You're confident you can find your way to Redmont?"

Will nodded. He touched the pocket where he kept his own copy of the chart, and glanced at the sun for direction.

"Northwest," he said tightly, indicating the direction he had chosen. Halt nodded, satisfied.

"You'll strike the Salmon River before dusk, that will give you a good reference point. And the main highway is just a little way west of the river. Keep to a steady canter all the way. Don't try to race the horses—you'll just tire them out that way and you'll be slower in the long run. Travel safely now."

Halt swung up into Abelard's saddle and Will mounted Tug. Gilan pointed to Will and spoke in Blaze's ear.

"Follow, Blaze. Follow." The bay horse, intelligent as all Ranger horses were, tossed its head as if in acknowledgment of the order. Before they parted, Will had one more question that had been bothering him.

"Halt," he said, "the Gorlan Ruins . . . what exactly are they?"

"It's ironic, isn't it?" Halt replied. "They're the ruins of Castle Gorlan, Morgarath's former fiefdom."

28

THE RIDE TO CASTLE REDMONT SOON SETTLED INTO A BLUR of weariness. The two horses maintained the steady lope for which they had been bred. The temptation, of course, was to urge Tug into a wild gallop, with Blaze following behind. But Will knew that such a course would be self-defeating. He was moving at the horses' best speed. As Old Bob, the horse trainer, had told him, Ranger horses could maintain a canter all day without tiring.

It was a different matter for the rider. Added to the physical effort of moving constantly to the rhythm of whichever horse he was riding—and the two had distinctly different gaits, due to their difference in size—was the equally debilitating mental strain.

What if Halt were wrong? What if the Kalkara had suddenly veered to the west and were heading now on a course that would intercept his? What if he made some terrible mistake and failed to reach Redmont in time?

That last fear, the fear of self-doubt, was the hardest one of all to deal with. In spite of the hard training he had undergone over the past months, he was still little more than a boy. What was more, he had always had Halt's judgment and experience to rely on in the past. Now he was alone—and he knew how much depended on his ability to carry out the task he had been set.

The thoughts, the doubts, the fears crowded his tired mind, tumbling over each other, jostling for position. The Salmon River came and went beneath the steady rhythm of his horses' hooves. He paused to water the horses briefly at the bridge, then, once on the King's Highway, he made excellent time, with only short halts at regular intervals to change his mount.

The day's shadows lengthened and the trees overhanging the road grew dark and menacing. Each noise from the darkening trees, each vaguely seen movement in the shadows, brought his heart to his mouth with a lurch.

Here, an owl hooted and stooped to fasten its claws around an unwary mouse. There, a badger prowled, hunting its prey like a gray shadow in the undergrowth of the forest. With each movement and noise, Will's imagination worked overtime. He began to see great black figures—much as he imagined a Kalkara would look—in every patch of shadow, in every dark clump of bushes that stirred with the light breeze. Reason told him that there was almost no chance that the Kalkara would be seeking him out. Imagination and fear replied that they were abroad somewhere—and who was to say they weren't close by?

Imagination and fear won.

And so the long, fear-filled night passed, until the low light of dawn found a weary figure hunched in the saddle of a sturdy, barrel-chested horse that drove steadily onwards to the northwest.

Dozing in the saddle, Will snapped awake with a start, feeling the first warmth of the sun's rays upon him. Gently, he reined Tug in and the little horse stood, head down, sides heaving. Will realized he had been riding far longer than he should have been, his fear having driven him to keep Tug running through the darkness, long after he should have rested him. He dismounted stiffly, aching in every joint, and paused to rub the horse's soft nose affectionately.

"Sorry, boy," he said. Tug, reacting to the touch and the voice that he now knew so well, tossed his head and shook his shaggy mane. If Will had asked it, he would have continued uncomplaining until he dropped. Will looked around. The cheerful light of early morning had dispelled all the dark fears of the night before. Now, he felt slightly foolish as he remembered those moments of choking panic. Stiffly, he dismounted, then loosened the girth straps on the saddle. He gave his horse ten minutes' respite, until Tug's breathing seemed to settle and his sides ceased heaving. Then, marveling at the recuperative powers and endurance of the Ranger horse breed, he tightened the girths on Blaze's saddle and swung astride the bay, groaning softly as he did so. Ranger horses might recover quickly. Ranger apprentices took a little longer.

It was late morning when Castle Redmont finally came in sight.

Will was riding Tug again, the small horse seemingly none the worse for the hard night he'd put in, as they crested the last row of hills and the green valley of Arald's barony stretched out before them.

Exhausted, Will stopped for a few seconds, leaning tiredly on the pommel. They'd come so far, so quickly. He looked with relief on the familiar sight of the castle—and the tidy little village that nestled contentedly in its shadow. Smoke was rising from chimneys. Farmers were walking slowly home from their fields for their midday meal. The castle itself stood solid and reassuring in its bulk at the crest of the hill.

"It all looks so . . . normal," Will said to his horse.

Somehow, he realized, he had been expecting to find things changed. The kingdom was about to go to war again for the first time in fifteen years, but here, life went on as normal.

Then, realizing he was wasting time, he urged Tug forward until he was stretched out in a gallop, both boy and horse eager to finish this final leg of their journey.

People looked up in surprise at the rapid passing of the small, green and gray clad figure, hunched low over the neck of his dusty horse, with a larger, bay horse following behind. One or two of the villagers recognized Will and called a greeting. But their words were lost in the rattle of hooves.

The rattle turned to an echoing drumming as they swept across the lowered drawbridge into the foreyard of the castle itself. Then the drumming became an urgent clattering on the cobblestones of the yard. Will drew back lightly on the reins and Tug slid to a halt by the entrance to Baron Arald's tower.

The two men-at-arms on duty there, surprised by his sudden appearance and breakneck pace, stepped forward and barred his path with their crossed pikes.

"Just a moment, you!" said one of them, a corporal. "Where do you think you're off to in such a clatter and a rush?"

Will opened his mouth to reply, but before words could form, an angry voice boomed from behind him.

"What the hell do you think you're doing, you idiot? Don't you recognize a King's Ranger when you see one?"

It was Sir Rodney, striding across the courtyard on his way to see the Baron. The two sentries stiffened to attention as Will turned, gratefully, to the Battlemaster.

"Sir Rodney," he said, "I have an urgent message from Halt for Lord Arald and yourself."

As Halt had observed to Will after the boar hunt, the Battlemaster was a shrewd man. He took in Will's disheveled clothing, the two dusty horses, standing, heads drooping tiredly, and realized this was no time for a lot of foolish questions. He jerked a thumb at the doorway.

"Best come in and tell us then." He then turned to the sentries. "Have these horses looked after. Feed and water them."

"Not too much of either, please, Sir Rodney," Will said quickly. "Just a small amount of grain and water, and maybe you could have them rubbed down. I'll be needing them again soon."

Rodney's eyebrows rose at that. Will and the horses looked as if they could use a long rest.

"Something must be urgent," he said, adding to the corporal, "See to the horses then. And have food brought to Baron Arald's study— and a jug of cold milk."

The two knights whistled in astonishment as Will told them the news. Word had already come that Morgarath was mustering his army, and the Baron had sent out messengers to assemble his own troops—both knights and men-at-arms. But the news of the Kalkara was something else entirely. No hint of that had reached Castle Redmont.

"You say Halt thinks they may be going after the King?" Baron Arald asked as Will finished speaking. Will nodded, then hesitated before he added:

"Yes, my lord. But I think there's another possibility."

He was loath to go further, but the Baron gestured for him to continue and he finally gave voice to the suspicion that had been building inside him through the long night and day.

"Sir . . . I think maybe there's a chance that they're after Halt himself."

Once the suspicion was voiced, and the fear was out in the open to be examined and evaluated, he felt the better for it. Somewhat to his surprise, Baron Arald didn't dismiss the idea. He stroked his beard thoughtfully as he digested the words.

"Go on," he said, wanting to hear Will's reasoning.

"It's just that, Halt felt Morgarath might be looking for revenge—looking to punish those who fought him last time. And I thought, probably Halt did him the most harm of all, didn't he?"

"That's true enough," said Rodney.

"And I thought, maybe the Kalkara knew we were following them—the Plainsman had plenty of time to find them and tell them. And maybe they were leading Halt on, until they found a place for an ambush. So while he thinks he's hunting them, he's actually the one being hunted."

"And the Gorlan Ruins would be an ideal place for it," Arald agreed. "In that tumble of rocks, they could be on him before he had a chance to use that longbow of his. Well, Rodney, there's no time to waste. You and I will go. Half armor, I think. We'll move faster that way. Lances, axes and broadswords. And we'll take two horses each—we'll follow Will's example there. We'll leave in an hour. Have Karel gather another ten knights and follow us as soon as he can."

"Yes, my lord," the Battlemaster replied.

Baron Arald turned back to Will.

"You've done a good job, Will. We'll take care of this now. As for you, you look as if you could use eight hours' solid sleep."

Wearily, aching in every muscle and joint, Will drew himself erect.

"I'd like to come with you, my lord," he said. He sensed that the Baron was about to disagree and added hurriedly, "Sir, none of us knows what is going to happen, and Gilan is out there somewhere on foot. Besides . . ." He hesitated.

"Go on, Will," the Baron said quietly and, when the boy looked up, Arald saw the steel in his eyes.

"Halt is my master, sir, and he's in danger. My place is with him," Will said.

The Baron assessed him shrewdly, then came to a decision.

"Very well. But at least you can get an hour's rest. There's a cot in that annex over there." He indicated a curtained-off section of the study. "Why don't you use it?"

"Yes, sir," said Will gratefully. His eyes felt as if he'd had handfuls of sand rubbed into them. He had never been happier to obey an order in his life.

29

THROUGH THAT LONG AFTERNOON, WILL FELT AS IF HE HAD lived his entire life in the saddle, his only respite being the hourly changes from one horse to another.

A brief pause to dismount, loosen the girth straps of the horse he had been riding, tighten those on the horse which had been following, then he would remount and ride on. Again and again, he marveled at the amazing endurance shown by Tug and Blaze as they maintained their steady canter. He even had to rein them in a little, to keep pace with the battlehorses ridden by the two knights. Big, powerful and trained for war as they might be, they couldn't match the constant pace of the Ranger horses, in spite of the fact that they were fresh when the small party had left Castle Redmont.

They rode without speaking. There was no time for idle talk and, even if there had been, it would have been difficult to hear one another above the drumming thunder of the four heavy battlehorses, the lighter rattle of Tug and Blaze's hooves and the constant clank of equipment and weapons that accompanied them as they rode.

Both men carried long war lances—hard ash poles more than three meters in length, tipped with a heavy iron point. In addition, each had a broadsword strapped to their saddles—huge, two-handed weapons that dwarfed the swords they normally wore in day-to-day use—and Rodney had a heavy battleax slung at the rear right pommel of his saddle. It was the lances on which they would place greatest trust, however. They would keep the Kalkara at a distance, and so reduce the chance that the knights might be frozen by the terrifying stare of the two beasts. Apparently, the hypnotic gaze was only effective at close quarters. If a man couldn't see the eyes clearly, there was little chance of their paralyzing him with their gaze.

The sun was dropping fast behind them, throwing their shadows out before them, long and distorted by the low angle light. Arald glanced over his shoulder at the sun's position and called to Will.

"How long before dusk, Will?"

Will turned in his saddle and frowned at the descending ball of light before answering. "Less than an hour, my lord."

The Baron shook his head doubtfully. "It'll be a close run to get there before full dark then," he said. He urged his battlehorse onward, increasing speed a little. Tug and Blaze matched the increase without effort. None of them wanted to be hunting the Kalkara in the dark.

The hour's rest at the castle had done wonders for Will. But it seemed that it had happened in another lifetime now. He thought over the cursory briefing that Arald had given as they mounted to leave Redmont. If they found the Kalkara at the Gorlan Ruins, Will was to hold back while the Baron and Sir Rodney charged the two monsters. There were no complex tactics involved, just a headlong charge that might take the two killers by surprise.

"If Halt's there, I'm sure he'll take a hand too. But I want you well back out of harm's way, Will. That bow of yours won't make any impression on a Kalkara."

"Yes, sir," Will had said. He had no intention of getting close to the Kalkara. He was more than content to leave things to the two knights, protected by their shields, helmets and half armor of chain mail shirts and leggings. However, Arald's next words quickly dispelled any overconfidence he might have had in their ability to deal with the beasts.

"If the damn things get the better of us, I'll want you to ride for more help. Karel and the others will be somewhere behind us. Find them, then go after the Kalkara with them. Track those beasts down and kill them."

Will had said nothing to that. The fact that Arald even contemplated failure, when he and Rodney were the two foremost knights within a two hundred kilometer radius, spoke volumes of his concern about the Kalkara. For the first time, Will realized that in this contest, the odds were heavily against them.

The sun was trembling on the brink of the world, the shadows at their longest, and they still had several kilometers to go. Baron Arald raised a hand and brought the party to a stop. He glanced at Rodney and jerked a thumb at the bundle of pitch-soaked torches each man carried behind his saddle.

"Torches, Rodney," he said briefly. The Battlemaster demurred for a moment.

"Are you sure, my lord? They'll give away our position if the Kalkara are watching."

Arald shrugged. "They'll hear us coming anyway. And among the trees, we'll move too slowly without the light. Let's take the chance."

He was already striking his flint and steel together, igniting a spark that set his small pile of tinder smoking, then flaring into flame. He held the torch in the flame and the thick, sticky pine pitch with which it was impregnated suddenly caught and burst into yellow flame. Rodney leaned toward him with another torch and lit it in the Baron's flame. Then, holding the torches high, their lances held in place by leather thongs looped around their right wrists, they resumed their gallop, thundering into the darkness beneath the trees as they finally left the broad road they had been following since noon.

It was another ten minutes before they heard the screaming.

It was an unearthly sound that twisted the stomach into knots of fear and turned the blood cold. Involuntarily, the Baron and Sir Rodney reined in as they heard it. Their horses plunged wildly against the reins. It came from straight ahead of them and rose and fell, until the night air quaked with the horror of it.

"Good God in heaven!" the Baron exclaimed. "What is that?" His face was ashen as the hellish sound soared through the night toward them, to be answered immediately by another, identical howl.

But Will had heard the terrible noise before. He felt the blood leave his face now as he realized his fears were being proven correct.

"It's the Kalkara," he said. "They're hunting."

And he knew there was only one person out there that they could be after. They had turned back and were hunting Halt.

"Look, my lord!" Rodney said, pointing to the rapidly darkening night sky. Through a break in the tree cover, they saw it, a sudden flare of light reflecting in the sky, evidence of a fire in the near distance.

"That's Halt!" the Baron said. "Bound to be. And he'll need help!"

He rammed his spurs into the tired battlehorse's flanks, urging the beast forward into a lumbering gallop, the torch in his hand streaming flame and sparks behind him as Sir Rodney and Will galloped in his tracks.

It was an eerie sensation, following those flaming, spitting torches through the trees, their elongated tongues of flame blowing back behind the two riders, casting weird and terrifying shadows among the trees, while ahead of them, the glow of the large fire, presumably lit by Halt, grew stronger and nearer with each stride.

They broke out of the trees with virtually no warning, and before them was a scene from nightmares.

There was a short space of open grass, then the ground beyond was a litter of tumbled rocks and boulders. Giant pieces of masonry, still held together by mortar, lay scattered on their sides and edges, sometimes half buried in the soft grassy earth. The ruined walls of Castle Gorlan surrounded the scene on three sides, nowhere rising to more than five meters in height, destroyed and cast down by a vengeful kingdom after Morgarath had been driven out of his keep and back into the Mountains of Rain and Night. The resulting chaos of rocks and sections of tumbled wall was like the playground of a giant child—scattered in all directions, piled carelessly on top of one another, leaving virtually no clear ground at all.

The whole scene was illuminated by the leaping, twisting flames of a bonfire some forty meters in front of them. And beside it, a horrific figure crouched, screaming hatred and fury, plucking uselessly at the mortal wound in its chest that had finally brought it down.

Over two and a half meters tall, with shaggy, matted, scale-like hair covering its entire body, the Kalkara had long, talon-clad arms that reached to beneath its knees. Relatively short, powerful hind legs gave it the ability to cover the ground at a deceptive speed in a series of leaps and bounds. All of this the three riders took in as they emerged from the trees. But what they noticed most was the face— savage and apelike, with huge, yellowed canine teeth and red, glowing eyes filled with hatred and the blind desire to kill. The face turned toward them now and the beast screamed a challenge, tried to rise, and stumbled back into a half crouch again.

"What's wrong with it?" Rodney asked, reining in his horse. Will pointed to the cluster of arrows that protruded from its chest. There must have been eight of them, all placed within a hand's breadth of each other.

"Look!" he cried. "Look at the arrows!"

Halt, with his uncanny ability to aim and fire in a blur of movement, must have sent a volley of arrows, one after the other, to smash into the armorlike matted hair, each one widening a gap in the monster's defenses until the final arrow had penetrated deep into its flesh. Its black blood ran in sheets down its torso and again it screamed its hatred at them.

"Rodney!" yelled Baron Arald. "With me! Now!"

Dropping the lead rein to his spare horse, he tossed the flaming torch to one side, couched his lance and charged. Rodney was a half second behind him, the two battlehorses thundering across the open space. The Kalkara, its lifeblood saturating the ground at its feet, rose to meet them, in time to take the two lance points, one after the other, in the chest.

It was all but dead. Even so, the weight and strength of the monster checked the onward rush of the battlehorses. They reared back on their haunches as both knights leaned forward in the stirrups to drive the lance points home. The sharp iron penetrated, smashing through the matted hair. The force of the charge drove the Kalkara from its feet and hurled it backward, into the flames of the fire behind it.

For an instant nothing happened. Then there was a blinding flash, and a pillar of red flame that reached ten meters into the night sky. And quite simply, the Kalkara disappeared.

The two battlehorses reared in terror, Rodney and the Baron only just managing to retain their seats. They backed away from the fire. There was a terrible reek of charred hair and flesh filling the air. Vaguely, Will remembered Halt discussing the way to deal with a Kalkara. He had said that they were rumored to be particularly susceptible to fire. Some rumor, he thought heavily, trotting Tug forward to join the two knights.

Rodney was rubbing his eyes, still dazzled by the enormous flash.

"What the devil caused that?" he asked. The Baron gingerly retrieved his lance from the fire. The wood was charred and the point blackened.

"It must be the waxy substance that mats their hair together into that hard shell," he replied, in a wondering tone of voice. "It must be highly flammable."

"Well, whatever it was, we did it," Rodney replied, a note of satisfaction in his voice. The Baron shook his head.

"Halt did it," he corrected his Battlemaster. "We merely finished him off."

Rodney nodded, accepting the correction. The Baron glanced at the fire, still pouring a torrent of sparks into the air, but settling back now from the huge explosion of red flame.

"He must have lit this fire when he sensed they were circling back on him. It lit up the area so he had light to shoot by."

"He shot all right," Sir Rodney put in. "Those arrows must have all struck within a few square centimeters."

They looked around, searching for some sign of the Ranger. Then, below the ruined walls of the castle, Will caught sight of a familiar object. He dismounted and ran to retrieve it and his heart sank as he picked up Halt's powerful longbow, smashed and splintered into two pieces.

"He must have fired from over here," he said, indicating the point below the ruined wall where he had found the bow. They looked up, imagining the scene, trying to re-create it. The Baron took the shattered weapon from Will as he remounted Tug.

"And the second Kalkara reached him as he killed its brother," he said. "The question is, where is Halt now? And where is the other Kalkara?"

That was when they heard the screaming start again.

30

INSIDE THE RUINED, OVERGROWN COURTYARD, HALT CROUCHED among the tumbled masonry that had once been Morgarath's stronghold. His leg, numb where the Kalkara had clawed him, was beginning to throb painfully and he could feel the blood seeping past the rough bandage he had thrown around it.

Somewhere close by, he knew the second Kalkara was searching for him. He heard its shuffling movements from time to time and once even its rasping breath as it moved close to his hiding place between two fallen sections of wall. It was only a matter of time before it found him, he knew. And when that happened, he was finished.

He was wounded and unarmed. His bow was gone, smashed in that first terrifying charge when he had fired arrow after arrow into the first of the two monsters. He knew the power of his bow and the penetrative qualities of his razor-sharp, heavy arrowheads. He couldn't believe that the monster had continued to absorb that hail of arrows and still come on, seemingly undaunted. By the time it faltered, it was already too late for Halt to turn his attention to its companion. The second Kalkara was almost upon him, its massive, taloned paw smashing the bow from his grasp, so that he barely had time to scramble for safety onto the ruined wall.

As it clawed its way after him, he had drawn his saxe knife and tried to strike at the terrible head. But the beast had been too fast for him and the heavy knife merely glanced off one of its armored forearms. At the same time, he had found himself confronted by its red, hate-filled eyes and felt his mind leaving him, his muscles freezing in terror as he was drawn to the horrific beast before him. It took an immense effort to wrench his eyes away from the creature's gaze, and he staggered back, losing the saxe knife as the bearlike claws swiped at him and ripped down the length of his thigh.

Then he had run, unarmed and bleeding, trusting to the maze-like confusion of the ruins to evade the monster behind him.

He had sensed the change in the Kalkara's movements around late afternoon. Their steady and previously undeviating path to the northeast suddenly changed as the two beasts abruptly separated, each turning through ninety degrees and moving in different directions into the forest that surrounded them. Their trails, up until then so easy to follow, also showed signs of concealment, so that only a tracker as skilled as a Ranger would have been able to follow them. For the first time in years, Halt felt a cold stone of fear in his belly as he realized that the Kalkara were now hunting him.

The Ruins were close by and he elected to make a stand there, rather than in the woods. He knew the Kalkara would come after him once night fell, so he prepared as best he could, gathering deadfall wood to form the bonfire. He even found half a jar of cooking oil in the ruins of the kitchen. It was rancid and foul smelling, but it would still burn. He poured it over the pile of wood and moved back to a spot where he could place the wall at his back. He had fashioned a supply of torches and kept them burning as darkness fell and he waited for the implacable killers to come for him.

He sensed them before he saw them. Then he made out the two

shambling forms, darker patches against the darkness of the trees. They saw him immediately, of course. The flickering torch jammed into the wall behind him made sure of that. But they missed the pile of oil-soaked wood—and that was what he had been counting on. As they screamed their hunting cries, he tossed the burning torch into the pile and the flames leaped up instantly, flaring yellow in the darkness.

For a moment, the beasts hesitated. Fire was their one fear. But they saw the Ranger was nowhere near the flames and they came on—straight into the hail of arrows that Halt met them with.

If they'd had another hundred meters to cover, he might have managed to stop them both. He still had over a dozen arrows in his quiver. But time and distance were against him and he had barely escaped with his life. Now, he huddled beneath two pieces of masonry that formed an A-shaped refuge, hidden in a shallow indentation in the ground, his cloak concealing him, as it had for years. His only hope now was that Will would arrive with Arald and Rodney. If he could evade the creature until help came, he might have a chance.

He tried not to think of the other possibility—that Gilan would arrive before them, alone and armed only with his bow and sword. Now that he had seen the Kalkara close-up, Halt knew that one man had little chance of standing against it. If Gilan arrived before the knights, he and Halt would both die here.

The creature was quartering the old courtyard now like a hunting dog in search of game, adopting a methodical search pattern, back and forth, examining every space, every cranny, every possible hiding place. This time, he knew, it would find him. His hand touched the hilt of his small throwing knife, the only weapon left to him. It would be a puny, almost useless defense, but it was all he had left.

Then he heard it: the unmistakable heavy drumming of battlehorses' hooves. He looked up, watching the Kalkara through a small gap between the rocks that concealed him. It had heard them too. It was standing erect, its face turned toward the sound outside the ruined walls.

The horses stopped, and he heard the ringing scream of the mortally wounded Kalkara outside as it challenged these new enemies. The hoofbeats rose again, gaining speed and momentum. Then there was a scream and a gigantic red flash that towered for a moment into the sky. Dimly, Halt reasoned that the first Kalkara must have been thrust into the fire. He began to inch back, wriggling out of his hiding place. Perhaps he could outflank the remaining Kalkara, moving to the side and scaling the wall before it noticed him. The chances seemed good. Its attention was drawn now to whatever was happening outside. But even as he had the thought, he realized it was no option. Though the Kalkara had apparently forgotten him for the moment, it was moving stealthily toward the tumbled masonry that formed a rough stairway to the top of the wall.

In a few more minutes, it would be in position to drop on his unsuspecting friends on the other side, taking them by surprise. He had to stop it.

Halt was clear of the hiding place now, the small knife sliding free of the sheath almost of its own volition as he ran across the courtyard, dodging and weaving among the scattered rubble. The Kalkara heard him before he had gone half a dozen paces and it turned back on him, terrifying in its silence as it loped, apelike, to cut him off before he could warn his friends.

Halt stopped suddenly, stock-still, eyes locked on the shambling figure coming at him.

In another few meters, its hypnotic gaze would seize control of his mind. He felt the irresistible urge to look into those red eyes growing stronger. Then he closed his own eyes, his brow furrowed in

fierce concentration, and brought his knife hand up, back and forward in one smooth, instinctive memory throw, seeing the target
moving in his mind's eye, mentally aligning the throw and the spin
of the knife to the point in space where knife and target would arrive simultaneously.

Only a Ranger could have made that throw—and only one of a
handful of them. It took the Kalkara in its right eye and the beast
screamed in pain and fury as it stopped to clutch at the sudden lance
of agony that began in its eye and seared all the way to the pain sen-
sors in its brain. Then Halt was running past it for the wall, scram-
bling up the rocks.

Will saw him as a shadowy figure as he scrambled onto the top of the
ruined wall. But shadowy or not, there was something unmistakable
about it.

"Halt!" he cried, pointing so that the two knights saw him as
well. All three of them saw the Ranger pause, look back and hesitate.
Then a huge shape began to appear a few meters behind him as the
Kalkara, whose wound was painful but nowhere near mortal, came
after him.

Baron Arald went to remount. Then, realizing that no horse
could pick its way through the tumble of rocks and masonry beside
the wall, he dragged his huge broadsword from its saddle scabbard
and ran toward the ruins.

"Get back, Will!" he shouted as he advanced and Will nervously
edged Tug back to the fringe of the trees.

On the wall, Halt heard the shout and saw Arald running forward. Sir Rodney was close behind him, a huge battleax whirring in
circles around his head.

"Jump, Halt! Jump!" the Baron shouted, and Halt needed no further invitation. He leaped the three meters from the wall, rolling to

break his fall as he landed. Then he was up on his feet, running awkwardly to meet the two knights as the wound in his leg reopened.

Will watched, his heart in his mouth, as Halt ran toward the two knights. The Kalkara hesitated a moment, then, screaming a blood-curdling challenge, it leaped after him. But, whereas Halt had rolled to recover, the Kalkara simply transformed the three-meter drop into a huge, bounding leap, its unbelievably powerful rear legs driving it up and forward, covering the ground between it and Halt in that one movement. The massive arm swung, catching Halt a glancing blow and sending him rolling forward, unconscious. But the beast had no time to finish him off, as Baron Arald stepped up to meet it, the broadsword humming in a deadly arc for its neck.

The Kalkara was wickedly fast and it ducked the killing blow, then slammed its talons into Arald's exposed back before he could recover from the stroke. They slashed the chain mail as if it were wool and Arald grunted in pain and surprise as the force of the blow drove him to his knees, the broadsword falling from his hands, blood streaming from half a dozen deep slashes in his back.

He would have died then and there had it not been for Sir Rodney. The Battlemaster whirled the heavy war ax as if it were a toy, and crashed it into the Kalkara's side.

The armor of wax-matted hair protected the beast, but the sheer force of the blow staggered it so that it reeled back from the knight, screaming in fury and frustration. Sir Rodney advanced, placing himself protectively between the Kalkara and the prone figures of Halt and the Baron, his feet set, the ax drawing back for another crushing blow.

And then, strangely, he let the weapon fall from his grasp and stood before the monster, totally at its mercy as the power of the Kalkara's gaze, now channeled through its one good eye, robbed him of his will and his ability to think.

The Kalkara screamed its victory to the night sky. Black blood
streamed down its face. Never in its life had it felt such pain as these
three puny men had inflicted on it. And now they would die for pre-
suming to stand against it. But the primitive intelligence that drove
it wanted its moment of triumph and it screamed again and again
over the three helpless men.

Will watched, horrified. A thought was forming, an idea was
lurking somewhere at the edge of his mind. He looked to one side,
saw the flickering torch that Baron Arald had discarded. Fire. The
one weapon that could defeat the Kalkara. But he was forty meters
away . . .

He whipped an arrow from his quiver, slipping from the saddle
and running lightly to the flickering torch. A good supply of sticky,
melted pitch had run down the handle of the torch and he quickly
rolled the arrowhead in the soft, clinging stuff, forming a huge gob-
bet of it on the arrow. Then he placed it in the flame until it flared
to life.

Forty meters away, the huge evil creature was satisfying its need
for triumph, its screams rolling and echoing through the night as it
stood over the two bodies—Halt unconscious, Baron Arald in a
daze of pain. Sir Rodney still stood, frozen in place, hands dangling
helplessly by his side as he waited for his death. Now the Kalkara
raised one massive, taloned paw to strike him down and all the
knight could feel was the paralyzing terror of its gaze.

Will brought the arrow back to full draw, wincing at the pain as
the flames singed against his bow hand. He raised his aim point a little to allow for the extra weight of the pitch, and released.

The arrow soared in a spark-trailing arc, the wind of its passage
subduing the flame to a mere coal. The Kalkara saw the flash of light
coming and turned to look, sealing its own fate as the arrow struck
it square in its massive chest.

It barely penetrated an inch into the hard, scale-like hair. But as the arrow came to a halt, the little flame flared again, the bonding material in the hair around it caught, and the flame began to spread with incredible speed.

Now the Kalkara's screams had terror in them as it felt the touch of fire—the one thing in life it feared.

The monster beat at the flames on its chest with its paws but that served only to spread the fire to its arms. There was a sudden rush of red flame and in seconds the Kalkara was engulfed, burning from head to toe, rushing blindly in circles in a vain attempt to escape. The screams were nonstop, piercing, reaching higher and higher into a scale of agony that the mind could barely comprehend as the rush of flames grew fiercer with each second.

And then the screaming stopped and the creature was dead.

31

THE INN AT WENSLEY VILLAGE WAS FULL OF MUSIC AND laughter and noise. Will sat at a table with Horace, Alyss and Jenny, while the innkeeper plied them with a succulent dinner of roast goose and farm fresh vegetables, followed by a delicious blueberry pie whose flaky pastry won even Jenny's approval.

It had been Horace's idea to celebrate Will's return to Castle Redmont with a feast. The two girls had agreed immediately, eager for a break in their day-to-day lives, which now seemed rather humdrum compared to the events that Will had been part of.

Naturally, word of the battle with the Kalkara had gone around the village like wildfire—an appropriate simile, Will thought as it occurred to him. As he entered the inn with his friends that evening, an expectant hush had fallen over the room and every eye had turned toward him. He was grateful for the deep cowl on his cloak, which concealed his rapidly reddening features. His three companions sensed his embarrassment. Jenny, as ever, was the quickest to react, and to break the silence that filled the inn.

"Come on, you solemn lot!" she cried to the musicians by the fireplace. "Let's have some music in here! And some chatter if you please!" She added the second suggestion with a meaningful glace at the other occupants in the room.

The musicians took their cue from her. Jenny was a difficult person to refuse. They quickly struck up a popular local folk tune and the sound filled the room. The other villagers gradually realized that their attention was making Will uncomfortable. They remembered their manners and began talking among themselves again, only occasionally casting glances his way, marveling that one so apparently young could have been part of such momentous events.

The four former wardmates took their seats at a table at the back of the room, where they could talk without interruption.

"George sent his apologies," Alyss said as they took their seats. "He's snowed under with paperwork—the entire Scribeschool is working day and night."

Will nodded his understanding. The impending war with Morgarath, and the need to mobilize troops and call in old alliances, must have created a mountain of paperwork.

So much had happened in the ten days since the battle with the Kalkara.

Making camp by the ruins, Rodney and Will had tended to the wounds of Baron Arald and Halt, finally settling the two men into a restful sleep. The following morning saw the arrival of a leg-weary Gilan, riding a sway-backed plow horse. The tall Ranger gratefully reclaimed Blaze. Then, after being reassured that his former master was in no danger, he set off almost immediately for his own fief, after Will promised to return the plow horse to its owner.

Later in the day, Will, Halt, Rodney and Arald had returned to Castle Redmont, where they were all plunged into the nonstop activity of preparing the castle's fighting men for war. There were a thousand and one details to be handled, messages to be delivered and summonses sent out. With Halt still recuperating from his wound, a great deal of this work had fallen to Will.

In times like these, he realized, a Ranger had little chance for relaxation, which made this evening such a welcome diversion. The innkeeper bustled importantly to their table and set down four glass tankards and a jug of the nonalcoholic beer he brewed from ginger root before them.

"No charge for this table tonight," he said. "We're privileged to have you in our establishment, Ranger."

He moved away, calling to one of his serving boys to come and attend the Ranger's table, "And be quick smart about it!" Alyss raised one eyebrow in amazement.

"Nice to be with a celebrity," she said. "Old Skinner usually holds on to a coin so tight, the king's head suffocates."

Will made a dismissive gesture. "People exaggerate things," he said. But Horace leaned forward, his elbows on the table.

"So tell us about the fight," he said, eager for details. Jenny looked wide-eyed at Will.

"I can't believe how brave you were!" she said admiringly. "I would have been terrified."

"Actually, I was petrified," Will told them with a rueful grin. "The Baron and Sir Rodney were the brave ones. They charged in and took those creatures on at close quarters. I was forty or fifty meters away the whole time."

He described the events of the battle, without going into too much detail in his description of the Kalkara. They were dead and gone now, he thought, and best forgotten as soon as possible. Some things didn't need dwelling on. The three others listened, Jenny wide-eyed and excited, Horace eager for details of the fight and Alyss calm and dignified as ever, but totally engrossed in his story. As he described his solo ride to summon help, Horace shook his head in admiration.

"Those Ranger horses must be a breed apart," he said. Will grinned at him, unable to resist the jibe that rose to his mind.

"The trick is staying on them," he said, and was pleased to see a matching grin spread over Horace's face as they both remembered the scene at the Harvest Day Fair. He realized, with a small glow of pleasure, that his relationship with Horace had evolved into a firm friendship, with each viewing the other as an equal. Eager to slip out of the spotlight, he asked Horace how life was progressing in Battleschool. The grin on the bigger boy's face widened.

"A lot better these days, thanks to Halt," he said and, as Will adroitly plied him with more questions, he described life in the Battleschool for them, joking about his mistakes and shortcomings, laughing as he described the many punishment details he attracted. Will noticed how Horace, once inclined to be boastful and a little arrogant, was far more self-effacing these days. He suspected that Horace was doing better as an apprentice warrior than he let on.

It was a pleasant evening, all the more so after the strain and terror of the hunt for the Kalkara. As the servers cleared their plates, Jenny smiled expectantly at the two boys.

"Right! Now who's going to dance with me?" she said brightly and Will was just too slow in responding, Horace claiming her hand and leading her to the dance floor. As they joined the dancers, Will glanced uncertainly at Alyss. He was never quite sure what the tall girl was thinking. He thought that perhaps it might be good manners to ask her to dance as well. He cleared his throat nervously.

"Um . . . would you like to dance too, Alyss?" he said awkwardly. She favored him with the barest trace of a smile.

"Perhaps not, Will. I'm no great shakes as a dancer. I seem to be all legs."

In fact, she was an excellent dancer but, a diplomat to the core, she sensed that Will had only asked her out of politeness. He nodded several times and they lapsed into silence—but a friendly sort of silence.

After some minutes, she turned toward him, placing her chin on her hand to consider him closely.

"A big day for you tomorrow," she said, and he flushed. He had been summoned to appear before the Baron's entire court the following day.

"I don't know what that's all about," he muttered. Alyss smiled at him.

"He possibly wants to thank you in public," she said. "I'm told barons tend to do that to people who have saved their lives."

He began to say something, but she laid one soft cool hand over his and he stopped. He looked into those calm, smiling gray eyes. Alyss had never struck him as pretty. But now he realized that her elegance and grace and those gray eyes, framed by her fine blond hair, created a natural beauty that far surpassed mere prettiness. Surprisingly, she leaned closer to him and whispered, "We're all proud of you, Will. And I think I'm proudest of all."

And she kissed him. Her lips on his were incredibly, indescribably soft.

Hours later, before he finally fell asleep, he could still feel them.

32

WILL STOOD, TRANSFIXED BY STAGE FRIGHT, JUST INSIDE THE massive doors to the Baron's audience hall.

The building itself was enormous. It was the main room of the castle, the room where the Baron conducted all his official business with the members of his court. The ceiling seemed to stretch upward forever. Shafts of light poured down into the room from windows set high in the massive walls. At the far end of the room, seeming to be kilometers away, the Baron sat, wearing his finest robes, on a raised, throne-like chair.

Between him and Will was the biggest crowd Will had ever seen. Halt propelled his apprentice gently forward with a shove in the back.

"Get on with it," he muttered.

There were hundreds of people in the Great Hall and every eye was turned toward Will. All of the Baron's Craftmasters were there, in their official robes. All of his knights and all the ladies of the court—every one in their best and finest clothes. Farther down the hall were the men-at-arms from the Baron's army, the other apprentices and the trademasters from the village. He saw a flutter of color as Jenny, uninhibited as ever, waved a scarf at him. Alyss, standing beside her, was a little more discreet. She unobtrusively kissed her fingertips to him.

He stood awkwardly, shifting his weight from one foot to another. He wished that Halt had let him wear his Ranger's cloak, so he could blend into the background and disappear.

Halt shoved him again.

"Get a move on!" he hissed.

Will turned to him. "Aren't you coming with me?" he asked. Halt shook his head.

"Not invited. Now get going!"

He shoved him once more, then limped, favoring his injured leg, to a seat. Finally, realizing he had no other course to follow, Will began to walk down the long, long aisle. He heard the muttering voices as he went. Heard his name being whispered from one mouth to another.

And then the clapping started.

It began with one knight's lady and rapidly spread throughout the entire hall as everyone joined in. It was deafening, a thundering, echoing roar of applause that continued until he reached the foot of the Baron's chair.

As Halt had instructed him, he dropped to one knee and bowed his head forward.

The Baron stood up and raised his hand for silence and the clapping died away to echoes.

"Stand up, Will," he said softly, and reached out a hand to help the boy to his feet.

In a daze, Will obeyed. The Baron rested a hand on his shoulder and turned him to face the huge throng before them. His deep voice carried effortlessly to the farthest corner of the hall when he spoke.

"This is Will. Apprentice to the Ranger Halt of this fiefdom. See him now and know him, all of you. He has proven his fidelity, courage and initiative to this fief and to the Kingdom of Araluen."

There was a murmur of appreciation from the people watching. Then the clapping began again, this time accompanied by cheering. Will realized the cheers had begun in the section of the crowd where the Battleschool apprentice warriors stood. He could make out Horace's grinning face, leading the chorus.

The Baron held up a hand for silence, wincing as the movement brought pain to his cracked ribs and the carefully bandaged and sutured gashes in his back. The cheering and clapping slowly died away.

"Will," he said, in a voice that echoed to the farthest corners of the massive room, "I owe you my life. There can be no thanks adequate for that. However, it is in my power to grant you a wish that you once made of me . . ."

Will looked up at him, frowning.

"A wish, sir?" he said, more than a little puzzled by the Baron's words.

The Baron nodded. "I made a mistake, Will. You asked me if you could train as a warrior. It was your wish to become one of my knights and I refused you.

"Now, I can rectify that mistake. It would do me honor to have one so brave and resourceful as one of my knights. Say the word now and you have my permission to transfer to the Battleschool as one of Sir Rodney's apprentices."

Will's heart pounded in his ribs. He thought how, all his life, he had yearned to be a knight. He remembered his deep and bitter disappointment on the day of the Choosing, when Sir Rodney and the Baron had refused his request.

Sir Rodney stepped forward, and the Baron gestured for him to speak.

"My lord," said the Battlemaster, "it was I who refused this boy as an apprentice, as you know. Now, I want all here to know that I was wrong to do so. I, my knights and my apprentices all agree that there could be no more worthy member of the Battleschool than Will!"

There was a great roar of approval from the assembled knights and apprentice warriors. With a slithering clash of steel they unsheathed their swords and clashed them together above their heads, shouting Will's name. Again, Horace was one of the first to do so, and the last to stop.

Gradually, the tumult died down and the knights resheathed their swords. At a sign from Baron Arald, two pages stepped forward, bearing with them a sword and a beautifully enameled shield, which they laid at Will's feet. The shield was painted with a representation of a fierce boar's head.

"This will be your coat of arms when you graduate, Will," said the Baron gently, "to remind the world of the first time we learned of your courage and loyalty to a comrade."

The boy went down on one knee and touched the smooth, enameled surface of the shield. He drew the sword slowly and reverently from its scabbard. It was a beautiful weapon, a masterpiece of the swordsmith's art.

The blade was razor keen, and slightly blued. The hilt and crosspiece were inlaid with gold and the boar's head symbol was repeated on the pommel. The sword itself seemed to have a life of its own. Perfectly balanced, it seemed light as a feather in his grasp. He glanced from the beautiful, jeweled sword to the plain leather grip of his Ranger knife.

"They're a knight's weapons, Will," the Baron urged. "But you've proved over and again that you're worthy of them. Just say the word and they're yours."

Will slid the sword back into its scabbard and stood slowly up. Here was everything he had ever wished for. And yet . . .

He thought of the long days in the forest with Halt. The fierce satisfaction that he felt when one of his arrows struck home, exactly where he had aimed it, exactly as he had seen it in his mind before releasing it. He thought of the hours spent learning to track animals and men. Learning the art of concealment. He thought of Tug, of the pony's courage and devotion.

And he thought of the sheer pleasure that came when he heard Halt's simple "Well done" as he completed a task to his satisfaction. And suddenly, he knew. He looked up at the Baron and said in a firm voice:

"I am a Ranger, my lord."

There was a murmur of surprise from the crowd.

The Baron stepped closer and said in a low voice, "Are you sure, Will? Don't turn this down just because you think Halt might be offended or disappointed. He insisted that this is up to you. He's already agreed to abide by your decision."

Will shook his head. He was more certain than ever now.

"I thank you for the honor, my lord." He glanced at the Battlemaster, and saw, to his surprise, that Sir Rodney was smiling and nodding his head in approval. "And I thank the Battlemaster and his knights for their generous offer. But I am a Ranger." He hesitated. "I mean no offense by this, my lord," he finished awkwardly.

A huge smile creased the Baron's features and he gripped Will's hand in his enormous grip.

"And I take none, Will. None at all! Your loyalty to your craft and your Craftmaster does honor to you and to all of us who know you!" He gave Will's hand one final, firm shake and released him.

Will bowed and turned away to walk down that long, long aisle again. Again, the cheering started and this time, he kept his head high as the cheers rolled around him and echoed to the rafters of the Great Hall. Then, as he neared the massive doors once more, he saw a sight that stopped him in his tracks, stunned with surprise.

For, standing a little aside from the crowd, wrapped in his gray and green mottled cloak, his eyes shadowed by the cowl, was Halt.

And he was smiling.

EPILOGUE

LATER THAT AFTERNOON, AFTER ALL THE NOISE AND CELE-brations had died down, Will sat alone on the tiny verandah of Halt's small cottage. In his hand, he held a small bronze amulet, shaped like an oak leaf, with a steel chain threaded through a ring at the top.

"It's our symbol," his teacher had explained as he handed it to him after the events at the castle. "The Rangers' equivalent of a coat of arms."

Then he fumbled inside his own collar and produced an identically shaped oak leaf, on a chain around his neck. The shape was identical, but the color was different. The oak leaf Halt wore was made of silver.

"Bronze is the apprentice color," Halt told him. "When you finish your learning, you'll receive a silver oak leaf like this one. We all wear them in the Ranger Corps, either silver or bronze." He looked away from the boy for a few minutes, then added, his voice a little husky, "Strictly speaking, you shouldn't receive it until you've passed your first Assessment. But I doubt anyone will argue about it, the way things have turned out."

Now the curiously shaped piece of metal gleamed dully in Will's hand as he thought of the decision he'd made. It seemed so strange to him that he had voluntarily given up the one thing that he had spent most of his life hoping for: the chance to go through Battleschool and take his place as a knight in Castle Redmont's army.

He twirled the bronze oak leaf on its chain around his index finger, letting it wind right up to the finger, then spiral loose again. He sighed deeply. Life could be so complicated. Deep within himself, he felt he had made the right decision. And yet, way down deeper still, there was a tiny thread of doubt.

With a start, he realized that there was someone standing beside him. It was Halt, he recognized as he turned quickly. The Ranger stooped and sat beside the boy on the rough pine planking of the narrow verandah. Before them, the low sun of the late afternoon filtered through the luminous green leaves of the forest, the light seeming to dance and gyrate as the light breeze stirred the leaves.

"A big day," he said softly, and Will nodded.

"And a big decision that you made," the Ranger said, after several more minutes' silence between them. This time, Will turned to face him.

"Halt, did I make the right decision?" he asked finally, the anguish clear in his voice. Halt placed his elbows on his knees and leaned forward a little, squinting into the dappled glare through the trees.

"As far as I'm concerned, yes. I chose you as an apprentice and I can see all the potential you have in that role. I've even come to almost enjoy having you around and getting under my feet," he added, with the barest hint of a smile. "But my feelings, my wishes, aren't important in this. The right decision for you is the one you want most."

"I always wanted to become a knight," Will said, then realized, with a sense of surprise, that he'd phrased the statement in the past tense. And yet he knew that a part of him still wanted it.

"It is possible, of course," said Halt quietly, "to want to do two different things at the same time. Then it just becomes a choice of knowing which one you want most."

Not for the first time, Will felt that Halt had some way of reading his mind.

"If you can sum it up in one thought, what's the main reason you feel a little disappointed that you refused the Baron's offer?" Halt continued.

Will considered the question. "I guess . . . ," he said slowly, "I feel that by turning down Battleschool, I'm somehow letting my father down."

Halt's eyebrows shot up in surprise. "Your father?" he repeated, and Will nodded.

"He was a mighty warrior," he told the Ranger. "A knight. He died at Hackham Heath, fighting the Wargals—a hero."

"You know all this, do you?" Halt asked him, and Will nodded again. This was the dream that had sustained him through the long, lonely years of never knowing who he was or what he was meant to be. The dream had become reality for him now.

"He was a man any son would be proud of," he said finally, and Halt nodded.

"That's certainly true."

There was something in his voice that made Will hesitate. Halt wasn't simply agreeing out of politeness. Will turned quickly to him, realizing the full implications of the Ranger's words.

"You knew him, Halt? You knew my father?"

There was a light of hope in the boy's eyes that cried out for the truth and the Ranger nodded soberly.

"Yes. I did. I didn't know him for long. But I think I could say I knew him well. And you're right. You can be extremely proud of him."

"He was a mighty warrior, wasn't he?" said Will.

"He was a soldier," Halt agreed, "and a brave fighter."

"I knew it!" Will said happily. "He was a great knight!"

"A sergeant," Halt said softly, and not unkindly.

Will's jaw hung open, the next words he had been about to say frozen in his throat. Finally, he managed, in a confused voice:

"A sergeant?"

Halt nodded. He could see the disappointment in the boy's eyes and he put an arm around his shoulders.

"Don't judge a man's quality by his position in life, Will. Your father, Daniel, was a loyal and brave soldier. He didn't have the opportunity to go to Battleschool because he began life as a farmer. But, if he had, he would have been one of the greatest of knights."

"But he . . . ," the boy began sadly. The Ranger stopped him, continuing in that same kind, soft, compelling voice.

"Because without taking any of the vows or the special training that knights have, he lived up to the highest ideals of knighthood and chivalry and valor. It was actually a few days after the battle at Hackham Heath, while Morgarath and his Wargals were fighting their way back to Three Step Pass. A sudden counterattack took us by surprise and your father saw a comrade surrounded by a troop of Wargals. The man was on the ground and was within a second of being cut to pieces when your father took a hand."

The light in the boy's eyes had begin to shine again.

"He did?" Will asked, his lips just framing the words, and Halt nodded.

"He did. He left the safety of the battle line and leaped forward, armed only with a spear. He stood over his injured comrade and protected him from the Wargals. He killed one with the spear, then another smashed the head of the spear, leaving Daniel with only a spear shaft. So he used it like a quarterstaff and knocked down two others—left, right! Just like that!"

He flicked his hand to left and right to demonstrate. Will's eyes were intent on him now, seeing the battle as the Ranger described it.

"He was wounded then, as the spear shaft broke under another attack. It would have been enough to kill most men. But he simply took the sword from one of the Wargals he'd killed and struck down three more, all the time bleeding from a massive wound in his side."

"Three of them?" Will asked.

"Three. He had the speed of a leopard. And remember, as a spearman, he had never really trained with the sword."

He paused, remembering that day so long ago.

"You know, of course, that there is almost nothing that Wargals fear? They're called the Unminded Ones, and once they begin a battle, they almost always finish it.

"*Almost* always. This was one of the few times I saw Wargals afraid. As your father struck out to either side, still standing over his wounded comrade, they began to back away. Slowly at first. Then they ran. They simply turned and ran.

"I have never seen any other man, no knight, no mighty warrior, who could send Wargals running in fear. Your father did. He may have been a sergeant, Will, but he was the mightiest warrior I ever had the privilege to watch. Then, as the Wargals retreated, he sank down on one knee beside the man he'd been protecting, still trying to shield him, even though he knew he was dying himself.

"He had taken half a dozen wounds. But it was probably the first that killed him."

"And was his friend saved?" Will asked in a small voice.

Halt looked a little puzzled. "His friend?" he asked.

"The man he protected," Will explained. "Did he survive?"

Somehow, he thought it would have been a tragedy if his father's valiant attempt had been unsuccessful.

"They weren't friends," said Halt. "Up until that moment, he had never laid eyes on the other man." He paused, then added, "Nor I on him."

The significance of those last four words sank deep into Will's consciousness.

"*You?*" he whispered. "You were the man he saved?"

Halt nodded. "As I said, I only knew him for a few minutes. But he did more for me than any other man, before or since. As he was dying, he told me of his wife, and how she was back at their farm alone, with a baby due any day. He begged me to see that she was looked after."

Will looked at the grim, bearded face he had grown to know so well. There was a deep sadness in Halt's eyes as he remembered that day.

"I was too late to save your mother. It was a difficult birth and she died shortly after you were born. But I brought you back here and Baron Arald agreed that you should be brought up in the Ward— until you were old enough to become my apprentice."

"But all those years, you never . . ." Will stopped, lost for words. Halt smiled grimly at him.

"I never let on that I had placed you in the Ward? No. Think about it, Will. People are . . . strange about Rangers. How would they have reacted to you as you grew up? Wondering what sort of strange creature you were? We decided it would be better if nobody knew of my interest in you."

Will nodded. Halt was right, of course. Life as a ward had been difficult enough. It would have been far more so if people had known he was somehow connected to Halt.

"So you took me as your apprentice because of my father?" said Will. But this time Halt shook his head.

"No. I made sure you were looked after because of your father. I chose you because you showed you had the abilities and the skills that were needed. And you also seem to have inherited some of your father's courage."

There was a long, long silence between them as Will absorbed the story of his father's amazing battle. Somehow, the truth was more stirring, more inspiring than any fantasy he could have made up over the years to sustain himself. Eventually, Halt stood up to go and he smiled gratefully up at the grizzled figure, now silhouetted against the sky as the last light of day died.

"I think my father would be glad I chose the way I did," he said, slipping the bronze oak leaf on its chain over his head. Halt merely nodded once, then turned away and went inside the cottage, leaving his apprentice to his own thoughts.

Will sat quietly for some minutes. Almost unthinkingly, his hand went to touch the bronze oakleaf symbol hanging at his throat. Faintly, the evening breeze carried the sounds of the Battleschool drill yard to him, and the nonstop hammering and clanking from the armory that had been going on, night and day, for the past week. They were the sounds of Castle Redmont preparing for the coming war.

Yet strangely, for the first time in his life, he felt at peace.

Turn the page for a preview of

RANGER'S APPRENTICE

BOOK TWO: THE BURNING BRIDGE

1

IT WAS CLOSE TO MIDNIGHT WHEN THE SINGLE RIDER REINED in his horse outside the small cottage set in the trees below Castle Redmont. The laden pack pony trailing behind the saddle horse ambled to a halt as well. The rider, a tall man who moved with the easy grace of youth, swung down from the saddle and stepped up onto the narrow verandah, stooping to avoid the low-lying eaves. From the lean-to stable at the side of the house came the sound of a gentle nickering and his own horse's head rose as he answered the greeting.

The rider had raised his fist to knock at the door when he saw a light come on behind the curtained windows. He hesitated. The light moved across the room and, a second or so later, the door opened before him.

"Gilan," Halt said, without any note of surprise in his voice. "What are you doing here?"

The young Ranger laughed incredulously as he faced his former teacher. "How do you do it, Halt?" he asked. "How could you possibly know it was me arriving in the middle of the night, before you'd even opened the door?"

Halt shrugged, gesturing for Gilan to enter the house. He closed the door behind him and moved to the neat little kitchen, opening the damping vent on the stove and sending new life flaring into the wood coals inside. He tossed a handful of kindling into the stove and set a copper kettle on the hot plate over the fire chamber, shaking it first to make sure there was plenty of water in it.

"I heard your horse some minutes ago," he finally said. "Then, when I heard Abelard call a greeting, I knew it had to be a Ranger horse." He shrugged again. Simple when you explained it, the gesture said. Gilan laughed again in reply.

"Well, that narrowed it down to fifty people, didn't it?" he said. Halt cocked his head to one side with a pitying look.

"Gilan, I must have heard you stumbling up that front step a thousand times when you were studying with me," he said. "Give me credit for recognizing that sound once more."

The younger Ranger spread his hands in a gesture of defeat. He unclasped his cloak and hung it over the back of a chair, moving a little closer to the stove. It was a chilly night and he watched Halt measuring coffee into a pot with some anticipation. The door to the rear room of the house opened and Will entered the small living room, his clothes pulled on hastily over his nightshirt, his hair still tousled from sleep.

"Evening, Gilan," he said casually. "What brings you here?"

Gilan looked from one to the other in something like despair. "Isn't anybody surprised when I turn up in the middle of the night?" he asked, of no one in particular. Halt, busy by the stove, turned away to hide a grin. A few minutes earlier, he'd heard Will moving hurriedly to the window as the horses drew closer to the cottage. Obviously, his apprentice had overheard Halt's exchange with Gilan and was doing his best to emulate his own casual approach to the unexpected arrival. However, knowing Will as he did, Halt was sure that the boy was burning with curiosity over the reason for Gilan's sudden appearance. He decided he'd call his bluff.

"It's late, Will," he said. "You may as well go back to bed. We have a busy day tomorrow."

Instantly, Will's nonchalant expression was replaced by a stricken look. The suggestion from his master was tantamount to an order. All thought of appearing casual departed instantly.

"Oh, please, Halt!" the boy exclaimed. "I want to know what's going on!"

Halt and Gilan exchanged a quick grin. Will was actually hopping from one foot to another as he waited for Halt to rescind the suggestion that he should go to bed. The grizzled Ranger kept a straight face as he set three steaming mugs of coffee on the kitchen table.

"Just as well I made three cups then, isn't it?" he said and Will realized that he'd been having his leg pulled. He shrugged, grinning, and sat down with his two seniors.

"Very well, Gilan, before my apprentice explodes with curiosity, what is the reason for this unexpected visit?"

"Well, it has to do with those battle plans you discovered last week. Now that we know what Morgarath has in mind, the King wants the army ready on the Plains of Uthal before the dark of the next moon. That's when Morgarath plans to break out through Three Step Pass."

The captured document had told them a great deal. Morgarath's plan called for five hundred Skandian mercenaries to make their way through the swamps of the fenlands and attack the Araluen garrison at Three Step Pass. With the Pass undefended, Morgarath's main army of Wargals would be able to break out and deploy into battle order on the Plains.

"So Duncan plans to beat him to the punch," Halt said, nodding slowly. "Good thinking. That way we control the battlefield."

Will nodded in his turn and said in an equally grave voice, "And we'll keep Morgarath's army bottled up in the Pass."

Gilan turned slightly to hide a grin. He wondered if he had tried to copy Halt's mannerisms when he was an apprentice, and decided that he probably had.

"On the contrary," he said, "once the army's in place, Duncan plans to withdraw the garrison, then fall back to prepared positions and let Morgarath out onto the Plains."

"Let him out?" Will's voice went up in pitch with surprise. "Is the King crazy? Why would . . ."

He realized that both Rangers were looking at him, Halt with one eyebrow raised and Gilan with a quizzical smile playing at the corners of his mouth.

"I mean . . ." He hesitated, not sure if questioning the King's sanity might constitute treason. "No offense or anything like that. It's just—"

"Oh, I'm sure the King wouldn't be offended to hear that a lowly apprentice Ranger thought he was crazy," said Halt. "Kings usually love to hear that sort of thing."

"But Halt . . . to let him out, after all these years? It seems . . ." He was about to say "crazy" again, but thought better of it. He thought suddenly of his recent encounter with the Wargals. The idea of thousands of those vile beasts streaming unopposed out of the Pass made his blood run cold.

It was Halt who answered first. "That's just the point, Will—*after all these years*. We've spent sixteen years looking over our shoulders at Morgarath, wondering what he's up to. In that time, we've had many of our forces tied up patrolling the base of the cliffs and keeping watch over Three Step. And he's been free to strike at us any time he likes. The Kalkara were the latest example, as you know only too well."

Gilan glanced admiringly at his former teacher. Halt had instantly seen the reasoning behind the King's plan. Not for the first time, he understood why Halt was one of the King's most respected advisers.

"Halt's right, Will," he said. "And there's another reason. After sixteen years of relative peace, people are growing complacent. Not the Rangers, of course, but the village people who provide men-at-arms for our army, and even some of the barons and Battlemasters in remote fiefs to the north."

"You've seen for yourself how reluctant some people are to leave their farms and go to war," Halt put in. Will nodded. He and Halt had spent the past week traveling to outlying villages in Redmont Fief to raise the levies of men who would make up the bulk of the army. On more than one occasion, they had been met with outright hostility—hostility that melted away as Halt exerted the full force of his personality and reputation.

"As far as King Duncan is concerned, now is the time to settle this," Gilan continued. "We're as strong as we'll ever be and any delay will only weaken us. This is the best opportunity we'll have to get rid of Morgarath once and for all."

"All of which still begs my original question," Halt said. "What brings you here in the middle of the night?"

"Orders from Crowley," Gilan said crisply. He placed a written dispatch on the table and Halt, after an inquiring look at Gilan, unrolled it and read it. Crowley was the Commandant of the Rangers, Will knew, the most senior of all the fifty Rangers in the Corps. Halt read, then rolled the orders closed again.

"So you're taking dispatches to King Swyddned of the Celts," he said. "I assume you're invoking the mutual defense treaty that Duncan signed with him some years ago?"

Gilan nodded, sipping appreciatively at the fragrant coffee. "The King feels we're going to need all the troops we can muster."

Halt nodded thoughtfully. "I can't fault his thinking there," he said softly. "But . . . ?" He spread his hands in a questioning gesture. If Gilan were taking dispatches to Celtica, the sooner he got on with it the better, the gesture seemed to say.

"Well," said Gilan, "it's an official embassy to *Celtica*." He laid a little stress on the last word and suddenly Halt nodded his understanding.

"Of course," he said. "The old Celtic tradition."

"Superstition, more like it," Gilan answered, shaking his head. "It's a ridiculous waste of time as far as I'm concerned."

"Of course it is," Halt replied. "But the Celts insist on it, so what can you do?"

Will looked from Halt to Gilan and back again. The two Rangers seemed to understand what they were talking about. To Will, they might as well have been speaking Espanard.

"It's all very well in normal times," Gilan said. "But with all these preparations for war, we're stretched thin in every area. We simply don't have the people to spare. So Crowley thought . . ."

"I think I'm ahead of you," said Halt, and finally, Will could bear it no longer.

"Well, I'm way behind you!" he burst out. "What on earth are you two talking about? You are speaking Araluen, aren't you, and not some strange foreign tongue that just sounds like it, but makes no sense at all?"

THE ADVENTURE CONTINUES IN . . .

RANGER'S APPRENTICE

BOOK TWO: THE BURNING BRIDGE

On a special mission for the Rangers, Will discovers all the people in the neighboring villages have been either slain or captured. But why? Could it be that Morgarath has finally devised a plan to bring his legions over the supposedly insurmountable pass? If so, the king's army is in imminent danger of being crushed in a fierce ambush. And Will is the only one who can save them.

978-0-14-240842-1

RANGER'S APPRENTICE

BOOK THREE: THE ICEBOUND LAND

Kidnapped and taken to a frozen land after the fierce battle with Lord Morgarath, Will and Evanlyn are bound for Skandia as captives. Halt has sworn to rescue his young apprentice, and he will do anything to keep his promise—even defy his King. Expelled from the Rangers he has served so loyally, Halt is joined by Will's friend Horace as he travels toward Skandia. But will he and Halt be in time to rescue Will from a horrific life of slavery?

978-0-14-241075-2

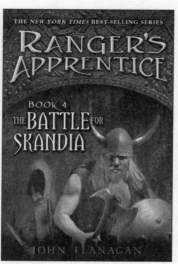

RANGER'S APPRENTICE

BOOK FOUR: THE BATTLE FOR SKANDIA

Still far from home after escaping slavery in the icebound land of
Skandia, young Will and Evanlyn's plans to return to Araluen are
spoiled when Evanlyn is taken captive, and Will discovers that
Skandia and Araluen are in grave danger. Only an unlikely union can
save the two kingdoms, but can it hold long enough to vanquish a
ruthless new enemy?

978-0-14-241340-1

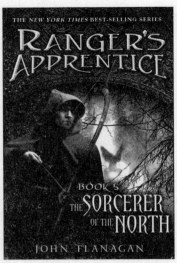

RANGER'S APPRENTICE

BOOK FIVE: THE SORCERER OF THE NORTH

Will is finally a full-fledged Ranger with his own fief to look after. But when Lord Syron, master of a castle far in the north, is struck down by a mysterious illness, Will is suddenly thrown headfirst into an extraordinary adventure, investigating fears of sorcery and trying to determine who is loyal to Lord Syron. . . .

978-0-14-241429-3

RANGER'S APPRENTICE

BOOK SIX: THE SIEGE OF MACINDAW

The kingdom is in danger. Renegade knight Sir Keren has succeeded in overtaking Castle Macindaw. The fate of Araluen rests in the hands of two young adventurers: the Ranger Will and his warrior friend, Horace. . . .

978-0-14-241524-5

BOOK SEVEN: ERAK'S RANSOM

In the wake of Araluen's uneasy truce with the raiding Skandians comes word that the Skandian leader has been captured by a dangerous desert tribe. The Rangers—and Will—are sent to free him. Strangers in a strange land, they are brutalized by sandstorms, beaten by the unrelenting heat; nothing is as it seems. Yet one thing is constant: the bravery of the Rangers.

978-0-14-241525-2

BOOK EIGHT: THE KINGS OF CLONMEL

When a cult springs up in neighboring Clonmel, people flock from all over to offer gold in exchange for protection. But Halt is all too familiar with this group, and he knows they have a less than charitable agenda. Secrets will be unveiled and battles fought to the death as Will and Horace help Halt in ridding the land of a dangerous enemy.

978-0-14-241857-4

BOOK NINE: HALT'S PERIL

The renegade outlaw group known as the Outsiders may have been chased from Clonmel, but now Rangers Halt and Will, along with the young warrior Horace, are in pursuit. The Outsiders have done an effective job of dividing the kingdom into factions and are looking to overtake Araluen. It will take every bit of skill and cunning for the Rangers to survive. Some may not be so lucky.

978-0-14-241858-1

BOOK TEN: THE EMPEROR OF NIHON-JA

Months have passed since Horace departed for the eastern nation of Nihon-Ja on a vital mission. Having received no communication from him, his friends fear the worst. Unwilling to wait a second longer, Alyss, Evanlyn, and Will leave and venture into an exotic land in search of their missing friend.

978-0-14-241859-8

Look for John Flanagan's newest series

BROTHERBAND
CHRONICLES
BOOK ONE: THE OUTCASTS

Outcasts for a moment. Heroes for life.